Hunger for You

ISLAND EMBERS, Book 1

CHERYL BARTON

About the *Island Embers* Series:

Join me on this journey into a new sexy, romantic series called, Island Embers. How, do you ask, would embers be used to describe something like a budding romance when its definition means something that's burning away, fading even? Well, that's true, but in this series, embers signify a place where love and desire, which could be fading, actually flourish again as the embers are ignited hotter and fiercer than ever.

In this series of three books, *Hunger for You, Desire for You* and *Thirst for You*, three brothers, Tellum, Byrum and Callum Blackstone have enjoyed their lives as bachelors, never thinking that there would be a woman for each of them who could stoke the desires of their hearts as they do their bodies.

In the business of building romantic resorts, *Secret Whisper, Silent Whisper*, and *Quiet Whisper*, each brother will discover that the heart wants what it wants. Their lives are no longer only about intoxicating, lust-filled needs. The grown and sexy in them have found it's about everlasting love.

We're starting with, *Hunger for You*, with the location being *Secret Whisper*, somewhere in the Dominican Republic.

Come on and have a taste of Tellum and Cheyenne, coming up in book 1.

About – *Hunger for You*, Book 1

Tellum Blackstone was entranced the moment his eyes landed on Cheyenne Reddick and her magnetic beauty. In her eyes, arms, and heart, he thought he'd found forever. A rift between their fathers had him questioning what kind of real love could be torn apart with a line drawn in the sand.

Cheyenne never thought that she would meet the perfect man until she did in Tellum. He exuded the kind of charm, kindness, and simmering heat that had her mind, body, and soul sizzling like no man had ever done before. To her dismay, a ticking time bomb of epic proportion, in the form of her father, brought about an ultimatum for her to choose a man she loves from a family he detests or lose his love and support forever.

At *Secret Whisper*, a romantic island resort owned by Tellum, Cheyenne finds that his passion-infused hunger for her easily penetrated her paper-thin resistance. Their desire for each other reignited an insatiable appetite that no woman in her right mind could fight.

Tellum put his all into their red-hot kisses and explosive days and nights of seduction. He needed to find a way to overshadow the risk they were taking in discovering if their love was worth fighting for.

Welcome to Secret Whisper!

Also by Cheryl Barton

www.cherylbarton.net

*Upcoming Novels

Romance Series

The Sullivans of Montana

Home for Thanksgiving, Book 1
The Way You Love Me, Book 2
On the Right Track, Book 3
Three's a Crowd, Book 4
The Law of Love, Book 5

Sister Act

An Unexpected Destiny, Book 1
For You I Will, Book 2
More Than Friends, Book 3

Bachelor Series

Bachelor Not for Sale
A Designed Affair
A Perfect Combination
Love at Last

A Lovers' Heart Series

Heartthrob
Heartbeat
Heartbreaker

Brothers of Chi-Town Series

I Can't Let Go, Book 1
Swagger and Baggage, Book 2
Claiming His Child, Book 3
Always Bet on Black, Book 4
It Takes Two to Tangle, Book 5
Crashing into Love, Book 6
*Leaks, Lies, Lust and Love, Book 7 -
Valentine's Day, 2024

Stand Alone Romance

Snowbound
Cupid's Arrow
One Wish
His Halloween Promise
Holly for Christmas
A Better Man
Bossy
Un-Break My Heart
Love on Top
Take a Knee
Love at First Sight
My First Love
Black Love
A Younger Man
The Lake House
True Lies or True Love
When I Think of You
And Then There Was You
Baby, Come Back
Unforgettable
The Power of Seduction
Seize the Moment
A Christmas Wish
It Should Have Been You
The Christmas Layover
The Sweetest Revenge
The Sweetest Temptation
The Diner
Mister Christmas
Love Therapy

1

Tellum Blackstone's purposeful strides slowed as he reached the red door with gold accents at the far end of the hall that included the entrance to four condominiums on the fifth floor of the luxury building. Behind that one door could be something great or something really bad. The latter of those didn't sit well with him.

Where he would usually be happy to be arriving at this door, he had an inkling that on the other side of it, was not the future he had been hoping for. It was the tone that was used to get him here that had him weary of the answers that awaited him. Tellum knew something was wrong, as he suspected, the moment he used his key to enter his girlfriend, Cheyenne Reddick's three-bedroom, three-full, one-half bath condo in Rochester, Michigan. She'd given him the key months ago after their relationship had quickly become serious. They had fallen in love; a first for him at thirty-four years old.

After dating for six-months and while out on one of their many date nights, they surprised each other with the same act of trust and commitment. He and Cheyenne had settled into a routine of spending most of their nights together either at her condo or at his lavish six thousand square foot, three-level condominium in the heart of Detroit. He loved the city he'd grown up in. He couldn't see himself living or working anyplace else.

At dinner that night, he presented Cheyenne with a key and the code to his place. He never wavered in giving her full access to him. For the first time after years of dating a plethora of women, he knew instantly that Cheyenne was the one for him. She was so happy that night. Her electric smile lit up the room. His love for her grew even deeper. To his surprise, she reached into her small *Louis Vuitton* handbag and pulled out a small box. When she slid it over to him, he opened it and laughed. Wide eyed, he looked across the table at her when he saw what was inside. She had given him a key to her place. They laughed out loud together. He remembered telling her a few months back that he loved how in sync they were with each other on most things. It had been that way from the start.

The excitement of that night was nothing like the dread he felt today as he entered her quiet space. His idea of them being in sync had dissipated. He knew Cheyenne had to hear him enter the condo since he could see her standing in front of the large glass bay window where rain beat softly against it. Her back was to him. She didn't turn around.

Now that he was here and before he even closed the door behind him, he knew things between them had changed. There were days when he couldn't wait to get to her knowing she would run and leap into his arms, kissing him fervently like a woman who couldn't wait to get her hands on him. He loved those moments. Today was not that type of day. There was no running or leaping. He sensed that they were as far apart as two people could be. He feared the moment of them getting here. He saw it coming in the past few weeks.

Watching Cheyenne stoically staring out at nothing other than the rain on the darker than blue night wasn't his only clue, but it was one of his top five. Her lack of movement told him that things were still icy between them; something he hated. They never fought when it came to their relationship. This in-fighting was because of a rift between their fathers.

Her father, Joseph Reddick, whom everyone called Captain Joe, and his father, Dennis Blackstone, had quickly turned into fierce enemies over a business deal that didn't happen. It wasn't on his father's part, but Captain Joe took everything, including sensible business decisions, personal. The latest one happens to be the reason behind why he and Cheyenne were moving into a lane in their relationship reserved for strangers. The issue between the two dads had found its way into the loving bond they shared.

Closing the door, he didn't walk to pull her into his arms. The chilly vibe in the air told him, now wasn't the time for anything lovingly. Tellum lowered his shoulders in defeat. This wasn't a stance he was familiar with, but he'd heard stories. He knew what was coming without hearing her say it; he just knew.

Leaning back against the door, he crossed his long legs and put his hands in his pockets. He wanted to hold her. He wanted to kiss her. He had to resist doing anything other than standing still. She had the floor. From the looks of things, Cheyenne didn't want to be touched or kissed. He was here because she had asked him to come. This was her show. He would follow her lead.

Tellum was upset knowing what would happen before he left back out. Still, he spoke in a low, calm tone. The situation of the moment didn't seem like Cheyenne would speak first.

When she still hadn't acknowledged his presence, he said, "we're doing this?"

Her stance stiffened right before his eyes. Her arms were wrapped tight around her body. She was still wearing her black *Essential* trench coat from Banana Republic that he'd bought her a month ago. He looked down at her staple type of shoe, heels. Cheyenne was sexy, especially when she wore high heels, making the coat look amazing on her beautiful body. He could see some of the rain that still covered it. She must have arrived home shortly before he showed up. He'd rushed over through the rain to get to her building from the parking lot across the street.

He looked at her closely. No way was Cheyenne her usual self. Wearing a rain covered coat on her wood floors? He braced himself for the conversation.

"He's my dad, Tellum. What am I supposed to do?" she asked without turning to look at him.

"Not throw away what we have because our fathers are having a problem."

Cheyenne slowly turned toward him. Tellum's heart sank when he saw tears in her eyes. He started to walk in her direction to comfort her, but her hand going up stopped him. She knew, like he did, that if they touched, she wouldn't be able to make the hard decision that he feared she was about to make.

"It's a big problem. That business deal could have helped my father out. It could have resulted in a major financial boost for him. He needed that. You have no idea how much he needed that. I've never seen him so angry. Why couldn't your dad just help him out?" she pleaded.

Her passion was clear. Tellum wished he could wipe it all away, but the end result of what happened was out of his reach. He wanted to be angry that she continued to push him on this as she had been doing for weeks. Though his own anger could boil over at her not understanding how his hands were tied, he kept his calm. He didn't raise his voice. He wanted this moment to go away. He wanted their love to get back to normal.

"Baby, are you serious? You want me to question my father about his business decisions when I have nothing to do with that?" he inquired.

"How are we to survive what's happening? The entire Blackstone family is now his enemy. I'm so confused."

Cheyenne wiped away the new tears on her cheek. Tellum's heart sank even more. His love for her couldn't take her crying. Seeing her in pain hurt him to his heart.

"Cheyenne, don't," he said softly. He never wanted to see her cry. He'd spent months loving her. He only wanted to see her happy. He especially hated that she was directing her anger at him as the tears continued to flow. He felt like it was his fault even though deep down, he knew it wasn't. He had no stake in what happened between their fathers. He didn't get why she couldn't see that.

"My father has made it very clear that he will disown me if I continue to see you. He doesn't want me to fraternize with your family in any way. He blames all of you for the amount of money he has lost not getting that deal."

"Baby, it's business. It's their business, not ours. These types of things happen every day."

"It didn't have to!" she shouted.

Tellum put his hands up in surrender. This is what he never wanted for them. The day her father came to him to ask if he could sway his father on a business deal, Tellum knew there would be problems with him and Cheyenne. Things got worse when one night, just as they were about to make love, she brought up the business deal. She wanted to know if he was going to help her father out. That brief conversation had interrupted the lasciviously intimate atmosphere. He'd been waiting all day to get home knowing she would be in something silky and sexy just for his eyes. Instead, they ended up fighting. He had watched, with dismay and a lack of patience, as Cheyenne rushed to get dressed just before storming out of his condo. He tried for a week to get her to answer his calls and texts, to no avail. Then, the next week, she showed up unexpectedly at his office with an apology that he knew didn't come from her. It's not that she wouldn't apologize for the nasty way she spoke to him when he wouldn't do what she wanted. Her apology was laced with requests for him to reconsider helping her father, which he did not. There was no doubt the words were planted in her head by Captain Joe. It didn't work. Her father would not get a contract that would bring millions of dollars his way.

"Cheyenne, look at us? We're fighting, not about anything that has to do with us, but about something that is out of our control. I don't have a hand in this just as you don't."

"You could have talked to your father. You could have shown him what this means to Captain Joe."

Tellum exhaled in despair every time she mentioned his name. His skin crawled every time Cheyenne referred to her father that way instead of calling him dad or daddy. He couldn't believe that the man made his only child call him Captain Joe.

"Listen, I stay in my own lane. I have enough work issues to deal with when it comes to my own company. What I don't have time to do is fight someone else's battles in a business arena that does not involve me. My father doesn't need my insight into deals he should stand behind or not. He works for *General Motors*, I don't."

"You wouldn't even read Captain Joe's proposal. You could have given my father some advice about how to best approach your father."

Tellum laughed silently. As much as he respected Cheyenne's father because he was her father, not when it came to business, he hated times when she spoke as if she were reading from a script that he prepared for her. He heard her father's voice in place of hers when she spoke.

"I'm not going to go back and forth with you about this. We've been arguing for weeks, and why? Why do we have to crash and burn because of outside forces?" he questioned avidly.

"He's my *father*! He's not you or your father or anyone else in your family. Your family has a lot of money. You grew up in wealth. You've acquired your own wealth. My father is trying hard to succeed. You did nothing to help."

Tellum was losing patience. He knew he was all business and could be brutal around the table when he had to make decisions that could make or break his company. When it came to women, he focused on his softer, more sensitive side. He'd been fighting an uphill battle for a while now. It was getting old. They couldn't focus on where they were going to travel to, what restaurant they were going out to or even what movie on Netflix or Hulu they wanted to chill and relax to. Instead, every time they talked, they had to fight about their fathers. He had never put as much time and energy into loving a woman before her. To his consternation, their only disagreements involved anything but them.

"I get it. You love your father. You respect him. I love my father and respect him just as you do yours. What does all of this mean? He's given you an ultimatum and what? You asked me over here to end our relationship over this mess? Is that what this is? You're throwing us away because Captain Joe said so. He threatened your entire relationship with him because you're fraternizing with me, someone he considers the enemy? This can't be my reality right now," he spoke, exasperated and throwing his hands in the air in frustration.

Cheyenne's eyes locked with his. When she was about to tear into him, he saw her open her mouth and then stopped. She closed her lips tight. He waited for what was coming next.

Cheyenne was his first serious relationship. Women have been his weakness since his teenage years. He never saw himself getting serious about any one woman because there were so many that he wanted to indulge in. For as long as he could remember, back to when he lost his virginity at the age of sixteen, he kept his heart on lock and only offered his body. Women enjoyed how attentive he could be when it was just the two of them seeking pleasure. Some tried to put him under lock and key, but he easily charmed his way out of any kind of commitment. He was all about business and not personal. There were tricks with his tongue that he knew had them crawling up the walls and pounding on his bedroom door for more. He loved that kind of existence. There were no hurt feelings. Everyone was on the same page. Life was good. One day, into his life walks Cheyenne. From day one, every force-field he'd built up around his heart was torn down by her beauty, inside and out. She was the complete package for him. He fell hard and fast. How he got to this minute of her dumping him, he still didn't understand.

The moment the words left his mouth about this being his reality, he already knew the answer.

"My father is hurting. I can't go against him. He and my mother are all I have. How can we continue with this between us? He hates your father. He blames Mr. Dennis for everything that he won't get as a result of him not backing my father's plan."

"Captain Joe is a big boy. This is not his first failed business deal. It won't be his last. He will continue to bounce back," Tellum suggested, trying to make light of it all while also working hard to show her that this was a ridiculous conversation.

"Not this time. This will do him in. I don't know why you don't understand that. Everything he had was put into this deal. All he needed was the support from the *great* Dennis Blackstone. Your father didn't even give it a chance. I know you don't want to understand this. This is my father. I can't go against him."

"Cheyenne, you cannot be serious right now. Did our relationship mean so little to you? How can you walk away without a second thought?"

"You think I'm not struggling with this? I can't eat. I can't sleep. I can barely function at work every day because I have him in one ear and you in the other. I don't deserve to be in the middle of this," she asserted.

"And I do? You're putting me in the middle of this. I deserve this? I deserve you ending things? We have an amazing relationship. We are *that* couple and you know it. This is how it ends?"

"It impacts me. It impacts my life with my father, Tellum. Do you hear that? It's my *father*!"

Tellum exhaled loudly. There was no way he was going to win this battle. He saw it all over her.

"That's it then? We're done? Just like that? We're done because your father has drawn a line in the sand and has dared you to cross it? You're not a little girl. You're a grown ass woman who can make her own decisions. You're telling me that everything you and I have shared means nothing if I don't bend to your father's wishes as you have?"

"I'm not bending to anything. I'm supporting my father. Don't you do the same thing? Wouldn't you side with your father if the tables were turned?"

"I wish I could answer that because I can't. The reason is because our fathers are different. Dennis Blackstone would never, *ever* make my relationship with you the bargaining chip for keeping or ruining my relationship with him. A father's love doesn't do that. It's terrible that yours is placing you in a position to either choose him or choose me. You're choosing him," Tellum relented.

Cheyenne's body jerked with the heart-filled crying that came to the surface. A steady stream of tears raced down her face and splattered onto her raincoat, joining the remnants of rainwater from being outside.

"This isn't easy for me. There is no way to make this work. My father meant what he said. He is my family. Despite the fact that he's not perfect like your father, he's still my father."

Tellum heaved a heavy breath with dire anguish. He didn't want to lose Cheyenne for anything. He saw a future with her that was slowly fading away. The worst part of it all was that he couldn't persuade her to believe that what they shared was worth the fight. He'd been fighting for them for weeks. It was clear to him that as they stared each other down, she was letting go.

"Say it, Cheyenne. I'm not going to assume that we're done. Baby, you're going to have to say it," he said, still full of hope.

A few seconds, then a few minutes went by. He could hear the storm getting worse outside. The rain was coming down harder. He could even see debris flying through the air five stories up. No storm was greater than the one that rose between them in this very room. It was as powerful as they came. The fate of their relationship, of their love, was in her hands. He couldn't fight or come between the love she had for her father. He knew the man was vile, but still, he was her father.

"I'm sorry. Our relationship is over," she said softly.

When Cheyenne's eyes moved from his as she looked around at everything already familiar to her in her own home, he knew. Her words were saying goodbye to him. Before her eyes turned away, they showed him that she wanted to choose him; she wanted to choose love.

"You're leaving me? We're done?" he asked one last time.

"We're done."

Tellum needed some space. This was not the outcome he saw when he'd first met her.

He couldn't think of anything else to say. He'd been begging and pleading with her for too long already. The drama was impacting his daily life in a bad way. His brothers, Byrum and Callum, had made reference to that many times as they sat around the conference room of their office discussing new business ventures. He was far from focused. He hated to see Cheyenne torn like this every time he saw her. He loved her too much to be a part of her struggle when it came to whether her father or him was pulling on her arm the hardest. To free her from the heartache that he knew she was experiencing every time they saw each other, he let go. His love held on, but his mind let go. It wasn't easy. In fact, walking away was about the hardest thing he has ever had to do.

"I love you, Cheyenne. I won't dismiss the love your father has for you by saying I love you more. I will say that I love you enough to not have a part in you being this despondent. I won't play tug-of-war with your heart. You know where I stand. If you don't know, understand or believe anything else in this world, know that I *love* you," he stressed keenly.

Tellum turned and reached for the door handle, not waiting for her to answer. He took his key to her place off of his keyring and sat it on the table next to the door. Without hesitating any longer, he opened the door.

"I have your key in my..." Cheyenne said, but he cut her off without looking back.

"You keep it for now. If you change your mind, use it."

"Eventually, some other woman won't want me having a key to your place."

Her words cut him deep. Cheyenne was actually trying to make light of their end. He turned and made sure she could see his eyes. There was nothing light in them; he knew that for a fact.

"Don't ever dismiss how much I love you. The hurt that's in my heart doesn't have me thinking about another woman being in your place right now. I'm disappointed that you would even put that in the air between us. You should know me better than that by now."

When she nodded, he knew she was about to apologize for demeaning their relationship as if it was a flippant passage of time for them. He didn't give her a chance to say anything. He stepped out of her place and closed the door behind him. He could hear her openly sobbing through the door. He wanted to go to her, but he wasn't a fool. She'd ended things. He walked down the hall to the elevator like a lost soul. For the first time in his life, a woman had broken his heart, ripped it from his chest and stepped all over it in high-heeled Dior Slingbacks, her favorite shoes.

"This is one hell of a day," he sighed out loud as the elevator took him down to his car.

2

6 Months Later

There was something amazing about the view from the top of the thirty-ninth floor of the Renaissance Center complex in downtown Detroit. Not many sights compared to having an office that looked out over the Detroit International Riverfront or down to the covered pedestrian skywalk. In the years that he's been walking the earth with his brothers, Byrum, two years older than him and Callum, who was two years younger than him, his family has always been a staple in the Detroit area.

His father and his uncle Hyman Blackstone, still worked as top executives for *General Motors*. GM owned the building where the company that he and his brothers built together, *Blackstone Real Estate Investment Trust Corporation* now rented on the top three floors of one of the six, thirty-nine story buildings. Their executive offices were at the very top. Their large staff occupied the other two floors. This was the ideal location for the major moves they were making.

Prime real estate was hard to come by in the Detroit area, which is where they wanted to stay. They were already planning on scouting out locations for their own building now that their company was a huge success in the business of developing and owning their own luxury resorts. For now, this location was a perfect as they come.

He enjoyed getting to the office earlier than most of his staff. That was, of course, made easier by having a penthouse condominium a few blocks away. In fact, a week ago, he had gone out with friends and celebrated the fact that he had purchased his condo three years ago. He lived in the top floor loft penthouse, a newly renovated old warehouse building. It had been expertly overhauled with top quality materials. There were six condos in the nine-story building with each covering an entire floor. His condo was an exception with three levels, the top included the entire roof of the condo. That was his entertainment hub when he hosted friends and family. The lowest level housed an in-building gym and several black owned small businesses. There was a clothing boutique, a juice bar, a beauty salon and a twenty-four-hour, seven day a week convenience store. Thankfully security was extremely tight. They never had any issues.

On the two floors directly below him, there were two married couples. Under them was Byrum. He had purchased a unit a year ago after some additional renovations were made to his liking. The level below Byrum was owned by one of the top R&B singers in the country. She was from Detroit. She didn't spend a lot of time in it, but when she did, she considered her condo as her place of peace away from the rat-race that was the life of a celebrity. The level above the businesses was currently for sale. Callum had thought about it, but he had come to love the house he purchased out in the quiet suburbs. It was where he hosted pool parties too many times throughout the year. Tellum chuckled at the wildness that was his little brother.

Tellum knew that nothing could be more perfect than his loft with its built into the brick walls of his kitchen refrigerator along with a wine cooler. His kitchen also boasted a chef-style kitchen in black, white and gold with an island that sat eight, two on each side and four along one length. What he loved the most was the fully exposed brick and wood beams throughout. He loved the rustic, yet chic style. He also enjoyed windows from the floor to the ceiling in every room. His home was perfectly perfect just for him.

Living not too far from the office building, some days when the mood struck him, he walked, taking in everything he loved about Detroit. He was living in the city that was home to the famous Motown sound. He was in the town they called Motor City. Being a music enthusiast, the history of the city meant a lot to him. This morning wasn't a walk to work kind of day. He used his car service to get him the few blocks to the office.

Turmoil drove him to get up earlier than usual. Six hours into his day and his mood hadn't changed. That was made known to him by his first executive assistant, Lisa-Marie McMann. She kept his business life in perfect running order. She's been with him since moving into the office park building from much smaller office space a few miles away two years ago.

His company had reached unimaginable profits since they began investing in and building vacation resorts around the world. Their first location purchased three years ago in Denver, Colorado, was bought as is. With investor money and business loans, they updated the resort, changed the name to *White Whisper* and renovated it with alluring upgrades. An unimaginable number of reservations over the past few years turned out to be a platinum level investment. Shortly after, he and his brothers were able to purchase an already-standing resort in Miami, Florida, which they renamed, *Palm Whisper*. With these two locations and other investments, they were able to pay back their father and uncle for the start-up money they gave them. They made profits sooner than anyone expected. There were already plans in place to expand both of those locations. The reservations were already booked for the next few years.

On the heels of such great success, he was excited about their latest venture, a romantic resort in the Dominican Republic called *Secret Whisper*. It was the first of their three new resorts opening over the next two years. Following this first one, they would be launching *Quiet Whisper* opening in Hawaii and *Silent Whisper* being built from the ground up on a private island in the Mediterranean. *Silent Whisper* was coming up next. They were able to purchase the island from a billionaire who wanted to unload it after realizing he hadn't done much with it. The island was its own small city with schools, major shopping outlets, restaurants and smaller hotels and communities. The resort was bringing the opportunity for more tourists as well as those who were looking to move to an exotic location. They were also partners in two resorts in the South of France, *Ultra* and *Wave*. Their business profile was expanding at record speed. That was well known after several news stories were released on their business acumen. Together and individually, they were making moves by leaps and bounds.

Tellum enjoyed his position as the company's chief executive officer. His brother Callum was the chief operating officer and Byrum served as chief financial officer. Byrum's three degrees in finance helped get them to where they are along with their father and their uncle's investments into their vision.

Owning their own company had always been the dream of the three Blackstone boys from Detroit. Local start-ups like how Motown began had inspired them from birth. Thankfully, their father believed in them too. He had made them a promise to help them start a company and get it off the ground if they each handed him their high school and college degrees. They fulfilled their end of the bargain and so did their father. There had never been a time when he didn't have the backs of his sons. Nothing could stop them. Their father often bragged about how his sons were powerful men in the business world due to their hard work. Their staunch determination drove them straight ahead into success. Their father had been their role model as one of the major players who helped push *General Motors* to the top.

Tellum remembered one day asking his father why he didn't use his own knowledge, skill and money to start his own company. His father's reply was simple. He didn't want to spend all of his time running a company when he had three sons at home that he wanted to give his attention to as they were coming up. His father's plan had always been to foster an environment that would feed into his sons. He knew it would allow them to have and see dreams come to fruition. He worked hard and invested well. Tellum appreciated that he and his brothers were benefactors of their father's lifelong financial planning. They never took any of that for granted. They grew up, as some would say, with a silver spoon in their mouths. Still, their father demanded hard work and respect from them. They gave both to him ten-fold.

Sitting behind his all glass-top desk in an office with windows on all sides but one, Tellum turned around left and then right in his chair, spinning it, not able to concentrate on anything other than the current state of his now ended relationship with Cheyenne. He knew he was risking a lot being involved with her knowing the scammer her father was. There weren't many in the business world who didn't know to be careful of Captain Joe. He hated the moment her father found out who his daughter was dating. From day one, he knew the man plotted to use their relationship to his own advantage. In the end, there wasn't a winner. The biggest loser was Cheyenne. She spent months being torn between her love for him and her love for her father. Tellum's constant foul mood was the result of his personal life crashing and burning around him.

Once office staff began arriving, he made his way down to the floor below to check in on a few details about his upcoming time away. In a few weeks, he and his brothers would soon be heading out of the country to *Secret Whisper* to oversee the planned week-long launch of the resort. This location took two years to upgrade. In his opinion, it was their most spectacular resort so far.

Secret Whisper was his baby. He put all the feels into the resort, especially with changes he made over the last year since he'd met and fallen in love with Cheyenne. He had been thinking about all of the plans they had made together to spend quality time at the resort. He thought about all of the things missing from the other resorts that he would like to see in a place where he wanted to spend all of his time with the woman he loved.

Besides the resorts, each brother had their own investment properties as well. Building wealth was the name of their game. Second to that, he had thoughts of building a life with the first woman he ever declared his love for. Today, his world was different. He wasn't happy about it.

He hated that he wouldn't be spending any time with Cheyenne in what he would often refer to as their personal paradise island. *Secret Whisper* was going to be their home away from home as often as they wanted. Knowing that wasn't going to happen had him snapping at members of his team since they began arriving. He didn't have just cause; no reason at all for doing so. Realizing he was too deep in his feelings over Cheyenne and having no contact with her since the breakup, he found his way back up to his office. Once inside, he slammed his office door, closing himself off from everything and everybody. He needed time to reign his terrible attitude back in. In a few short moments, he had turned into a tyrant. He seemed to be doing that a lot lately.

He then heard a slight knock on his office door. He thought that it may be Lisa-Marie checking to see if his mood had improved. When he called to her to come in, he was surprised to see, the first love of his life, his mother, Felicia Blackstone, enter his office ahead of Lisa-Marie.

He stood quickly to greet her. She was the person with the real power in their family. She had to be that way when it came to raising three rambunctious boys.

"I'm sorry to interrupt you, Tellum, since you didn't want to be disturbed today. I assumed that didn't apply to your mother," Lisa-Marie explained.

He hugged his mother a second time, tighter this time. It wasn't often that she came to the office. Seeing her today was a welcomed surprise.

"Thanks Lisa-Marie. Of course, always interrupt me for my mother, you know that. Mom, you're here in the middle of the week," he said, kissing her on the cheek.

He walked her further into his office once they were alone.

"I thought I would stop by to see how you were doing. Your father and I are having lunch with some friends today in about an hour. He's in a meeting right now, so I thought I would see if you had a few minutes for your mother. You're still leaving in a few days, right? This isn't the trip to the resort, is it?" she questioned.

"No. This is a business trip to Atlanta. I'm meeting with our main architect, Duron Knight of Pioneer Architecture and Design. His company will have the job of designing the Denver concert venue, if that deal goes through soon. I'll be gone for a few days. Duron has an actual model of it that I'd like to see in person. The 3-D diagram he sent us to look at was nice, but I want to see what it will actually look like."

"You're going by yourself? Without your brothers?"

"I'm taking our design team with me and one of my assistants. Byrum and Callum have other business priorities to attend to."

"That means I won't get to see you for our usual Sunday visit this weekend."

"I promise to make it up to you. You look amazing for your lunch date, mom. I don't think I've seen this dress before," he said, walking her over to the plush navy-blue leather sofa that matched the two single chairs in front of it.

"It's new. Your aunt Sara came by last week for a day of shopping and lunch. I got it that day."

"How are she and uncle Hyman doing? I heard Carmalita was in town last week to see them. Their only daughter living in New York must be hard for them. I know how close she is to them."

"They're fine. Carmalita mentioned she was going to the opening of the resort. Your aunt and uncle are fine. They do miss her. Thankfully, she comes to town often."

"Yeah, she's coming. She actually going to perform for us. She's going to be the next big R&B artist to come out of Detroit by way of New York. She reached out to Lisa-Marie last week to ask about accommodations for a few friends. You know it will be a party if she's there," he quipped.

"I don't doubt it."

"I guess no longer working gives you much more time for midday dates with her and your sister. How is aunt Angel doing? I still can't fathom why you worked as long as you did. Dad always said he encouraged you to quit years ago, but you were determined to stay on as director of marketing for GM."

"My sister is stubborn and onery, but I love her. I know what your father wanted. I needed to do it in my own time. I got that degree for me. I wanted to use it. After staying home for so long with you boys, it was time I did more for myself. Now that he has reduced his hours, I love all the time we get to spend together with you boys being grown and finding your own legs in the business world."

Tellum watched her relax back on the sofa. When she focused on rubbing her hands across the soft leather seating, he knew what was coming next.

"We are who we are because of how hard you and dad worked to help get us here. After that week or so at *Secret Whisper*, I'll have about four months before I'll head off to Hawaii to check progress of *Quiet Whisper*. Byrum will be heading to *Silent Whisper*, which will be the launch after *Secret Whisper*. It'll be almost a year away before that launch. There is still a lot to do. The Hawaii location is just getting started."

"All of you stay so busy. I hope you're making time for fun. You know, I must say that I love this sofa. The leather is so rich looking in color and softness. It's like sitting on a cloud. Is it new? I don't remember it being here the last time I was here. I really like it," she said.

Tellum knew that was code for she wants a set.

"There is a lot going on that I need to stay on top of. Byrum is in the Dominican Republic right now checking on the progress there."

"Didn't Callum just get back from being out of town?" she asked.

"He did. He took two business trips that Byrum and I couldn't make it to in-person. He was good having his team with him."

"You boys work so hard."

"We love being successful. That comes with hard work."

Sitting on the other end of the sofa, he crossed his legs and turned to her. He loved his mother, but something was up regarding her impromptu visit.

"Before we drag this out, what color would you like?" he asked, patting her hand where it rested on chair.

"What?" she smiled acting as if she didn't know what he was talking about. She knew him just as well as he knew her.

"Mom, I know you. You've fallen in love with this sofa in the five minutes that you've been sitting on it. I also know that you'd like one. I'm asking what color so that I can have it made and delivered to the house."

"I'm thinking burnt orange. That would fit wonderfully in my new home office. Now that I spend a lot of time fundraising for Detroit public schools, I'll be spending more time at home working. Something like this would fit nicely in the new space your father had reconfigured for me. The office is larger than my bedroom, but it's missing a nice chair like this."

"A full set, I presume?" he asked, pointing to the two side chairs.

"Oh, that would be wonderful. I have the perfect tables I'd like to complement it with."

Tellum chuckled. He already knew.

"Sofa and two chairs, it is. I'll talk to your assistant, Carmen, to make sure she's aware it's coming. Should only take about a month, maybe two. It's all custom made. Remember I mentioned Duron Knight out of Atlanta? His sister, Loren Knight-Bailey owns an amazing interior design company. She's based out of Los Angeles. These are from her. I'll have someone reach out to her today."

"You and your brothers spoil me so," she beamed.

"You're our mother. Anything you want, we got you."

She sharply turned to him. Tellum knew he was about to hear the real reason she stopped by.

"Good, then I need something else," she stated.

"I knew there was something special to this visit."

Here it comes, he thought. When she sat her red Hermès Birkin bag in the space between them, he prepared for her latest request.

"Cheyenne."

She said that one name, surprising him. He prepared himself for more.

He exhaled loudly. He then closed his eyes and dropped his head down toward his chest. He'd dated a lot of women over the years, but none had ever gotten a hold of his mother's heart the way Cheyenne had. He didn't want to talk about with his mother. As much as he loved Cheyenne, his mother did as well. With his parents having only sons, Cheyenne was the closest his mother got to having a daughter. He and his brothers all loved the bachelor life. He was the only one, apparently, who had been ready for more.

"Mom, I can't get into this with you," he said harshly while standing and walking over to his desk, sitting down. He was hoping to avoid the upcoming discussion. He was still trying to come to terms that they were over. Talking about her with his mother was never a good conversation of late. She pressed him often over the past few months about what he was going to do about it. He still had no answer.

"Don't use that tone with me," she said sternly. "You know better. You went from being soft and loving to being cold and distant in a matter of seconds. All that from me mentioning her name. I don't like it. This can't be who you are now."

"I'm sorry, mom. I meant no disrespect. I didn't catch my tone before I opened my mouth. I didn't mean it. I just can't talk about her right now," he huffed softly.

"So, you're not going to fix things? It's been months. I miss her. I know you do too," she said.

Tellum was surprised that, even though he and Cheyenne were no longer a couple, that she would push away from his mother as well. There were many times when he would call either his mother or Cheyenne only to find that they were either out somewhere together or at his parents' home having a great visit. Not wanting to see or be with him, he understood. Giving his mother the cold shoulder was something totally different. It surprised him to hear that she hadn't seen or heard from Cheyenne either.

"You mean she hasn't called or come to see you? That surprises me about her," he asserted.

"Oh, of course she has. She broke up with you, not me," Felicia kidded. "It's just not the same is all."

Tellum chuckled. He pulled back on what he thought was something negative about Cheyenne.

"Very true. I get that, mom."

"I talked to her yesterday. She called me for my short-rib recipe. She wanted to know how I make the au jus for the beef. You know that cannot be bought in any store. I really need to do a cookbook. She also stopped by two weeks ago when you were in Miami speaking at the airline conference about your new resort. She stayed a full day. We got the chance to have a late breakfast, late lunch and dinner before she left. She helped me plant some new flowers in my garden. We even baked scones."

"Ah, she came by knowing I was out of town. That conference had been planned back when we were dating, so she knew."

"Don't make her visits about you. That's not fair."

"Ma, I'm surprised she's anywhere around us. Her father didn't find out and drag her out of the house? I mean, his demand that she stays away from the Blackstones didn't include the family in general?" he sneered.

"Captain Joe wouldn't dare!" Felicia proclaimed firmly.

"She told me it's what he demanded. Stop calling him that, mom. He is not a captain of anything simply because he likes to be at the helm of a boat. That's a self-proclaimed name he gave himself."

"Don't be disrespectful. I get it. You hate the man because of the hold he has over his daughter."

"No, he dislikes me being with Cheyenne because of what's going on between him and dad. He hates dad and blames him for the loss of that contract with *General Motors*. He even blames me because I didn't stand behind him. It wasn't my place," Tellum explained.

"Son, your father was to blame, in a way."

Tellum opened his mouth to counter what his mother said and then stopped. He didn't think the words would come out right. He thought before he spoke knowing if he said something the wrong way, he would have to apologize again.

"It was business, mom. There is no blame. Dad had to do what he needed to do for the company he has worked for, for over forty years. He's spent the last twenty of those in an executive position. They expect him to make the right decisions based on business, not personal stakes. It is his job to seek out great partnerships. One with Cheyenne's father's company was not a good one. Her father has been involved in some shady business deals. Dad couldn't keep that hidden. The fact that he turned that situation into Cheyenne doing, what he calls, sleeping with the enemy, is beyond me. She has a right to be involved with whomever she chooses."

"Yet, in the end, she chose to honor her father's wish. I don't think she made her decision lightly. You know how Joe can be. Like you said, he's had some shady and quite ruthless business dealings. As a result, he lost out on an opportunity that would have netted him millions. I understand he's in financial distress these days," Felicia explained.

"He counted on my relationship with his daughter to pave the way to the golden nugget for himself. When he didn't get it, he blamed us without facing his own fault in this, his past practices. I love her, mom. Other than the first week when I first met her, I have not been with another woman. That's a lot for me. She was the woman I wanted and needed in my life," he explained.

"Yes. Don't remind me," Felicia chuckled.

"I know, too much information sharing. I get it. You don't want any more exposure to my life as a bachelor than you already knew about. I love her with all of me."

"You expected her to choose you over her father?"

"Yes," he shot back instantly.

"Would you choose someone over me?" she asked.

Hearing the words shocked Tellum. He'd never thought about that.

"No, never. You or dad would never ask any of us to make such a choice. You would allow us to choose who we wanted to choose."

"I am not Joe, and neither is your father. He isn't the most likable man, but he is her father."

"He has an unhealthy hold on Cheyenne. I would never be able to break through that. I didn't ask her to choose. I simply stood by and waited for her to love our love as much as I did."

"Despite who he is in the business world, she loves him. Most girls do love their fathers unconditionally. I think she chose devotion to him. I don't think she chose leaving you as much as it was something that ate away at her. She is hurting. She still loves and misses you. I saw it and heard it in her voice when she came to visit me. I don't believe it's completely over with the two of you. She couldn't breathe. She was being pulled in a million directions. She didn't choose you or her father; she chose peace; she chose herself."

"Why did choosing herself have to mean not choosing me? Cheyenne and I are perfect together. Well, we were perfect together. We're not together, so you know what, in my eyes, I lost."

"So, you've given up?"

Tellum was frustrated. Why was everyone asking him about giving up? His brothers, his father and his two best friends, Omari Clark and Tommy Johnson had been hitting him left and right with the same question.

"What am I supposed to do? It's been months. For weeks, I called, texted, emailed, sent her flowers and tried to talk to her. She won't talk to me."

"Son, I'll ask you again, are you giving up?"

Felicia stood, ready to leave.

"She spoke the words that we were through. I am respecting her decision."

"That's all I asked. Now I have my answer," she said.

Tellum rushed over to help her. He guessed their chat was over.

"Everyone has questions but no one's offering any suggestions about what I may be missing," he said, softly.

As they walked toward his office door, Felicia turned and faced him, reaching up to place her hands on both sides of his face.

"Son, I love you. I want nothing for you, but the greatest happiness life can bring. Right now, you are miserable because for the first time in your life, you feel like you lost at something. You have lived a life of always winning, coming out on top. You excelled in school, in sports, in business and yes, I shudder to say it, even with women over the years. Nothing escaped me with my sons and all the women. You're a catch, so I expected that. You are a winner at everything you have ever touched. You've always had a handle on your interactions with women, controlling that narrative. The heart can't and won't be controlled. You can search within it to find the answer. I don't care how many people ask you that question. If you truly believe Cheyenne is the woman for you, and I hope you still do, you will fight for her. I heard you once tell your brother that your hunger for her was nothing like you'd ever experienced with another woman. Prove it. I know you had originally planned this time away at the new resort with her. You were going to spend a week in paradise with her. Figure out how to still do that."

Tellum was stunned. His mother was telling him to cross the line in the sand.

"Away with me? I can't even get her to talk to me. You think she would share a romantic week with me at *Secret Whisper*? Did she tell you that?" he questioned.

"You're thinking too hard about this. It's not complicated. She doesn't have to share your bed with you. I swear, you men have a one-track mind. You can share your resort with her. You would have a week with her away from Captain Joe. There would be no tug-of-war on her loyalty. Figure it out. I have to run before your father comes looking for me. Call me when you are leaving and when you land in Atlanta. Be safe and most of all, get my Cheyenne back. I've had some time with her since your break-up, but not like before. I can tell that she wants to ask me questions about you, but she's afraid to. That woman loves you like crazy. She shouldn't have to choose between you and the hatred her father now has for this family. Be patient with what she is going through. It can't be easy. The heart is the most sensitive organ in the body. Yours is broken, but remember, so is hers."

"It's not easy for me either, but I hear you. I feel my wheels turning already. Thanks for always bringing the fire I always need for motivation," he said smiling.

"There it is. There is that smile I love to see on my son's handsome face. I have some issues with this beard, though. I get it's the thing now. I'll work on letting it grow on me."

Felicia kissed his cheek and then wiped off the pink lipstick she left there.

"I will call you when I get to the airport."

"Great."

"I love you, mom. I'm glad you paid me a visit."

"Good. Then stop being an ogre to your staff and get it together. Yes, I heard murmurs as I walked through the office to speak to everyone. One day, I'm going to need a lot of beautiful grandchildren from you and Cheyenne."

"A lot?" he chuckled.

"A whole lot. I don't encourage out of wedlock children, so don't misunderstand what I'm about to say. I really do not understand how there aren't a million little Blackstones running around. I know how my sons are. I have heard the stories, to my chagrin."

Tellum laughed so hard, tears flowed down his face.

"That's a lot more than I want to hear from my mother," he exclaimed.

"Grandchildren, Tellum. Lots and lots of grandchildren. I'm ready to spend all of my time with them. That's all I have to say."

Tellum was ready to respond, but her words had come out too quick. Before he could say a word about her reference to grandchildren, she was through the door and chatting up Lisa-Marie. She left him standing in his office doorway with his mouth hanging open.

He had no words when she winked at him. He smiled and winked back. No one had a more beautiful and caring mother than he did.

When his cell phone, which sat on his desk, pinged, he knew it was Byrum calling from the resort. He was expecting his call. He raced back to his desk, grabbed it and found himself in a better mood. His mother was right – it was time he got his woman back. He already knew how to do it. His plan was playing over in his mind as he answered the phone.

"Byrum, let me hear it. We're good to go for the launch?" he asked.

With new enthusiasm running through his body, Tellum sat behind his desk. He leaned back in his chair, raised his feet up on the desk and crossed them on the corner. He kicked himself for not thinking of a master plan before now. He was feeling good about it already. To encourage himself even more, he reached for the remote to the sound bar in his office.

It was connected to speakers in all four corners of the room. He searched his iPad for the perfect song.

Seconds later, his office was filled with the sound of the classic rap song, *Thinking of a Master Plan*, by Eric B. and Rakim. He rapped along with the lyrics while Byrum ran the latest down to him.

3

Cheyenne couldn't believe the late hour. Her plan after teaching her high-velocity steppers aerobic dance class was to get back to her office. Working as a marketing executive for a pharmaceutical company kept her busy with early mornings and sometimes, late evenings. Most days, she didn't leave the office until ten or eleven at night. With all the extra time on her hands since her relationship with Tellum ended, she needed the classes she taught to help fill her days. They also helped to occupy her mind. The impact of how much she missed him weighed on her heavily day in and day out. Today, was an especially hard day. By now, she was supposed to be shopping and picking out as many sexy bathing suits and elegant yet suggestively intimate underwear as she could afford for a week in paradise with him. Instead, she was making a mental note to give back the week of vacation she would have been on during that time, a little over a week away. She and Tellum were no longer a couple and would not be going away together.

"Great class, Cheyenne!"

She heard that sentiment, in the midst of her daydreams, from several class participants as they walked by her to leave the early evening class. Her evening classes were two times a week. She also hosted a different type of session for the morning. Three days a week before the sun rose and before she headed into the office, she was at, *The M-O Spot*, teaching her yoga classes at one of two Detroit locations her best friend, Melodi O'Neal owned. Working out was her second favorite activity after her first love of dance.

This evening, when she arrived, she looked around for Melodi only to find that she was out at a business meeting regarding expanding her gym into several office parks around town. Her gyms were two of the most popular because they catered to women only. There were no men allowed, which took the pressure off of woman feeling the need to always be *'on'* in the presence of men. Here, they could let their hair down, come with no make-up and not worry about the few extra pounds being seen that they were working on losing. Luckily, Melodi's partner in life, love and business, Stephen, had an option for men with his two all-male gym locations, each directly across the street from Melodi's gyms. That way, men and women were not too far apart from each other, especially couples who enjoyed working out. One night a week, Stephen's gym did host a couples workout night, but not a Melodi's locations. They were also in the center of a lot of dating hotspots in Detroit that satisfied anyone's cravings for meeting and hanging out with the opposite sex.

"Thanks everyone!" she happily replied as they filed out. Tonight, she had a full class of over forty people.

She met Melodi five years ago when she was on the hunt for a gym to have a yoga party for her twenty-fifth birthday. The popular *M-O Spot*, named for Melodi's initials, had been recommended to her by another friend. The night of her party at the gym had been an amazing one.

Joining the gym a month later led to them becoming best friends. Four months later, she had stepped in for the yoga instructor of the class she participated in, who was leaving to help out with her sister who had a terminal illness. At first, she declined due to her hectic work schedule. Melodi offered her the chance to make her own schedule after her popularity soared once she began filling in for the original instructor. She decided to give it a try for a few weeks to see how things would go. It didn't take long for her to decide she loved the outlet. Not only did she continue teaching yoga, but she created several other classes that became just as popular. More instructors and more classes were added. Membership at the gym grew, which allowed Melodi to open her second location.

Her own yoga class was moved from the smaller workout room to the largest room when her class number outgrew the smaller space. She now taught classes three times a week at six in the morning before work and two times at the end of the workday, around dinner time. Once a month, she held a class on Saturday evening, which was her most popular time with members. There was a long list of people waiting to get in. Though she initially refused Melodi's offer to put her on the payroll, she finally agreed when her one class a week grew to a crazy size.

Her love for the gym started back in college where she was a member of the dance team. She also played volleyball. She had to stay in shape. Yoga came about after graduating from Morgan State University in Baltimore, Maryland. She needed the outlet to get through her wild homelife, something she rarely shared with people. Being the daughter of Joseph Reddick was not an easy one; not for her or her mother, Ramona, who had more patience than she could ever have.

Her father was a lot. It took a lot to be his daughter. Still, she loved him. He made sure she had everything she needed. He also provided most of what she wanted in life. He had never let her down.

When she wanted a car in high school, he didn't do like most fathers would do. He didn't get her a used clunker to get her back and forth. He took her to a BMW car dealership. She drove away with a brand new, white with cream interior BMW 328Xi. That was unheard of in the heart of Detroit. Her father enjoyed giving her the best. When she decided on Morgan for college, he never batted an eye when it came to the out-of-state tuition. He even allowed her to move off campus in her sophomore year and into her own apartment with a friend from their hometown. He easily paid all the bills for undergraduate and graduate school at Morgan. Not once did she have to worry about anything.

Cheyenne checked the time as she grabbed the broom to sweep up her dance room. She turned the music up a little louder. Now that she was alone, she turned it to one of her favorite songs by Daniel Caesar featuring H.E.R., *Best Part*. She moved about the room swinging her hips as she swept. She wondered where Melodi was. They had plans to connect before she ran back to her office. She didn't mind that Melodi was a little late. She knew that, eventually, their conversation would turn to Tellum. She wasn't ready for that. She was still suffering from the impact of not waking up in his arms several times a week. That was their norm when they were together. She still remembered the day they met over a year ago while she was out with friends enjoying a much-needed ladies' night out. Usually, she was against being picked up by men on a night when she only wanted to enjoy her girlfriends. That night was different. The moment she saw that Tellum only had eyes for her, she couldn't resist falling for his charm. There wasn't a woman alive who didn't know who Tellum Blackstone was. Whenever all of that sexiness he exuded entered a room, he owned it. Tellum commanded attention without asking for it. The man was gorgeous. Women made plays for him the entire night, but every time she looked up, his eyes were on her. Her girlfriends joked her about it for an hour. When she wasn't paying attention, he sauntered up behind her as she moved on the dance floor. He didn't get too close, but close enough to whisper an invitation to dance in her ear. She nodded yes and turned around to face him. For the rest of the night, they were inseparable.

There was one thing about Tellum that she was well aware of just as other women had been, his prowess in bed was legendary, and not just around Detroit. Women always talked sexually about men. That wasn't just a conversation that men had with each other about women. Even now, she shivered at the way he loved on her almost to the point of exhaustion. She could never seem to get enough of him. The only way to escape craving him again and again was to go to sleep. He was that good at pleasuring her.

Before getting with him, she'd heard rumors about how his body played a woman's body like a saxophonist would his instrument. He was a man who knew his way around all the curves of her body. She missed him with everything in her. She also knew that the only person to blame that she only had memories, was herself. He was unforgettable.

Tellum was six-feet-six, all muscle and sexiness. His dark mocha complexion was without blemishes. Most times he was neatly shaved with a sexy goatee. Other times, he was raw and just as sexy after waking in the morning or after a few days without worrying about his appearance when they spent lazy weekends together. The man wore suits like they were made specifically for his gorgeous body. She enjoyed watching him walk with his long, self-assured strides. Though he often complimented her on how sexy her ass was, she enjoyed holding onto his steely behind when they made love. There wasn't a part of him that she hadn't enjoyed.

Cheyenne closed her eyes and remembered the first time they were together. After meeting that first night, he had called her at work the next day to ask her out to dinner. Two days later, they were out on their first date. They had enjoyed dancing before, so he chose a nice restaurant that had a live band where they could dance again. Tellum had mentioned that he couldn't wait to hold her in his arms again like he'd done the night they met. After dinner, they had danced the night away. Their bodies moved together as one to fast and slow songs. His eyes would capture hers and in them, she saw what she felt, lust. Her heady desire was immeasurable. She hadn't dated anyone in over a year. That meant she also had not been intimate with anyone. She had a rule about not jumping into bed with a man until she was sure there was more to what he offered besides sex. She broke her own rule that night with Tellum. Her vow to keep her legs closed until she knew she was going to invest time and energy in a man did not apply to Tellum. He was too irresistible.

When they left the restaurant, he drove her home. They parked in the condo parking lot for guests across the street. Once they walked to the elevator in her building away from prying eyes, he kissed her and stole away all means of thinking she'd ever had. Her mind could only focus on the feel of his lips and tongue as he loved her mouth with a scandalous hunger. She was so into the kiss that she lost all track of time standing there practically clawing at him to give her even more. It wasn't until the elevator doors opened for the fourth or fifth time that they finally moved away from each other. An older woman had exited the elevator, glared at them and cleared her throat, drawing their attention away from each other. She had taken a few moments to try and gather herself until, without words, Tellum's eyes found her lips. The way he looked at them was like a hunter setting eyes on his prey. His eyes conveyed a commanding look of desirous pleasure. The next thing she knew, before the elevator doors could close again, she stepped inside and signaled for him to join her with a welcoming finger. Tellum had moved with a quickness. Pulling her body snug against his, he lifted her up after the door closed behind them. Using both hands, he wrapped her legs around his waist and pressed her back against the wall. She was glad that the little red dress she wore to dinner gave her room to spread her legs. Boy, had she done that.

Cheyenne laid the broom against the wall of the gym and fanned herself while she reminisced about that night. The slow, seductive music wooed her mind back to that night with a fierce determination to not let her forget. This time, she closed her eyes and vividly saw Tellum's handsome face in her head.

In the elevator that night, the minute her womanhood encountered something very hard and long between them, her rule of no sex shortly after meeting someone was out of the door. They had known each other only a few days. The way he'd already mesmerized her had her mind racing with the most sexually shameful thoughts of what she'd like to do to him; to all of him. In the next moment, they were tearing at each other in an elevator. It was wild and crazy. She was a happy, willing participant.

As quickly as the kissing had started up in the elevator, it had stopped. Tellum slid her down from his body. That moment had her questioning if going at his mouth like a moth to a flame was the right move for her. She wanted him with desire that she'd never encountered before. She also wanted more than just amazing sex. Maybe he, for some reason, saw her in another light that wasn't impressive. After a few moments of silence, Tellum spoke before she could get words of an apology out for the way she turned into a she-devil the minute the elevator closed. He shared with her that he wanted her, but needed her to know that he wasn't offering her any kind of commitment. He wanted her to decide what would happen between them next knowing that it was all casual. He was a busy man and didn't make time for relationships. She knew about the business conglomerate he'd built with his brothers. She assumed he didn't have much time for anything else. There was no way she had gotten this hot and bothered to just walk away. She felt him. She wanted him. The kiss demanded that he leave her as satisfied as she'd heard he was good at. She wanted to know for herself. He said no commitment and she was down for that. She wasn't much for casual sex, but this was Tellum Blackstone. He was every woman's sexy dream man. Tonight, she would forget that she was looking for more than a man to stoke her desires. She would get a night with Tellum. Her body was telling her to forget about rules. She wanted hot, tempting and out of this world sex. Everything about Tellum said that she would get that with him. She would deal with the guilt of giving in once the morning hit. No one would know but them.

When the elevator doors opened on her floor, he let her decide. She didn't give it another thought when she nodded her head yes and took him by the hand to her door at the end of the hall. Once inside, she'd had the hottest sex of her entire life. The sex she'd had after losing her virginity while away at college was nothing compared to what Tellum had put on her that night. He was in a class by himself.

Before she could gather her thoughts after locking the door behind them, Tellum had her thong off in seconds. He then lifted her body high up on the wall as he buried his face between her legs. She'd never had a man go down on her in a way that sent her over the edge in rapid succession before. They had been in her place for a few minutes, and she had exploded faster than a fighter jet could fly. Before the night ended, she had lost count of the number of orgasms he'd given her. The first one against the wall was so powerful, that she still remembered hitting her head against the wall when her release slammed into her like the waves of a tsunami. Within seconds, his mouth on her had sent shock waves through her a second time. He had her screaming out her desire at the top of her lungs. Minutes later, as his mouth loved hers again, he'd had somehow, without her taking note, put on a condom, spread her legs while bracing her against the wall and entered her. When she felt his size, her legs tensed. He rubbed them to relax her, letting her know that he would fit. He damn sure did. Her legs felt like rubber afterward, but it was well worth it.

Cheyenne remembered the way he moved his body meticulously with expert precision. She wished like never before that she would have been able to see his body move in a mirror. She knew it had to be masterful. She looked down where their bodies were joined and watched his hips pump and grind slowly, hitting every spot on and in her body that needed to be stroked. Watching his movements alone had her on the brink of yet her next explosive release. Tellum was too damn sexy.

What she could never forget was the delicious soreness of the morning after. Sexually, she was out of shape. She barely made it through her early Saturday morning yoga class without images of Tellum filling her head. He was an experience that no woman could ever forget about even if she tried. She should know. That was how it started, and it never stopped.

Cheyenne stopped moving to the music remembering how everything with Tellum had come to an end. She spent the first month after not being with him crying herself to sleep every night. The only person who knew that she spent her nights like that was Melodi. Her father didn't care. He only wanted to know that she had done as he had commanded.

Her mother never said a word. She wasn't a fighter when it came to Captain Joe either. He controlled everything. He could be mean and abrasive. There were also times when he was mentally and emotionally abusive. Her mother had found a place of peace in their marriage that required her to just be quiet and let him have his way. Cheyenne knew that her way of dealing with him was just like that.

At the age of thirty, she was still allowing him to control her life. She didn't know what else to do. That was why she chose to work harder and longer at the office. Most of her free time was spent at the gym to avoid going home alone every night.

"What's got you looking so serious?"

Cheyenne put thoughts of her trauma behind her and turned to Melodi who had finally shown up.

"Nothing. I was about to give up on you. I thought you were going to take my class tonight," she mentioned.

"Girl, there is no room for me in your class. I wish there was a way to clone you and double the number of your classes. You have the most popular class at my gym. How was tonight?" Melodi asked.

"It was good. It was packed in here. After you made it clear that anyone who missed two classes without notification would be dropped so that another person could get in, no one has missed a class in a month. How did your business meeting go? I see you're still in your black and white power suit."

"It went great. I think things are going to work out with these two companies. Each are building in-office gyms and want to partner with me and Stephen. We're going to talk about it later tonight before and after sex and then decide!"

"That's more than I asked for. Why must you continue to throw your every night of sex in my face? You know my sex life right now is bone dry!" Cheyenne declared.

She reached for the broom again and faked like she was still sweeping.

"Because there was a time when I was jealous of all the nasty, sexy sex you and Tellum were having, though you would never talk about it. I would roll my eyes every time I saw you walking like you'd had a night of blissful love making. Now, you get to be jealous of me because you made a terrible life decision, but that's just my opinion."

Melodi huffed at her. Cheyenne crossed her arms over the black mini-bra portion of her yoga outfit. She tapped her foot annoyed that Melodi was still throwing that kind of shade in her face. If they weren't friends, she would have been pissed. The real point was, Melodi was right. She couldn't complain about that.

"You know why I did. You also know my father. He's Captain Joe. No one says no to him," she explained.

"Oh really? Well, Mr. Blackstone sure knew how to say no."

"Melodi!" Cheyenne shouted at the low blow.

"I'm sorry if that was disrespectful. Tellum's father had no problem using that word with conviction. Look, I'm not the biggest fan of your father and you know that. Hell, I'm not too big on your mother for allowing your father to bully you the way he does, but I get it. He does her the same way. I abhor his dismissive disrespect when it comes to the two of you. I say this with love as your friend, not to hurt your feelings. You and I both know you love Tellum like crazy. You miss him. I miss him for you. I loved your love. I don't like seeing you this miserable when you don't have to be. I hate that you avoid all the places the two of you loved to go to just so that you could avoid him. I've seen him out a few times when Stephen and I venture out on the town. I can tell he's always looking to see if you're with me. What are you afraid of if you see him?"

"Wanting him."

"You should want him. You're in love with him. You're always in the car playing the sappiest love songs. I heard the music when I first walked in."

Cheyenne felt the weight of her own words as she inhaled deeply and slid to the floor against the wall. Before she could stop herself, she cried softly. She was still doing that whenever she thought about how her heart hurt. She needed to know when the hurt would end. She watched Melodi close and lock the door to the room before joining her on the floor. Cheyenne laid her head on Melodi's shoulder.

"I hurt so bad. I miss him so much. I have to honor my father, though. He's the only one I have. He was ready to disown me if I didn't disassociate with Tellum and his family. Money wise, my father is in a bad way, according to my mother. She said he's always on a rampage. I try to visit her when he's at work. He's not broke or anything. He still does well, but he is looking at the wealth that Tellum, his brothers and their father have in comparison. He wants that. He won't say he's jealous of it. All he can see is that Mr. Blackstone blocked his way to bigger wealth. What he doesn't see is how he's hurt himself over the years. I know my father's business dealings haven't always been on the up-and-up. I think he thought the deal with *General Motors* would make him more legit."

"Sis, you chose wrong. Look, I know you thought you were doing what you should as his daughter. It was wrong for him to make your life about him. One had nothing to do with the other. I'm sad for you."

Cheyenne reached for her phone which vibrated in her gym bag next to her. When she reached for it, she looked to Melodi and then back to her phone.

"It's an email from Tellum," she said.

"Read it," Melodi demanded.

Cheyenne looked at her sideways at the strong tone and forcefulness behind the words.

She did and read it out loud.

"Hi Cheyenne. I hope you're well. It's hard not seeing or talking to you, but I do understand why. I'm not writing about that. I don't want to put any pressure on you. I love you way too much to ever do that. I am respecting the boundary you have set. I do want to extend an invitation to you that I hope you will consider. As you know, my brothers and I are launching the new Secret Whisper resort in the Dominican Republic next week. You were scheduled to join me for the week for that launch before the relationship ended. I'm writing to personally invite you to the launch. Before you delete the email, please read on. I'd like for you and Melodi to come as guests to check out the resort. You were already scheduled to have the week off and so did she. If you are still free, I hope you will come and check everything out. Next week is by invitation only because we are looking for honest feedback on all of our amenities. I would still love your feedback. I have two over the water bungalows reserved, one for you and one for Melodi. It's all expenses paid, including your first-class air travel. I've included information on everything you need to know. The flight is reserved, though you have to do your own check-in and security clearance. The resort is all inclusive and there is a lot to do, especially the spa, which I know you were looking forward to enjoying. I promise to not be in the way. I know you work hard and could use the time away. I hope you will consider it and join us. I still value your opinion. I know you would be honest in your review and survey responses. Everything is reserved under your two names. You don't have to reach to me directly if you plan to go. I promise, as I stated, I will stay out of your way. I think you will enjoy it. Think about it. Yes, I will be there. If you don't want to be bothered by me, which is your desire and I respect it, I will stay sight, but unseen. Thanks for all of the support you gave me as my brothers, and I continued to make our dreams come true. Having you in my corner meant everything to me; it still does. I missed you like crazy.
I still love you very much.
Love, Tellum."

Cheyenne didn't realize she was holding her breath in while she read until she finished and released it with a heavy sigh.

"Girl! You broke up with him and we still get a free week in the Dominican Republic? Are you serious? Tell me we're going. Please tell me we're going. A free week in paradise where we know a bunch of sexy men will be?"

Cheyenne leaned back and looked her up and down.

"You're involved with Stephen!" she shouted. "Why are you talking about sexy men!"

"It doesn't hurt to look and admire even if I don't dabble. Now, if by chance I do dabble, what happens in paradise, stays in paradise."

"You mean you're not taking Stephen with you?" she asked.

"Hell no! Besides, he needs to be here to look after the gyms. I need some time away. We could use time apart anyway."

"What about all your hot sex with him at night? You'll be gone for a week."

Cheyenne's eyes followed Melodi as she stood.

"I didn't say anything about missing out on hot sex. Didn't I just say what happens in paradise stays in paradise? Besides, you may find a hot, sexy man while you're there. Oh wait, we already know of one who will be there, don't we? His name is Tellum Blackstone, the love of your life! Then again, there is Reed Howard. He's a snake, but I know he has the hots for you. He has, especially since you and Tellum parted ways."

"Definitely not Reed. I saw him at my favorite coffee spot about a week ago. He was talking about the resort. His family owns one of the airlines that will be in partnership with the resort when it comes to flying guests there. He's going during the invitation-only launch week."

"Did he ask you to go with him? I hate that sneaky bastard. He's been pushing up on you hard since your breakup with Tellum. The two of them used to be friends. Not best friends, but still, friends. The way he's been trying to slide in is disgusting. I told you he was lusting after you the whole time you dated Tellum. Too bad he doesn't have charm and personality to go along with all that money."

Cheyenne bit her bottom lip. Everything Melodi was saying about Reed was true. The man was relentless in his pursuit of her. She kindly declined all of his advances. She wasn't ready to date. If she was, it would never be with him. There was a time when he and Tellum were cordial until Tellum discovered Reed had secretly lusted after her without caring that they were involved.

"He actually did, and I turned him down. He asks me out all the time. He even sent flowers to my office with a dinner invitation a few weeks ago. I never responded to that, though I did send a thank you note to his office for the flowers. He's persistent."

"But in the worse way. He knows your history with Tellum. His family's airline has done a lot of good partnerships with Tellum and his brothers' other resorts. He knows the two of you were involved. The minute he found out it was over, he was all over you. Admit it; he's the worst kind of pursuer."

"No worries. It never crossed my mind to go out with him or even go with him to the resort. That would be hella disrespectful to Tellum. I wouldn't do that to him. I wouldn't be with any man in his face. It's not time yet to even think about another man. Tellum is still very much in my system."

"See? Love. So, are we going? Do I need to let Stephen know how busy he will be while I'm away? If so, tell me right now. Then, let's hit up a few boutiques tomorrow for some sexy gear. We work on these gorgeous shapes every day. I want to show mine off! Well?" Melodi asked.

Cheyenne thought about it. Melodi's pleading wasn't for naught. She could definitely use the week off. She still hadn't told her team that she wasn't going to be off that week. She'd had it on the books since before she and Tellum broke up. That meant, her vacation week was still a go as far as the job was concerned. She still wanted to support Tellum. He worked hard for the wealth and status he'd built. She respected how he did it the honest way. Could she be at the resort for a week and not run into Tellum? Is that even possible? It was his resort. Still, she wanted to see all the work he'd put into it.

They had spent many sleepless nights talking about everything the resort would be. He had taken her on a few trips to other resorts to see what worked and didn't work at those locations. He wanted to provide the very best for his own guests. She'd even visited the new resort with him during the development stage. She loved all that she'd seen. During her last visit, she could see that a lot had been put into the luxury that the resort would provide. She wanted to see how it all turned out. She hadn't seen him in person in about six months. She had to find a way to exist in life without avoiding him. Perhaps, now was the time.

"I am already off that week. I could use some time away. We could have some fun. Besides, it's all paid for," Cheyenne said, working through the idea in her head and out loud.

"Chick, stop playing with me. I'm going home to start looking through what I'm taking. You may not go, but I'm going. He said I have my own private over-the-water bungalow. I hate to leave you behind, but I will if you make me. What will it be? Are you going?"

Cheyenne stood, turned off the music and whipped her neck around at Melodi in the playful way they sometimes responded to each other.

"Girl, you are not going to paradise without me. Yes, I'm going. I do need some new bathing suits. I took a quick look at the itinerary for the week that Tellum included in his email. We need some colors for different events. Shopping tomorrow after work?" she asked.

"I'm thinking of shopping all day tomorrow. Take a slick day and join me!" Melodi cheered.

Cheyenne loved the idea. She seldom did it but knew that the time was right to do so. She was going to paradise. She was going to see Tellum. They may not be together, but she still wanted to knock his socks off with what she planned to wear.

"I'm down! Slick day it is!"

4

"Leavin' on a jet plane…"

"Shut up Callum. I do not need to be serenaded while I'm on the plane," Tellum yelled playfully into the speaker phone in front of him. He was alone aboard one of their company's two private Gulfstream G280 jets as it glided thirty-eight thousand feet in the air. All he could see outside of the window were visions of clouds above and below. He was relaxed in one of the nine cream-colored leather seats on the single seat side of the plane. On the opposite side, the seats were double. In the back, there was a lounger for easier relaxing that splayed out like a bed for rest during much longer flights. In the front of the plane, Captain Smitty flew him effortlessly through the air toward the *Secret Whisper* resort. Both of his brothers were already there to work on last minute details for the official launch. He was the last of them to arrive because of meetings he wanted to handle in person back at the office.

"You mean you don't enjoy my singing voice? I hear some say I sound like Teddy Pendergrass. Remember him? Mom used to play his songs throughout the house when we were growing up," Callum said.

"Yeah, I do, but I've never heard you sound anything close to him. I do remember a few dogs howling when they heard you singing though. Didn't you get a restraining order once demanding that you stop riling up the neighborhood animals with that voice?" Tellum joked.

"Whatever. The neighbors were just jealous. I'm glad you're finally on your way. Everything kicks off tomorrow, so you'll have tonight to take a look around and make changes that you want. In my opinion, Byrum has done a great job with the launch details in your absence thanks to the best event planner in the world. You really know some people. Vivica, same name as and just as sexy as the actress, but in a different line of work, put her foot in this launch. From the cakes to the drinks to the decorations; it's all top of the line. Tell me, is she someone who's had the Tellum experience?" Callum kidded.

Tellum laughed, but not loud enough to be heard. He hated when his brothers referenced him that way. He knew he had a reputation with the ladies. The Tellum experience was one of several ways women referenced him. He was creeped out when his brothers brought it up. Besides the fact that his name was unique, so he couldn't be mistaken for another man when women spoke of him, he had hoped to outlive any name he was called other than his given name. He remembered the times of getting with women just for hookups. That was until he met Cheyenne. She changed the game for him without even trying. He was never going back to the bed hopper he was before her. He still wanted only her. Until he either got her back into his life or eventually moved on to another woman, he was steering clear of any casual encounters. He couldn't handle it right now. His heart still ached for the woman it still belonged to.

"The answer is no, I have never hooked up with Vivica. I don't do that with every woman I meet," he declared.

"Really? She's gorgeous. I was sure you had at some point. Not even after you and Cheyenne broke things off?"

"Callum, seriously, stop. No. We didn't break things off, she broke up with me; there is a difference. Yes, Vivica is gorgeous, but I'm not interested. Besides, have you seen her linebacker boyfriend? She's not available. Don't you even try sliding up next to her," Tellum warned.

"Okay, I won't keep poking the bear. That's code for you and her. I know how you can growl when you lose patience. Byrum, you're awfully quiet," Callum said.

"I was waiting for you two kids to finish chatting about women. How long until you get here?" Byrum asked him.

"We're about three hours out. I was delayed in taking off. There was also a delay in clearance to take off."

"It's the weekend, so that's expected," Byrum answered.

"How is everything going?"

Tellum had been trying to catch up with all of the emails with photos both brothers had been sending him over the past few days. He was impressed with it all.

"We are more than ready, bro. All of the transportation vehicles are cleared. We have twenty-five twelve passenger vans with plenty of space for luggage. Hosea, who has complete responsibility of transportation services and his team of forty, are all set to give our guest the best treatment available. All drivers are cleared with the proper credentials. The change in uniforms that you wanted, going from brown slacks to navy, was completed as well. That way, they are dressed completely different from the bell boys who will stay in the brown ones. We also have a fleet of ten limousines for special occasions that have all cleared inspection. We have the black smaller car service as well. Our SUV transportation vehicles are for our executive team only. There will be one at the airport to pick you up when you arrive. I want you to see what it feels like to ride in one of the new ones. Call or text me when you're thirty minutes out. The butlers are of course, in all white uniforms. We did work out the contracts for them to be in service from six in the morning until eight in the evening. Most resorts do a shorter day, but we wanted out services to our clients extended. Vivica and her team have the tropical theme on lock everywhere. She went above and beyond. How did you find her?" Byrum asked.

"I went to Essence Fest in New Orleans last year. She was the event planner for one of the events I had gone to. It was amazing and everyone gave her rave reviews. I reached out when I knew we were looking for that type of service. I didn't know if she traveled this far for work. When I passed her contact information to our marketing and promotion teams, they said she was immediately interested. The contract details worked on both sides. That included paying to cover her and her team to be at the resort for the past two weeks and for the upcoming week to handle the big events each night. I'm thinking that we should have our team talk to her about a long-term relationship with her company. If you like what she's done, I'm already sold," Tellum explained with jubilance.

"Yeah, wait until you see it all. There will be warm wet towels when each guest arrives. Wine, champagne and bottled water will be offered when they exit their transport vehicle. There are trays of cookies, cupcakes, fresh fruit and pastries upon arrival as guests are waiting to be checked in. That's an expedited process. I'm looking forward to seeing how everything unfolds. Our hospitality crew members are all smiles and teeth. I won't even start on the food. Wait until you see what we're offering. I am extremely impressed with our around-the-clock, no contact room service and concierge service," Byrum explained.

"All sounds good. The rooms are all complete with in-wall televisions which also double as computers for those who need it? Plenty of USB outlets, plugs and all the other amenities we added after conducting tons of surveys of what guests would like to see? This isn't our first resort, but I'm bucking for it to be our best. You both know that after this, we'll need to make some upgrades to our current resorts. These are top shelf accommodations with our over-the-water villas. I remember visiting when those were first constructed. I loved everything about them, especially the wider boardwalk that leads to each one. The best idea, without taking away from the beauty of the resort, is the fencing in the water that prevents wildlife from venturing close to the villas for those who love to swim in the ocean. I can't wait to see the final product," Tellum said.

He'd been up most of the evening the night before checking out videos and tons of other footage that had been sent over the past week. He happily signed off on everything, though he wasn't there to see it in person. His favorite part of the resort was definitely the landscaping and the eight individually designed swimming pools. They spared no expense when it came to *Secret Whisper*.

"You will be overly impressed, trust me. When I arrived two days ago and got my first whiff of a difference from when I was here a month ago, I couldn't believe my eyes," Callum acknowledged.

"We have the press all set for the entire week? I want them to capture everything," Tellum said.

"Yes. We had an overwhelming response from all media outlets. Every guest had to sign a release before travel arrangements were provided for them. They agreed that we can use their images in video and photo formats on any and all platforms. Some have already arrived and checked in. The entertainment for the next two nights has arrived. The rest will arrive throughout the week. Some of the hottest in music is here and ready for an incredible week. No stone was left unturned. Everything we thought of is here. You'll see shortly," Callum added.

Tellum was already impressed. He couldn't wait to land and see for himself. They had secured enough guests for every room. All were attending at no expense to them. He could hardly wait to get their reaction. Though that was high on his list, there was one guest in mind he particularly wanted to know about. He'd extended the invitation. He didn't expect to hear back directly but hoped that she would take him up on his offer.

The plan before the breakup had been for them to share the bungalow he reserved for himself with a rooftop mini pool for two overlooking the ocean. Now that things have changed between them, he had a romantic bungalow all to himself with no romance on the agenda. Imagine that. A man with his status and he will be spending the week in his bed alone.

"What about our other guests? How are those reservations going? Anyone decline? Have you heard from everyone who was invited?" Tellum asked.

He was trying to be subtle without actually coming out and saying her name. He could hear Callum chuckling on the other end. He knew why. The three of them were close, but Callum was the one who could read him like a book.

"Really, Tell? That's how you going to play me? I have the list right here. All you have to do is ask me," Callum jested playfully.

"Can you stop taunting him for once in your life?" Byrum interjected.

"No, I can't. Did you know he sent out a special invitation? I didn't even know we had two bungalows available. It appears our dear brother had requested that two of them remain available. Would you like to guess why and for who?" he questioned.

"Jackass!" Tellum yelled into the speaker phone.

"Yeah, but I have the information you want. You have to say it. Come on, you can do it. Say her name, say her name," Callum chanted and laughed. He knew he didn't sound like Destiny's Child, but those words came from one of their favorite songs of his.

Tellum waited knowing his brother wasn't going to let him off the hook.

"Why do you have to be this way? I don't understand it. Did mom or dad drop you on your head when you were little? Did you miss your chance at being a comedian? We know you weren't cut out to be an R&B singer no matter how good you think you sound trying to croon," Tellum said, trying to persuade him.

"Alright, big brother. You can continue to try and insult me if you want to, but I'll hang up this phone and not say a word. That means you'll have to wait until you get here to find out. What's that, three hours or so away, when I know it's eating at you right now?" Callum continued.

"Whatever. When I see you, you're going to wish that you'd told me without me having to jump through your annoying hoops," Tellum reprimanded.

"Say and do whatever you like. I can run as fast as you can. You weren't the only long-distance runner in this family in high school and college. You'd have to catch me. So, what's it going to be?"

Tellum felt his blood boiling. He was picturing his brother tapping on the face of his imaginary watch as if he was really counting down the minutes.

"Did she RSVP? Did Cheyenne reach out to reservations to say she accepted my invitation?" he finally asked and waited anxiously.

"Ugh, finally. Was it really that hard? We all know you have a Jones for that woman. We don't blame you. If there was ever a picture of perfection in looks, intelligence and overall incredible vibe, it would be you and Cheyenne. To answer your question, yes, she did reach out to reservations to confirm she would be here for the week. She arrives tomorrow morning, pretty early. She's coming with Melodi. Their bungalows are ready. I saw the list of what you wanted to be sure was in them. I checked into that the minute I heard she was coming. Everything is all set. They are getting the top-of-the-line treatment. And, their butlers are both women, per your request. What was the problem? Did you think one of our male butlers would make a play for her?" Callum joked.

"Not on your life. I just happen to know Cheyenne. She would want a woman."

"Besides, our butlers are not who Tellum needs to worry about. *Ain't* that right, brother?" Byrum asked.

Just like that, Tellum went from being happy to being aggressively angry. He wished there had been a way to uninvite someone, but this was about business. The visit of his foe was to help promote the resort on their airline website and in other marketing promotions.

"He's still coming, huh?" he asked.

"Yes, Reed is still coming. I heard that he sent a huge bouquet of flowers to Cheyenne not too long ago. He's still making a play for her?" Byrum said.

"What if he's made some progress? How will that turn out with you inviting her and him? Reed wasn't supposed to come, but he couldn't pass up the opportunity to show and prove. He'll be here showing off all week. I'm sure we'll hear him talking like a rich kid with his father's money," Callum suggested.

"That may be him, but his wealth is no different than ours," Tellum said.

"Oh, yes, it is. I know you're not taking up for this clown who is trying his hardest to make a play for your woman. Besides, we built our company through hard work and diligence. Yes, dad and our uncle gave us some seed money and loaned us more of our initial funding to get us started, but we paid them back even sooner than they expected. Reed has hardly worked a day in his life for his father's airline. He goes around from place to place, event to event to represent the company and reap the benefits of being rich, but it's not his riches. It's his daddy's money," Callum said.

"Sometimes wealth is just wealth," Tellum noted. "I would never take up for a man who goes after another man's woman. He was doing that even before Cheyenne broke up with me. I heard he's upped his game in making a play for her heart," he added.

Tellum heard himself say the words. He hoped against all hope that Cheyenne hasn't played into Reed's shenanigans. Like he had been, Reed was a playboy. What he did know was that Reed would never give up being that for Cheyenne or any other woman because that's just who he was. He knew that the guy he once called friend saw Cheyenne as a beautiful woman to conquer and to, of course, stick it to him. For some reason, Reed was in competition with him, and he didn't have a clue why. It had been like that for a few years. Tellum hated that he was now jealous of any man who may gain Cheyenne's attention. He still wanted her. He hoped that he would be able to convince her to give them another try despite her father's warning. He didn't know how he could compete against that. He was, however, willing to put his all into trying it.

"He better not try anything while he's at the resort. I don't want any drama. I'm picturing him trying to hit on her and you trying to literally tackle him. Promise me that there will be no fists thrown. You and I both know that Reed is not worth the effort. We're looking at a spectacular week of events, so no drama. Besides, you will have your woman on this island for an entire week. If you can't work your magic to get her back, perhaps you're not worthy," Byrum said.

Tellum nodded his head though neither brother could see him. Byrum had always been the voice of reason between the three of them. He spoke his truth because beating around the bush didn't amount to any reality.

"I hear you. More important than getting her back, I want her to have a good time. I know she could use this time of getting pampered. I would love a chance to talk to her about us, but I don't want to stress her out with it. It's all about letting her relax and enjoy the experience," he said.

"And if that includes the Tellum experience, that's all the better, right?" Callum exclaimed.

Tellum laughed this time. He knew that Callum never meant any hard, so it was all good.

"Yeah, that too. I can't lie. That woman does it for me. I've had women and you both know that. I've never had a woman like Cheyenne before, the full package. I would be a fool to let it all go."

"Hence the invite to her to come here. We know that was the purpose and it's all good. Do what you can to fight for your woman. Captain Joe is an even bigger clown than Reed is. That man may have money, but not much of it is honest money. Dad did what he had to do to make sure he didn't bring off-kilter business to his company. The trickle-down impact to his other business ventures was all his fault once it all came out. Not only should he not blame dad for that, but he should not have brought your relationship with his daughter into it. That came out of left field. Hasn't he always treated you well?" Byrum asked.

"He has, but he hasn't always been the nicest to Cheyenne or her mother. I think he was especially nice to me because he was always planning to use me to get to dad. He's a tyrant in all aspects of his life, not just business. There were many nights that she cried herself to sleep in my arms because of something he said or did. She feels an obligation to him that no child should ever experience. She'll be here with me for a week, even if it's not really with me. I'm going to shoot my shot with her again without her father around. Anyway, I'm going to get a little rest before we land. I only slept about an hour last night after looking over some work. I'll see you when I land."

The call ended and Tellum put all of the paperwork away. He turn-off and stored his laptop in his backpack. He set his watch to wake him in two hours before turning out all of the lights. He reclined his chair all the way back after turning the seat in front of him around so that he could rest his long legs on it. His last thoughts before sleep captured him were of Cheyenne. He was hoping he could get her to say yes again, this time to their love.

5

Deplaning and going through immigration and customs went as smooth as Cheyenne remembered it to be from the last time she had been in the Dominican Republic, Punta Cana to be exact. There was no way this trip was going to able to touch her last trip to the island with Tellum. The airport was hectic. She was ready to get to the resort to unpack and take it all in.

Wondering what was taking Melodi so long when she scuttered off to the ladies' room a few minutes ago. She was left looking after their luggage. She literally kept her eyes glued to them as one person after another offered to help her with everything. She declined and checked again for Melodi, finally seeing her rushing over.

"What took you so long? Was the bathroom line long?" she asked her as they walked up to the correct transportation line for the resort.

"No, not at all. I ran into a cute guy, and we chatted a little," she snickered.

"You've been here five minutes and you're already flirting?"

"Look at me, Cheyenne. I did not do all of this to not be approached by every hot-blooded man who sees me. Look at my ass in these jeans? I specifically wore a shorter, crop shirt so that my ass would pop! I got my hair, nails and makeup done to perfection. Trust me, I will milk this free trip for all it's worth. Not all of us is a natural, exotic like beauty like yourself. I have to work a little bit harder than you. I'm not complaining. Your beauty keeps me on my toes. I plan to be like this all week. Wait until you see the bathing suits I brought that really are just a bunch of strings strung together. I can't wait to get down to some skin. You know I'm not going to cheat on Stephen. A little flirting and being complimented won't hurt a thing."

Cheyenne wanted to comment, but all she could do was laugh. When she arrived at the airport in Detroit, she looked around for Melodi after texting her and not getting a response. She wanted to be sure she didn't miss their flight. She'd hardly recognized her when she finally did see her. If she didn't know better, she would have thought Melodi was preparing for a stroll down the runway for New York Fashion week. She had on movie star dark sunshades with diamond like frames. She'd gotten boxed braids, much like hers, but Melodi's were two-toned. When her friend strutted toward her in heels, she was done. She would have said it was too much if it wasn't Melodi she was looking at. She, herself chose a more lowkey look of a long flowing summer multi-colored skirt with a white tank top. She had her long-braided tresses pulled into a tight bun on the top of her head. Thankful for pre-check flight check-in, she wouldn't have to take her hair down for homeland security guards to check it for anything suspicious. She'd been through that before. She didn't like it, but she understood the need for extra security when flying.

"You'll have a lot of time for that. Remember, we have accommodations on the water. I have never experienced that before. I'm so ready to get there. I'm ready to unwind," Cheyenne said.

When Melodi nudged her, she turned in her direction.

"Is that the only reason you're excited to get there? Are you sure there isn't another reason?" Melodi so eloquently asked her.

"Don't start with me. We're here and all I want to do is relax," Cheyenne lied. She refused to share that with Melodi. She knew she would never hear the end of it if she admitted she desired to feel Tellum up close and personal again.

"You would relax even more with a little bit of Tellum in you, or perhaps a whole lot of him in you. Do you think you can really be in such a romantic setting with that man around and not make a beeline for even a little bit of him? I know you didn't pack a toy because of customs, which means, it's either Tellum, a hot guy from the island, Reed or the two or three finger express. If you want some of that man, get you some. You know you want to. I promise to not continue to bring it up, though. He's here, you're here. You miss him and I know he misses you. Do you, boo."

"Miss, step up," the officer asked her.

Before she could jump into yet another conversation about Tellum with her, Cheyenne moved forward and provided the information for their transportation to the resort. She was told that their limousine was waiting for them. Immediately, two men came over, dressed in the same navy-blue slacks and white shirts with the resort logo on them and gathered their luggage. Following them, she was surprised when an actual white limousine greeted them at the curb. She wondered if all guests got this kind of treatment or if this was all Tellum. She knew the latter was true. She was impressed as she stepped inside. There was champagne chilling along with chilled fruits and fresh vegetables with dip, her favorite. This was definitely a Tellum touch.

As they whizzed through traffic, she closed her eyes and enjoyed the silence that came with Melodi enjoying the champagne. Her thoughts turned to Tellum. After months of not seeing him, she couldn't wait to hopefully set her eyes on him again. She may have ended things, but nothing prevented him from living in her head all day and night. The nights were the worst. She had come to love waking up cocooned in his embrace in the morning. Nothing was better than having a man's strong arms holding her protectively close. They didn't spend every night together, but when they could, especially after work kept them away from each other for several days at a time, they would make the most of being together. Lately, the only company she had in bed were the many pillows on the opposite side. Men asking her out never changed, but not once had she even considered sharing a bed with another man when the only one she truly wanted was Tellum.

"Do you want any champagne?" Melodi asked. "We're a few minutes away from the resort according to the driver. His name is Manny. I think he likes you," she whispered.

"No thanks on all fronts. Do not spend the week trying to hook me up with anyone. Worry about yourself," she humorously declared.

"I already know I won't have to do that. You and I both know that given the opportunity, you and Tellum will be burning up some sheets. If not, you are out of your mind! You are in paradise. I can already smell love in the air. I'm thinking of calling Stephen to join me before the end of our time here. Don't tell me you're not thinking about riding your man from sun up to sun down. You don't have to answer. I already know."

Cheyenne didn't comment. They were best friends. They knew each other. Melodi hit that nail on the head. It was all she could think about. She didn't know if she should after being apart from him for so long. She didn't know what part of what they had she would be able to get back. For now, she just wanted to feel his arms around her again. She longed for the touch of his lips.

Silence rested between them as the car turned up into a long driveway. The large, massive gate of the resort came into view. As the car came to a stop, a man walked over to the driver before coming around to the back door and asking her and Melodi for their proof of reservation. He finally waved them through. Going up a white bricked driveway, they pulled up to the most magnificent entrance in white marble with gold accents.

The limousine door opened and two men helped them exit the car before going to get their luggage from the trunk. As they walked into the large open and welcoming lobby, two women walked over to them and again, they shared their reservation information. One of the women talked into a walkie talkie and just like that, people raced up to them to help with everything. She was informed that they were already checked-in and their bungalows were ready.

"I thought check-in wasn't until two," she questioned.

"Yes, usually it is. Mr. Blackstone said to make sure we showed you to your accommodations the minute you arrived. We have a golf-cart that will drive you to your home away from home. I am Maria. I will be the person you will call on all week for anything you need. Nothing is too great or too small. I will respond right away from seven in the morning until eight at night. After hours, if you call the concierge, you will still be able to get assistance."

"Can I get one of those colorful, fruity drinks before we head to the bungalow?" Cheyenne asked, pointing to the portable bar at the entrance to the lobby.

Maria nodded and walked her right over. She saw Melodi talking a mile a minute to the woman who would be her closer-than-skin female butler for the duration. She knew that by week's end, the poor woman would be sick of Melodi.

After ordering a daiquiri, she turned just in time to catch a glimpse of Byrum, who was too far away for her to call his name without having to yell. She missed each of them, not just Tellum. Byrum and Callum were like brothers she didn't know she needed. Since the breakup, there had been no communication with them either. She missed everything about all of them. There wasn't a time when she didn't feel their love. The only one of them she couldn't avoid was their mother. They had kept in touch.

Her eyes scanned for any sighting of Tellum, but she saw none. She didn't even know if he had already arrived. She was anxious to see him, even if it was just a quick look across a crowded room.

"Are you ready?" Melodi asked her walking up. "Our coach awaits!" she hollered, walking toward the festively decorated golf cart that pulled up just for them.

"I am. Isn't this place amazing? Everything is so beautiful and lively. I love all the bright colors. Most of all, this drink is the bomb!" Cheyenne yelled as she followed behind Melodi's quick steps.

She and Melodi were whisked away the minute they sat down. Neither said a word as they checked out the immaculate views along the way.

"There are a lot of pools here. Eight of them are public pools. You will each have a private pool at your bungalow. You also have direct access to the beautiful blue ocean just mere steps away from hour door. There are swim up bars, restaurants and around-the-clock room service," Maria explained as she drove them.

Melodi leaned over close to her as Maria continued to explain the amenities at the resort.

"Did you see him?" she asked.

Cheyenne shook her head from side to side. She knew who Melodi was talking about.

"No. I saw one of his brothers."

"Are you ready to see him?"

"Yes. More than ever."

Cheyenne watched the expression on her best friend's face and recognized the look. She waited patiently for what was next.

"I don't get it. You have forced yourself into an allegiance that's as unhealthy as they come. You know I love you even more than if we were real sisters. I don't understand a family dynamic where your happiness isn't the first thing on your father's agenda. I don't want you to just be excited about seeing Tellum again. I want you to take the seven days we will be here and consider what you're missing out on. Do not let Tellum Blackstone slip through your fingers and into another woman. As your best friend, I swear I will hate on you forever while still loving you as my sister. You wouldn't let me do this without a serious tongue lashing like I'm giving you. This is from my heart to yours," Melodi expressed.

Cheyenne couldn't think of any words to say. She felt the tears welling up in her eyes. When one dropped before she could stop it, her best friend reached over before she, herself, could reach up, and wiped it away.

"I hear you," she finally said.

"Remember what I always say?" Melodi asked, smiling from ear to ear in order to lighten the mood.

Cheyenne nodded again.

"I do. Friends don't let friends make stupid decisions without reminding them of how miserable their stupid decisions can make them," Cheyenne declared boldly.

"You got it, Clyde."

Cheyenne locked arms with Melodi. "Alright, Bonnie. Let's get out of here," she said.

6

Tellum tipped his butler who had just finished unpacking his luggage and putting everything away for him. Though this was his second day at the resort, he'd spent the first day of his arrival going from one end of the resort to the other checking things out. At the end of the night, he decided to relax in his private bungalow. He ordered dinner and stayed in for the night. The plan was to catch up on some paperwork. A few minutes of relaxing on the bed, he was asleep. He didn't wake until the morning. That's when his butler called about anything he needed. He asked him to come by and unpack.

Once he left, Tellum ventured out to the large balcony outside of his bedroom. The view was breathtaking. He could see clear to the ocean with nothing blocking his view. He looked to his left and saw that his balcony had an outdoor shower that was not visible to any other bungalows near him. He liked that. He could imagine enjoying a morning shower outside. The shower in his bathroom was perfect. There was still something about the morning air that appealed to him. To his right, he saw an outdoor jacuzzi along with a large round sectional that looked like he could cop a few naps on it undisturbed. Extra sleep was definitely a part of his plan for the week. Thankfully, they had a team in place, including four general managers who would take care of everything. He would not step in to try and run things since his life was back in Detroit. He enjoyed letting his team do what they are hired to do. For a week, he wanted to be a guest while taking in what everyone thought of their stay. Their input would go a long way to the additional resorts they were opening open over the next several years.

On the side of the jacuzzi were steps that led to the roof of the bungalow where he knew he would encounter an infinity pool. That was a touch he wanted added to the all-brick structure. He wanted guests to be able to relax in a pool without having to leave to go to any of the public pools around the resort. This one was for those more private moments with someone special. Taking the steps, he reached the roof and again, looked to the shoreline where the individual bungalows over the water were located. That's when he saw her. There was Cheyenne. The sight of her had his heart racing the way his feet wanted to race to get to her. He couldn't. He'd promised her. He wouldn't spend the day ogling her. He did have some work to do. He got his last look at her as she and Melodi were moving in. He was just glad she was here. Going down to his room, his phone rang He knew it was one of his brothers wondering if he was coming to the meeting that they rescheduled from the night before. Grabbing his backpack, he slipped on casual sandals to go with his casual attire and rushed out. Descending the outside stairs that led one level down to the ground, he rushed toward the main offices when he was stopped by someone calling his name. He cringed recognizing the voice. He turned around and fake smiled.

"Reed," he said without much effort.

When it came to Reed, he had to keep his composure.

The man, he was once friends with, now rubbed him the wrong way. Could he really say that they were friends? He was more Byrum's friend than his. Still, there hadn't always been the tension between them that now existed. Reed was here by invitation like the other guests. He had to remember that.

"Well, well, if it isn't Tellum Blackstone in the flesh. I know you're taking your bow because from what I've seen already, this place is beyond words. I've been here a few hours and I will admit, I didn't expect this high-quality resort. You have outdone yourself. Pier-Howard Airlines looks forward to our partnership to bring business both of our way," Reed said.

Your father's airline, Tellum corrected Reed in his head. He was on guard for whatever spewed from Reed's mouth; good or bad. Reed's cockiness was sure to rear its ugly head at any given moment. It was definitely his way of operating.

"Everything I touch comes out as pure gold. Haven't you figured that out by now? There was never a doubt that this place wouldn't be the mecca of resort locations for the grown and sexy. Secret Whisper will be the hub for luxury accommodations, delicacies and entertainment," he boasted.

"I can see that already. I'm looking forward to being mesmerized by all of that and more. Tonight's festivities starting with the welcoming party I'm sure will be fire. Besides, I've seen some of the single women who have been arriving and I must say, I would take them all home with me if I could. I'll leave a few for you since I know you're back on the market again; at least that's what I've heard."

Tellum knew that Reed would find a way to broach the subject of Cheyenne in record speed. He didn't disappoint. The man was also predictable.

"Oh? Is that what you heard?" Tellum slyly asked.

"The word on the street is that you and Cheyenne ended things some months back. I'm sorry to hear that. Your good looks and her beauty made for the perfect couple. I guess that means you won't one day make a bunch of beautiful kids together. Your genes combined with hers would monopolize the market on beautiful children."

Tellum knew Reed was attempting to be facetious while also complimenting him. His micro-aggressive technique would not work on him.

"You heard right. Trust me when I say, you don't need to leave a few women for me. My game doesn't need any help. If your ears are connected to the word on the street, you should know that as well," Tellum replied with his usual swagger.

"True, true. I hope Cheyenne took the break-up well. I never pegged you as the relationship type, you know, much like myself. Is she by chance coming to the resort this week? I so understand if she's not. After all, who wants an ex hanging around cramping their style? In other words, who brings sand to the beach. It is a beautiful beach, too. I checked that out when I first landed and checked in. I mean, how wild would that be for both of you to be here getting your separate grooves on. Do people still say that?" Reed said.

Tellum felt his spine straighten. He knew the man was trying to hit below the belt in order to get a rise out of him, but he wasn't going to bite; not now, not ever. There was an additional word on the street that Reed was being extra vigilant about making his own play for Cheyenne. Tellum had a feeling that he was fishing to see if he knew. The less Reed actually knew, the better.

"I'm sure Cheyenne is doing okay. She was invited. I believe she is already here."

The light in Reed's eyes almost blinded him. He was glad he mentioned Cheyenne's presence. He knew what he was up against when it came to wits.

"Really? I guess the wounds have healed if you invited her and she still accepted. I'm sure the men will be on her like a moth to a flame. Did I compliment her beauty?"

"Yes, you have a few times in the past few minutes alone."

When Reed slid his hand down his full beard and licked his lips, Tellum was ready to drop his bag and introduce him to the concrete. He knew Reed was trying to get under his skin. The man was obtuse. His personality also sucked. His family's airline was in a major partnership with him and his brothers and so he worked hard at keeping the peace. Reed often made that complicated.

"She is beautiful. I have no doubt every man at this resort will see that as well. She's a grown woman. I'm hoping, like everyone else, that she'll have a great time."

"Hmm, perhaps, I'll see if she'll make room for a dance or two. It is a party, right? You won't have an issue with that, will you? I'm not trying to stir up any trouble. You know me," Reed jested.

Tellum wasn't amused. He kept a straight face. He saw Reed studying him. He remained calm.

"Like I said, Cheyenne can do as she likes; she's a grown ass woman. I'm sure she'll have lots of dance requests. There was no doubt in my mind that you would be hot on her trail."

Reed leaned over closer to him.

"Did you mean hot on her tail? I think that's the slogan."

"Don't tempt me, Reed. I know what you're trying to do. It won't work. I need to get going. I do have a resort launching tonight. Since this is my company and not my father's company, say, as in your situation, I have a lot to do. I'm sure I'll catch you around the resort over the next few days."

Reed laughed flippantly. Tellum let it slide.

"Make sure you catch me later tonight at the party. I'll be the one on the dance floor with the most beautiful woman, oh, I meant, women here."

Before he could respond, Reed turned and walked away, giving him a slight wave over his shoulder. Tellum, not knowing if he was being watched or not, gave Reed a gesture of his own that the man didn't see.

"I saw that."

Tellum turned with the biggest smile on his face. His favorite cousin, Carmalita Blackstone, his uncle Hyman's daughter walked up to him. He pulled her into a tight hug. She and Callum were the same age at thirty-two. They had the same wild spirit. When they separated, he checked out her silvery outfit.

"Girl, where are you going? To a Beyonce concert? You look amazing, but it's early in the day for all that glitters!" he joked.

"Well, you know how I do. I'm always celebrity-ready."

"Celebrity?"

He loved how Carmalita walked around with her head in the clouds with visions of being the hottest R&B singer who hasn't quite made it to the big-time yet. He knew she had the talent. It was her lack of commitment that held her back. The fact that her father also funded her lavish lifestyle didn't have her dreaming of working hard at her craft. He was giving her an opportunity this week to share her talent at the resort. She was going to be sitting in with one of the live bands that were scheduled to play in a few days.

"I'm manifesting it as we speak, for sure. I appreciate the opportunity you're giving me by allowing me to sing this week. I'm excited."

Tellum placed his free arm around her shoulder as they walked.

"You deserve it. I know you're still trying to figure it out. This is your chance to shine. You came by yourself? Where are your girls you always travel with?"

"Oh, they coming, for sure. I didn't come alone. I came with Keiko, Byrum's executive assistant. You know that's my girl, right?" Carmalita asked.

"Yeah, I heard y'all hang out when you're in town."

"Yeah, I love living in Atlanta. It's good for my up-and-coming career, but I miss Detroit."

"Is it Detroit friends or Atlanta friends joining you here this week?"

"Detroit friends. We are looking forward to letting our hair down."

"And the men?"

"You know I'll be front and center for the men. I heard that quite a few celebrities are here this week. Some professional football and basketball players? Some top-tier actors and artists? Let me know something. I'm trying to get hooked up."

"Cuz, you are not looking to be settled down with anyone and you know it," Tellum laughed.

"I said hooked up, not booed up! What happens at the resort will stay at the resort. If you hear anything about me, don't tell nobody; don't even tell me. You can go ahead and assume it's all correct. Anyway, I need to check-in. Keiko went ahead of me. I had to take a few minutes to chat up our driver. He is fine!"

Tellum shook his head and waved her off. She was definitely the female version of Callum.

Running late for a quick meeting with Byrum, he hustled off in the direction of the executive offices only to have to stop again. This time, he was more than excited to do so. Cheyenne and Melodi were walking up a path on his right. Something told him to look that way. He locked eyes with her. There was no way they could avoid each other as they had done a good job of back in Detroit. He strolled closer to them.

"Cheyenne."

He spoke softly without making a move in her direction.

"Hi, Tellum."

"How are you?" he asked.

"I'm great."

"It's good to see you," he quickly added

"Hey, I'm here too you know!" Melodi said.

On that, any bit of tension was released and the three of them laughed it off.

"Hey, Melodi. I see you girl. I'm glad the two of you made it."

"Made it? I wouldn't have missed this."

"Neither would I," Cheyenne said.

Tellum turned his attention back to her.

"This place is amazing. We are on our way to check out the resort," Melodi remarked.

"I hope you'll both give us your feedback."

"I know I will. Was that your cousin I saw you talking to?" Cheyenne asked.

"Yes. Carmalita will be singing a few times this week. She's hoping to finally get her career off the ground. We thought that this would be a great opportunity for her to put feelers out about her talent. We've always known that she could sing. It's time the rest of the world knew too."

"I'll have to connect with her before the week is out. I haven't seen her since last Thanksgiving at your parents' house."

Tellum's mind raced back to that night. After dinner, they'd relaxed in the family room, falling asleep when they were supposed to be watching a movie. By the time they woke up, a blanket had been placed over them, the lights were out, but the television was still on. Rather than leave to go home knowing they were both exhausted, they slept on the large sectional all night. In the morning, they ate breakfast with his parents before going back to his place to change for dinner with her parents. That had been a wonderful time for them.

"It's been a while then. I'm sure she'll be glad to catch up with you."

"You look like you're in a rush. Was that Reed I saw you talking to?" Cheyenne questioned.

"I am and it was. It was Reed being Reed. I'm on my way to a meeting with my brothers."

"Oh, okay. I don't want to keep you," Cheyenne said.

"I hope we get a chance to talk again."

"You better. Why come all this way with you both here and not catch up on the past several months? I'm sure Cheyenne has a lot to share about her life as a single woman all these months," Melodi suggested.

Tellum chuckled when Cheyenne pinched Melodi on the arm to shut her up.

"Hey!" Melodi yelped.

"We won't keep you. Thanks for the invitation. I know you didn't have to do that."

"My pleasure. If you need anything, let me know. I better get going before Callum buzzes me again. Have a good time, ladies," Tellum said before he turned and hustled away.

7

The first night of celebrating the opening of the resort was in full swing. After Callum and Byrum walked up to the microphone in the middle of the outdoor nightclub party, Tellum had welcomed everyone, not only to the resort, but to the first night of seven days and nights of planned activities. There were people dressed in white and silver as far as he could see. The décor was impeccable.

There were hundreds of high tables covered in white tablecloths with silver and white décor accentuating the tops. Each high table had four highchairs. Thankful that the weather would be cooperating all week, there was no need for tents. Mixed throughout with the tables were plush sofas, single chairs and lounge chairs. The party was in the center of the resort around the main pool which was illuminated with blue and white lights under the water. Music flowed from speakers all around the perimeter. There were white and silver balloons and other decorations, making for a festive atmosphere. There were eight bars set up with non-stop drinks being made. Not only were all ten of the resort restaurants open and operating, there were food stations equally spaced throughout the party. Wait staff dressed in black with trays of food and alcohol were mixed throughout to make sure all guest requests for either were being met.

Before he finished giving his welcome, even in a sea of white, he was able to spot Cheyenne easily the moment she arrived. He almost lost his train of thought at the sight of her. He'd heard that she had arrived hours ago. He'd had several bouquets of flowers placed around her villa. He made sure she had accommodations that he knew would please her. Being a lover of the water, her lodging for the week was right on top of the ocean. The glass bottom pool on the deck of her villa, he knew, would have her falling in love with the place.

Having her at the resort was his first priority. Now that she was here, he would make the time to speak with her.

As he spoke to the guests, his eyes panned around the crowd. He made sure to let his eyes linger a little longer each time they landed on Cheyenne. The way she smiled at him had his heart melting. He was reminded of just how much he'd missed her over the last six months. Seeing her again, the wait was finally over. She was also more beautiful than he even remembered. Her long, thick curly hair was wild about her head the way he loved. Her white dress hit all of her curves perfectly.

That had been two hours ago. For the past hour, he and his brothers had been making their way through the throngs of party goers, meeting and greeting as many as they could. Moving off to the side after stopping at one of the bars to grab a beer, his eyes landed on a sight that had him boiling. He knew it was possible, but still, seeing it had caught him off guard.

His pulse raced rapidly at the sight of Cheyenne dancing with Reed. Everything about the man irked him. Now that he and Cheyenne were no longer an item, word around town was that Reed was making a play for her. He and Reed had been rivals for years. The man may be a friend of Byrum's but for Tellum, nothing about Reed spoke that he was a friend to anyone. His ego entered a room before he did. Seeing him and Cheyenne enjoying the live band that was playing while the DJ took a break tore at his patience. He could see the way Reed used his eyes to caress Cheyenne's curves as they danced. Tellum saw fire. He could almost feel it in his nostrils as he breathed in and out. Each time Reed tried to move close to Cheyenne, Tellum could feel his pressure rising. Reed knew what he was doing. Their eyes locked as Reed smirked at him mockingly as he danced around Cheyenne, laughing and enjoying himself. He wondered if the was something going on between them now that Cheyenne was no longer his lady? Something in the interaction he had with Reed earlier piqued his interest for the rest of the day. It was as if Reed had a secret that he couldn't wait for Tellum to find out.

There was a crowd of over five hundred people in attendance. Each day and night for the first seven days have a different theme. Tonight's theme was, *"All-White to Everyone's Delight"*.

The moment he saw Cheyenne and Melodi join the crowd, his eyes hadn't been on anyone else. A few times, they caught each other's gaze. He made sure if either of them looked away, it would be her. No way did he want her to think that he didn't still have eyes for her and only her. He needed her to know that for him, nothing about the way he felt about her has changed. Then he thought about it. He realized his thoughts had changed. He loved her even more now than he did when they were together. He was able to see what life without her would be like and he didn't like it one bit. Maybe, just maybe, there was still some part of her that still loved and wanted him.

Earlier in the day, not long after she had arrived, they were able to speak briefly. He wished he had more time to engage her, but there was still a lot that he wanted to check out before tonight's huge event. There were also three smaller events, each with a different theme. One was for couples or singles who wanted a quieter existence for the night. On the other side of the resort, near the entrance, there was light food, a jazz saxophone player with a small band accompanying him. This party was the largest event of the evening with most of the guests in attendance. They could all venture to any of the night's festivities. For now, this seemed to satisfy most. There were various food stations. Of course, the most popular attractions were the three large bars where alcohol flowed freely all evening. So far, everything was going extremely well. They only had one issue with an accommodation which was quickly remedied. A guest who had requested a ground floor room in the resort hotel due to mobility issues had been placed in the wrong room on the second floor. He had received word that the guest had been accommodated correctly within ten minutes. He liked that the hundreds of people they employed were on top of everything. That made his job a lot easier.

Tellum smiled as guest after guest walked up to him where he stood on the edge of the large pool in the center of the property with his favorite beer in his hand. If he was going to make it through of night of watching Cheyenne dance in the arms of one man after the other, he would need a lot more of these.

What he found after seeing her at the resort was that he hadn't thought about the impact of seeing her in this sexy, romantic element. Secret Whisper was his baby. Everything about it came from his idea of the perfect place for lovers. There were just as many singles as couples at the resort, but the bottom line was, this was a place where lovers could come and unite, rekindle and fall in love again and again. He was hoping for some spark to still be between him and Cheyenne even though it wasn't the lack of it that had broken them up. He still struggled with the choice her father made her make.

"It's a party, Tellum. Don't start nothing tonight. I see it in your eyes. Don't start anything with Reed. It's just a dance. As you can see, it's all fast songs. They aren't even touching."

Tellum didn't have to turn around to know Callum had walked up. He heard him before he saw him. Nothing would make him take his eyes off of Cheyenne. If Reed turned into a hands-on kind of dancer, he needed the liquid courage in him to not pick him up to toss him in the pool to cool him off. He knew he had no right, but he would do it anyway.

"Not now, Cal," he grumbled out.

"I know it hurts to see her having this much fun and she's not with you. When you invited her, did you expect her to show up and be bummed all week? That wasn't the point of this place or your invite. I get it that the last person you want to see her dancing with or engaging with in any way is Reed Howard. I get it. That man has had a thing for Cheyenne since the moment he first saw her with you. We all know it. She would never," he said.

Tellum turned to his right where Callum now stood next to him, also dressed in all white with a beer in his hand.

"Are you sure about that? Yeah, Reed is a clown, but Cheyenne is now a single woman. He's not every woman's cup of tea, for sure. Who knows what kind of line he's tossing at Cheyenne. Look at how he's looking at her. His eyes go from her breasts, to her ass. That's what he has in mind."

"Tell, stop doing this to yourself. I don't care what Reed has in mind. That doesn't mean that's what she has in mind."

"We're in a place that I have deemed the most romantic in the world. I created a lot of what people see from what I would want in a place I would bring her to. My heart is in every room, every event and even in every meal and drink. It's my place made for lovers. It's where love can begin," Tellum admitted.

"Bro, is that what you think? You think that because you put all of your dreams about romance into this place that Cheyenne would come here and fall in love with someone else that fast? She still loves you. This is just a trying time for her. Let her work through it. Don't put her in the realm of other women who will just go with any man, even for one night in a place like this. I see the fire in your eyes. I see the smolder of lust and love for Cheyenne while at the same time, I see fire and brimstone that you'd like to toss Reed into if you could. Pull it back. I don't want any incident to involve you at your own resort."

Callum chuckled. So did he. The idea of tussling with Reed was laughable. Reed wouldn't survive his rage against him.

"I detest that man," Tellum blurted out.

"That's because, number one, he has eyes for your woman. Two, y'all breaking up has made you think that there is room now in her life for him. That's a no. And three, Reed has been trying to compete with your popularity since high school when he and Byrum played football together. They became friends and the two of you became enemies."

"Byrum still considers him a friend?"

"Not like in the past before this rivalry between the two of you got intense over the past few years or so. Your brother's allegiance will always be with you. Reed doesn't give him a reason to choose because he already knows. The Howard family is a strong partner in business with our company. Their airline offers deep discounts to our destinations. Their marketing has us all over it. In turn, we promote their airline in all of our locations It's a win, win for us all."

"That's his father's doing. If it were left up to Reed, I don't think we would have the deal with them that we have. Thanks to our attorneys and the best money man in the business, Sheldon Sullivan out of Bozeman, Montana, we have garnered some major deals and endorsements."

"True. Keep in mind that one day, Reed will take over his family's airline. We will have to work with him. You will have to work with him. There can't be tension at every meeting with him in the room. He goads you and you fall for it."

"Only when it comes to Cheyenne. In business, I don't care about Reed. I do care about how close he's dancing to my woman."

"Tell?"

"Yeah, I know. She's not my woman anymore. She can be with anyone she chooses. I'm just hoping it's not Reed. You know he would walk all over her. He would mess around on her like does with every woman he sets eyes on. He's a clown."

"He is and Cheyenne knows it. I'm just glad she came. Look at her. She is having the time of her life. You said she could use a vacation. She could have said no. She didn't have to accept your invitation to still come. You put her and her friend up in one of our best over the water villas. It's right in the center of all the villas. The red carpet was laid out for her in her villa."

"I want fresh flowers delivered to her every day. Can you make that happen for me?" Tellum asked.

Earlier, he had ordered three dozen roses in three different colors along with a vase filled with her favorite flower, the Calla Lilly.

"I made sure they were delivered myself and placed in her room while she was checking in. I wanted to be sure she was actually going to show up before doing so. I promise you that I'm on top of her getting the flower you select for her each day," Callum admitted.

"You had doubts about her showing up?" Tellum asked.

"Not at all. I simply wanted them to be fresh just like you ordered."

"I appreciate it."

"She hasn't mentioned them? They each had a separate card with a handwritten note from you."

"I haven't had a chance to talk to her much other than saying hello in passing earlier. I was on my way to take care of some business when we walked up to each other on the same path. I told her I'd connect with her a little later. She shook her head, smiled and walked on with Melodi. Man, I swear, when I saw her, all I wanted to do was hold her and never let go. I know I need to give her space though."

"You're giving up?"

Tellum wasn't known as a man to give up and thrown in the towel on anything.

"Not on your life, bro. Not until I see that there is nothing left to fight for. I know she said we were over, but I'm holding on to hope that eventually our love will win."

"I'm already claiming it for you."

"This clown!" Tellum shouted. He was thankful that with the music being so loud, only Callum heard him.

Their eyes, together, landed on Reed who took one of Cheyenne's hands in his while they danced.

"Don't," Callum warned. "They are dancing. Look, he's even dancing with Melodi. It's innocent. Don't make more out of this than there is. Maybe you need to walk it off. Go mingle with more of our guests. Stay away from Cheyenne for now. Reed is playing. I saw him look at you. He knows what he's doing. Release your hand. I know it's balled up at your side. Let it go."

Tellum didn't speak. The only words prepared to come out of his mouth were all laced with profanity. Reed was challenging him. The only thing was that only he knew that Reed wasn't ready for him. Callum was right. He needed to take his focus off of Reed and Cheyenne and focus on all of their guests. He handed his half-empty bottle to Callum.

"I need a stronger drink. I'm going to go chat with a few of our guests to make sure everyone is having a good time."

"Don't stop and ask Reed though. It's clear he's having the time of his life."

Tellum walked away with Callum laughing behind him. He tossed his middle finger back at him as he walked and then laughed with him. He loved his brothers with everything in him. He and Callum were always closer due to their similar personalities. Byrum was always the steady, even-keel brother while he and Callum were the wild cards.

"Love you too, bro," Tellum then hollered.

"Right back atcha!" Callum replied as they parted.

Tellum hated the thought that in the past six months since they had been apart that Cheyenne had found enjoyment in being single again. He missed everything about her, he thought as he walked up to one guest after the other, smiling and shaking hands. He loved hearing the accolades from everyone about how much they are loving the resort. Against his better judgement, he did look in Cheyenne's direction and caught her eyes. Unlike earlier when he saw her and smiled from ear to ear, he couldn't muster up even the slightest smile. She smiled at him and then stopped. He knew why. She saw his eyes go from her to Reed and then back to her before he finally turned away. There was no way she missed the silent communication they shared. He wanted to be where Reed and any other man she had danced with and would dance with before the end of the night. The image before him was troublesome. True, he had no right. He invited her for the week. He wanted her to have a good time even if it meant he wasn't going to be a part of it. Deep down, what he wanted most of her was pure happiness. The fun he saw her having told him that she was well on her way. For that, he couldn't be upset. He could be jealous of every man who could and would garner her attention. He knew he had no right to be upset.

8

Cheyenne couldn't believe she was in paradise. It was just after midnight. The night sky was as black as it could be with the brightest moon she'd ever seen considering it wasn't a full moon, she was surprised it was a bright as it was. The reflection of it on the water mesmerized her.

After leaving the party a little earlier than she thought she would, she came back to her villa and decided to sit out on the deck that overlooked the ocean. She still couldn't believe the space was all hers. Melodi's villa was right next to hers. Not surprising her at all, Melodi was still at the party. After dancing with a countless number of people, eating to her stomach was content and sipping on a few non-alcoholic beverages, she'd had enough. Her plan for the week wasn't to party like it was 1999 all day and night. She wanted some time alone to relax, think and reflect.

It had been a long time since she and Melodi had taken a girls' trip together. Her last few vacations had been taken with Tellum, though she and Melodi had done some day trips either together or with other girlfriends. This trip was going to be her time away to slow down. What she hadn't planned on was the sad look on Tellum's face when he saw her dancing with Reed. Though she knew it was all innocent, she should have known that Tellum would feel some type of way about it if he saw her. She knew the two men didn't care for each other. When she and Tellum were out and about and would run into Reed, they were cordial. She's even danced with Reed before. What she forgot was that this time was different. In the past, they may have been out in a larger group of people and playfully they would have danced. Tellum had also danced with other women, but nothing close together and definitely not to a slow song. When Reed had asked her to dance when a slow song came on, she declined and took that time to sit down. She would have said yest if Tellum had asked her. She hadn't seen him again after the solemn look he had on his face. She watched him walk around greeting everyone. She was keen to the fact that he didn't come in her direction. That saddened her. She felt awkward. Tellum was within reach but they were so far apart. This was all her doing. If she ever had a regret in her life, it was the moment she told him that they were through.

She thought back to the conversation she'd had with her mother a week later when she told her that she did as Captain Joe had asked. She didn't know what her mother's reaction would be but their heart to heart surprised her.

Ramona Reddick was a slight and quiet woman. It was her father who made all of the decisions in the family. If she had to put her mother in a category, reluctantly, she would call her the little woman. Her mother was beautiful at five-foot four. Cheyenne at five-foot eight, took her height from her father. Her mother rarely raised her voice. She pretty much went along with whatever Captain Joe decided for their lives. It wasn't until Cheyenne had graduated high school that her mother had rejoined the work force as a nurse. Captain Joe liked having her at home where she took care of them and their home. What she also knew was that her mother loved doing all of that, especially being home anytime Cheyenne left for school, came home from school or had one event or another. It was her mother who signed her up for gymnastics, soccer, volleyball, basketball, dance and theater classes. Her own love of dance came from her mother who herself, had been a professional dancer when she had met Captain Joe. Never had she ever heard a stern word from her mother. If there was ever a need for her to be disciplined growing up, it always came from her father. Something in her mother had changed the night she confided that her relationship with Tellum was over.

After she laid everything out for her mother, who already knew what Captain Joe had asked, or rather demanded that she do, her mother inhaled deeply and then exhaled loudly. Her eyes lit up as they sat across the kitchen table from each other at her parents' house. Her father was out which left them alone to speak openly. Even now, the conversation plagued her. It was during that talk that she realized she'd made the biggest mistake of her life. She recalled the chat as if it had just happened.

"You did what?" her mother asked.

"I ended my relationship with Tellum. Captain Joe told me that I had to choose where my loyalty was; with him or with the Blackstone family."

"And you decided that there were only two choices?"

"Well, yes."

"Cheyenne Alicia Reddick! Have you lost your mind? Did you fall and bump your head and I don't know that it happened? Why would you do such a thing?"

"But…"

"But what? But what, Cheyenne?" her mother yelled.

Never had her mother ever raised her voice. Her mother's words were bouncing off of the kitchen walls.

"The deal. Tellum's dad wouldn't help Captain Joe with the deal. He could lose everything. How could I stay with Tellum knowing how much he hates them? What else was I supposed to do?"

"You were supposed to live your own life with that amazing man. Do you know how hard it is to find a man in this day and time who loves you as hard and deep as Tellum does? Anyone with clear or not so clear vision could see that. If there was ever a man that I would want for you it's him; it's Tellum Blackstone. From the very first day that you brought him here for me to meet him, I knew he was the one for you. He was so gracious and kind. He was loving to you. I will never forget that day. I made spaghetti. While we talked, he helped me in the kitchen. That has never happened with anyone else you've ever brought around. I hate to admit it, but not even your father has ever done that. We had the best time that night. What I remember most was once we were settled in to eat, he noticed something very key about dinner. Do you remember?" her mother asked.

Cheyenne thought about it and couldn't figure it out.

"What?" she asked.

"He knew that you liked to cut your long spaghetti noodles into really small ones. He asked where the small knives were. When I pointed, he got up without missing a beat in the conversation we were having about that Power television series I like. He got up, grabbed the knife and handed it to you. He knew. I could tell that he took the time to learn about you and not just of you. That's important in a relationship. He was all gentleman, yes. You said that was just naturally him. I found that little thing turned out to be big. I was around several times when he declared his love for you. That time when Captain Joe was in Florida for some convention or something, which I still doubt, but I'll let that go for now, Tellum invited me to join the two of you in New York for the weekend. He was there on business but made sure we had three full days of fun while he was busy. We saw a play. We went to museums, something you and I both love. I won't even mention that cheesecake place that stole my heart that he recommended we try out. I experienced some of the best food I've ever had at a fine dining restaurant. Those amazing accommodations where he provided me with my own suite. He took great care of us that weekend. He took great care of you all the time. You told me he would do little things like if he called you and you were overwhelmed at work, he would steal you away for some relaxation so that you could get through the rest of your day with a smile. I don't need to know the full extent of what that entailed. I will say that he has always put a smile on your face."

"That he did."

"And now he can't because your father said so? What are you, ten years old and doing whatever Captain Joe wants? I'm disappointed. For the first time in my life, I am declaring out loud that you have disappointed me. I know what he asked you to do, but I thought that you would see that it was time to cut that cord."

"I owe him," she stated softly while on the brink of crying.

"Owe him? What the hell do you think you owe your father? I'll answer that for you; you owe him nothing! Do you hear me? I know I haven't been much of an ally for you against him. For that, I am sorry. If my being quiet on most things has led you to this point in your life of choosing anything other than love, then I am sorry. I've also not done a very good job. You need to fix this. Tell him you made a mistake."

"I can't. I already told Tellum that we were done. He asked me if I was sure. I already said yes."

"Baby girl, why would you do that to yourself? Look at you? You're about to cry. I know you're miserable. You love that man with everything in you. You don't choose anything over that kind of love."

"But it's..."

"Stop it, Cheyenne! This isn't you. Don't you dare tell me that you did this for Captain Joe; for your father. I can't believe you did this. I can't believe he asked you to do it. I heard the two of you talking when he made that demand. I never, in my wildest thoughts, would have believed you wouldn't have fought harder for what you want."

"What was I supposed to do?" she cried.

"Love Tellum. That's the choice you were to make. You were to love the man who loves you the way he does."

Cheyenne shook off the thought when she heard someone coming down the wooden path on the side of her villa. Thinking it may be Tellum, she jumped up to open the locked gate.

Her heart sank when the visitor wasn't Tellum. Instead, she encountered someone else; an unexpected visitor.

"Reed?" she questioned, knowing the hour of the night.

"Hey there, beautiful. I know it's late. I hope I'm not intruding. I saw your friend and didn't see you. She said you decided to call it an early night. I didn't know if you were ill or something. I thought I would check on you," he replied.

"Oh, it's nothing like that. I wanted to enjoy this peaceful night. I also didn't want to fall asleep until Melodi was back in her villa. I'm just sitting here looking at the still of the water and this beautiful sky."

"I get that. I see you have one of the largest villas here on the water. Very nice. I remember touring these when my company and the Blackstones were working on the marketing plan. These villas were my second favorite outside of the large, two-level bungalows. I'm assuming that's where Tellum and his brothers put themselves up."

Cheyenne nodded but didn't let him in. She wasn't blind to his interest in her. Reed's family owned the largest airline out of the Detroit Metro Airport, with service across the world. Like the Blackstones, Reed's family was well known.

"I saw the floor plan for those two-level bungalows. They are very nice," she replied.

"So, you haven't actually seen one up close?" he asked.

Cheyenne knew that was Reed's way of trying to find out where things stood with her and Tellum. He was trying to find out if she'd been in one with him.

"No. The last time I was here, they weren't completed yet. The resort looks completely different than it had when Tellum and his brothers bought it. One of the first things they did was completely gut all of the villas and have them rebuilt. The hotel rooms were also all re-done. This place is amazing."

"Yes, I agree with you on that. I'm not sure I've been to a more romantic destination before. That's saying a lot considering my family owns an airline and I've been all over the world. This place is definitely top-tier. Are you here for the entire week?" he asked.

"I am. I needed a vacation; Melodi and I both did. I'm looking forward to doing something different and fun every day," she noted.

"Do you think we could have lunch or dinner either later today, since it's after midnight or perhaps the next day? I'm not here all week."

"You're going to miss all of the big fun at the end of the launch," she said.

"I know. I hate that I will. I'm meeting with a prospective new client. I need to get back to Detroit for that meeting."

"Sounds mysterious," she said.

It didn't but she needed something to say.

"Maybe I'll share more about it with you one day. Maybe we can go out one night when you return home."

There it was. For the past three months, at least, Reed has tried to wrangle his way into her life on a more personal level.

"Reed, I appreciate you asking, but that's not going to happen."

"Which part? Lunch and/or dinner here or in Detroit?"

"Neither will work for me. You know Tellum is my ex. My relationship with him may be over, but I wouldn't go from him to you."

"Would you have been interested if you had met me before Tellum?" he asked.

"I can't answer that because that didn't happen. All that I can tell you is that, I appreciate that you're interested in me, but I'm going to decline."

"Didn't you have fun dancing with me? I'm a fun guy, Cheyenne. One lunch or dinner date isn't going to hurt anything."

"I'm here at Tellum's resort."

"I also offered Detroit."

"Reed! Come on, now. Why?"

"Cheyenne, I don't know the ins and outs of what happened with you and Tellum. I will say that you can't long for that man forever. I bet he ended things with you. I never saw him as the commitment type. You do know that he has a reputation with the ladies, right?"

"Don't do that. You have a reputation too. Most men and women have some sort of reputation to contend with whether it's true or not."

"What has Tellum told you about me? Has he talked down about me? We've been battling each other a long time. It's all fun and games. It's nothing serious. We have things we like and don't like about each other. You could take the time to get to know me for yourself. Are you still single?"

"I am, but my status has nothing to do with it."

"You're still in love with Tellum? Are you really out here pining for a man who has clearly moved on? I'm only asking for a chance. I think you're beautiful. I want to get to know you. There is no harm in that."

"There is no harm anywhere. I'm aware that you like me. I'm hoping you will understand that I'm interested. I think you're a cool dude."

"And a great dancer?" he kidded.

They laughed together.

"Yes, and a great dancer," she acknowledged.

"I hope Tellum knows that he walked away from one of the most beautiful women I've ever set my eyes on. If you ever change your mind about dinner, I hope you'll reach out. I better let you get back to your star gazing. It truly is a beautiful night."

"Thanks for checking on me, Reed. I appreciate that."

"It's the gentlemanly thing to do. Have a good night, Cheyenne. If nothing else, I hope you'll save another dance for me before I leave."

"A dance I can do," she said.

When Reed turned to walk away, Cheyenne closed the gate. Walking barefoot back to the edge of the deck, she sat down, this time at the edge of the pool. Closing her eyes, she cleared her mind and focused on the words of her mother. She had chosen wrong and was now suffering because of it. Maybe, just maybe, this week, she could figure out a way to get Tellum to forgive her. She was hoping for a second chance.

Laughing to herself like a schoolgirl, she silently wished upon a star. At one time she did believe in fairy tales. Perhaps, she still did.

9

Reed walked slowly back toward his room, disappointed that his visit to Cheyenne didn't deliver much other than rejection yet again. He knew he was being devilish by approaching her while at Tellum's resort. He didn't owe the man anything. In fact, his fake like for him was starting to wear thin. Cheyenne was beyond beautiful. Tellum was stupid for letting her get away. Reed had no problem going after what the man didn't want anymore. No doubt, he would get another chance with Cheyenne. He had a meeting set up that would almost guarantee that he would.

Walking back across the wooden path from her villa, he looked up and knew that his timing could have not been more perfect. Standing on the balcony of his large owner's size bungalow was Tellum. Reed's lips turned up into a quirky smile. To his delight, he knew the moment that had come to his conclusion of where he was coming from. Tellum had put Cheyenne in the villa that was a direct line of sight to his own accommodations. He knew where reed was coming from. Best of all, Tellum's mind had to be racing with why he would be coming from that direction. It was the only path that led to where Cheyenne was. He hoped that Tellum hadn't been there when he walked down that path. If that was the case, then Tellum would know how much time he'd spent with Cheyenne. Those few moments wouldn't amount to much. If he'd just stepped out while he was leaving, that would leave a man with all kinds of questionable thoughts. Though there were trees that blocked a perfect view of Cheyenne's villa, Tellum wouldn't know if anything happened. Knowing that, Reed inwardly cheered. The timing couldn't be more perfect.

He continued walking but slowed down a bit. He kept his eyes on Tellum who was now gripping the edge of the long golden bar that surrounded the balcony that circled the entire second floor of the huge bungalow. To piss the man off even more, Reed chuckled and turned his head to look back at where he came from before centering his gaze back on Tellum. He knew he was relaying a silent, but false reality to the man. That made him feel good.

Adding fuel to the fire, he winked and mouthed the word 'thank you'. His hope was that Tellum would read more into what actually happened. He was happy to see that the usual smug, confident look on Tellum's face was replaced with bitter anger. He got a rise out of seeing the man actually stew over what he thought he was seeing. In response, Tellum gave him the middle finger. Reed laughed out loud and continued to walk like a man who'd just come from getting lucky. He'd just scored his first win against Tellum Blackstone, lie or not. It still felt good.

"Are you coming from Cheyenne's villa?"

Reed turned his face forward right before he would have bumped into Melodi. He saw her eyes look up to where he had just been looking. When she leaned forward slightly, she saw Tellum.

"Um, yeah. I went to check to be sure she was okay. You mentioned she left early."

"She was fine. I told you she was okay when you asked."

Reed tried to hold his composure over the aggressive way she was speaking to him. When she again looked up at Tellum, he had walked away from the rail. The look on her face told him everything. She knew what he'd just done to Tellum. She wasn't happy.

"I wanted to check for myself. She's doing wonderfully. Have a good night," he said walking around her. He could tell Melodi was the type to read someone. He wasn't in the mood. He'd got his win and that's all that mattered.

**

Melodi walked past Reed and headed straight for Cheyenne. She didn't know what was going on but she had an idea of what she'd just walked up on. Luckily, she knew her friend well enough to know that nothing happened, but still, the image that must be in Tellum's head bothered her. Reed knew what he was doing when she walked up.

Walking a little faster, she again looked up at Tellum's balcony and didn't see him. This was only the first day and already someone brought drama into Cheyenne and Tellum's life. She had hoped beyond all hope that this week could be the restart of the perfect love. Going on vacation wasn't the only reason she pushed to come on this trip. It's possible, Reed just destroyed all of that by the perception she knew he tried to toss up at Tellum.

Taking out her phone, she sent Cheyenne a text to tell her she was coming her way. She got back a quick okay right before she pushed the buzzer on the gate. Cheyenne was already standing at the opened gate when she walked up.

Melodi took in her attire of a bright pink two-piece, barely-there bathing suit. It wasn't one of the new ones she'd bought but it was familiar.

"Is this what you had on when Reed was here? What the hell, Chey!" Melodi yelled assertively.

When Cheyenne's neck snapped straight, Melodi knew she'd caught her friend off-guard.

"What the hell? Why are you yelling at me? What are you talking about? You saw Reed?"

Melodi stomped away beyond Cheyenne. She didn't go far before she turned around and faced her.

"Reed was here? Why? And with you looking like this? What are you *doing*?" she questioned loudly.

"First of all, lower your voice. Why are you yelling like a maniac? I was not dressed like this. I just put this on to take a dip in the pool. I was waiting up for you to tell me you were safely back. Yes, he was here, but I was still in my dress. We talked right here at the gate. I opened it but I didn't let him come in. What's wrong with you?"

"You do know that man is trying to get inside of your bathing suit? Inside of you? You get that right?"

"I know and I told him that I'm not interested. You know I wouldn't give him any part of me. I don't like him in that way. We danced to some music. I danced with a lot of guys tonight. It's not that big of a deal," Cheyenne explained.

"Look, I'm sorry for yelling. I didn't mean that. I will ask, did any of the other guys show up here faking like they were checking up on you? You know what Reed wants."

"I *didn't* invite him here. He stopped by for a few minutes."

"A few minutes was all it took."

"Melodi, what are you talking about?"

"Tellum," she blurted out.

"What about Tellum? Can you start from a better place than at the end of a thought? I'm not following."

Melodi heaved a heavy sigh, closed her eyes and then opened them when she was a little less angry and more focused on her thoughts.

"Okay. When I was on my way back, I ran into Reed."

"Okay, that's pretty clear."

"I also saw Tellum, who I believe saw Reed as well. Catch this and make sure you're following along. Tellum saw Reed coming from your villa. The path outside of the gate leads right to yours and only yours. We each have our own wooden path. I believe Reed put something in Tellum's head about why he would be coming from this direction at this late hour. He saw the two of you dancing. He knows the vile person Reed is. That man has no boundaries. Do you get it?"

Cheyenne's mouth opened as wide as her eyes, yet no words came out. She only shrieked.

"He didn't," she yelled.

"Oh, yes he did. You should have seen Reed's face. When I looked up at Tellum, I caught the end of him lowering his middle finger. I think he and Reed had words without having actual words. I'm sure none were needed. It was the image he put in Tellum's head that mattered," Melodi explained.

"Nooooo. Oh, my goodness. Tell me that did *not* happen. I swear, nothing happened with Reed."

"I know that. Tellum doesn't."

"Oh, my god!"

Cheyenne unlocked her phone with nervous fingers that wouldn't stop twitching. Melodi felt terrible for her.

"Now you get it. I told you Reed was horrible person. You can't give him an inch. You can't be nice to him in any way. I know it was just a dance, but that combined with him coming from here after midnight spoke volumes to the man who still loves you."

"I can only imagine what Tellum is thinking," she said dialing his number. He answered on the first ring.

"*Really* Cheyenne?" Tellum blurted out before she could say anything.

"Tellum, wait and let me explain," she said nervously.

"No need."

Just like that, the line went dead. Cheyenne stood there looking at her phone as if it were a foreign object.

"What happened?"

"He definitely saw Reed. He hung up on me before I could clear things up."

"He *what*?"

"He's never done that before. He hung up on me."

"Oh, damn. That fool Reed. Day one and things have already gone straight to hell," Melodi said. "I'm sorry. I wanted you to know what I saw."

Cheyenne couldn't think of any words to say. She couldn't take her eyes from the phone. He'd hung up on her. He's never done that before. He had to be pissed. Now, so was she. He didn't even let her speak.

"I know you did and it's okay. What's not okay is Tellum hanging up on me like that. Who does he think he is dismissing me like that?"

Melodi smiled. This was the part of her friend that she needed to see. She loved the feisty side of Cheyenne. She'd been waiting for this person to show up for a while.

Just that fast, Melodi knew that there was still hope for her friend and the man she loved.

"What are you going to do?"

"Change and go see Tellum. He actually hung up on me. We are never doing that to each other whether we're together or not. That sh…"

"Cheyenne!"

Melodi stopped that curse word from escaping her lips. It wasn't often that she cursed like a sailor, but when she did, she felt sorry for the person on the other end of her anger. Cheyenne could be nice, cool, calm and collect. It was that intolerable spirit that people had to watch out for.

"I know. I almost let one fly, didn't I? That's how pissed off I am. Hanging up on me? To not even let me talk? You know what, I'm sick of men and what I've been enduring lately from them all. From Captain Joe and his militant attitude to Reed and his ploy tonight, to Tellum and his fine ass hanging up on me as if I didn't deserve to be heard. I'm going to go see him and say what I want to say!"

"Now? At this hour? It's after one in the morning here."

"I don't care. Clearly, he's woke!" she shouted.

Melodi followed Cheyenne inside. She cheered for the fire inside of her friend. It was beyond time that Cheyenne let out everything that she'd been holding in. She should have gotten angry long ago. Melodi's inner demons were doing a happy dance. Cheyenne may be angry, but if nothing else, it was going to get her a face-to-face with Tellum. Sometimes, that's all love really needs.

Cheyenne paced around the room like a mad-woman. She grabbed an orange and white flowing dress before heading toward the shower.

"You don't want to calm down first?" Melodi questioned, praying that the answer was no.

"No, I do not. I'm going to see him. I'm going *right* damn now!" Cheyenne hollered back at her.

Even though Cheyenne was out of sight, Melodi pumped her hand in the air. This, she knew is the Cheyenne that needed to respond to her father when he told her to leave Tellum alone. Something told her that by the time the sun came up, all would be heading in the direction of setting Cheyenne's world back on the right path to happiness.

Melodi silently thanked Reed. He didn't know it but his antics just may have been what was needed to solidify Cheyenne and Tellum's love forever. At least, that's what she hoped. She continued to cheer as she listened to Cheyenne's continued rant through the sound of the water running in the shower. Oh, she was mad alright.

"Get your girl, Tellum. Now is your chance," she said out loud to no one because Cheyenne was in the shower cursing up a storm. "When a woman's fed up!" Melodi hollered.

10

Cheyenne didn't bother to check her hair or makeup in the mirror. She was too fired up. The nerve of Tellum to be that nasty toward her.

"Where is my key?" she questioned, looking around the living room area. She remembered sitting it on the cream chaise lounge.

"Here it is," Melodi said getting to the chair before she did.

"Thanks. I thought you would be gone by now," Cheyenne said looking at Melodi who seemed to be in an extra jovial move.

"No. I'm going to make sure you get there okay. Do you even know which bungalow he's staying in?"

Cheyenne stopped moving. She was so overheated with fury that the thought of where his place was never crossed her mind. She knew that he must be someplace close to her in order to see Reed as he was leaving.

"I don't, but I'll find him."

"What? By randomly knocking on doors? Perhaps walking around screaming his name until he came out on one of the patios? Girl, you need to cool down a minute. I'll walk you over."

"Then who will walk you back?"

"Trust me when I say you will be able to see me from his bungalow."

Cheyenne nodded and whizzed by Melodi toward the door.

"Um, Chey?"

"What?"

"Are you wearing underwear? Are you sure you're not going to see him for another reason?" Melodi laughed.

Cheyenne looked down. The top of the dress was down around her arms because of how it was made. It was clear she didn't have a bra on. She also didn't have any panties on.

"It's too hot for underwear. You know how I am about that. This dress isn't see-through. Besides, it flows almost to the floor. That's why I put this on. There was no other reason. Are you walking with me, or do you plan to stay here and just talk to yourself? Because I'm out!" she declared.

"I'm a half of a step behind you. You know, he has every right to be mad. He's probably jealous as hell," Melodi said locking the door behind them as they headed for the gate. "Do you have your phone?" she added.

Cheyenne raised her hand in the air to show her that she had her phone in one hand and her key in the other. That's all she needed.

"I know what he thinks he may have seen. I'll deal with Reed when I see him, too. Men are getting on my last nerve! I love Tellum but that will be the last time that he ever hangs up on me when I'm in the middle of talking. I don't ever want him to think that I'm the kind of woman who would disrespect him by messing around with Reed or any other man. For goodness' sake! He invited me here. Are you coming?" Cheyenne yelled behind her when she noticed Melodi wasn't close.

"I'm trying, but you're moving like you're running a marathon. I love when you get like this. It's a good look for you. You wouldn't be this mad if you weren't madly in love with him."

"You know I never stopped loving him. He knows I am. That's what pisses me off the most. Which bungalow is his?" she asked when they reached a clearing. In front of them were the four presidential suite bungalows. She assumed Tellum had to be in one of them.

"The one right in front of you with the number two on it."

"Okay, you go back so that I can see you get on the path. Text me when you're behind your locked gate. I'm going to go up the steps. It looks like the entry is on the top level. I remember seeing one of these and they all enter on the second level. You're good?"

"The question is, are you good?" Melodi chuckled.

Cheyenne knew she looked a mad mess. She probably mirrored a crazed woman on a war path.

"I'm good. I'll call you in a bit when I get back. This won't take long."

"Sounds good."

When Melodi turned and raced back, Cheyenne heard her mumble but dismissed it. They would have plenty of time to talk. First up was Tellum.

Turning to the steps, she made her way to the second floor and knocked on the door. That's when she saw the bell on the wall. Without thinking, she pressed it over and over without stopping. The door suddenly flew open. Before she could get a word out, her eyes took in Tellum's massive, muscled pecks, bare for her eyes to peruse. She resisted the urge to look down his body. Even though he was in black silk pajama bottoms, she knew what was behind them. She didn't want her body to betray her current state of anger, replacing it with desire. Too late, she thought. Damn, she said under her breath. No way could any woman in this world not have spicy thoughts with every gaze on his body.

"Cheyenne? What the hell? The bell works. Once will do. What are you doing here?" he questioned.

"What am I doing here? Why do you think?"

"It's one in the morning. You're not tired?" he asked.

The way his question came out hit the target it was intended to. She knew what he was alluding to. For the moment, she would let it fly because he was clueless.

"You're being an *asshole and I don't like it!* I commend you that it isn't taking you much effort to do so. I'll give you that. Why did you hang up on me?"

"You came here to ask me that? At this hour?"

"You hung up on me. I wasn't going to call you back and have you do it again. That was rude. That's not you."

"Well, there is a lot I didn't know was me. Is there a lot I don't know, is you?" he leaned down and asked.

His tone cut her deep. He was definitely acting and speaking out of character.

"You want to do this with me standing out here? I'm about to get really loud."

Cheyenne had to say the words through clinched teeth in order to not wake up everyone on the island. She wanted to. She was mad enough to do so. Tellum opened the door all the way and waved her inside. She stormed passed him and turned around to face him.

"Why are you yelling?" he asked before she could get a word out.

"Why did you hang up on me? I guess we both have a question."

"Did I need to hear what you had to say? I'm sure I didn't need an education at that moment. I have already been schooled."

"Since when are you rude like this?"

"I'm not; not usually. Some circumstances warrant it."

"Oh? You think you have a reason that involves me being the target of your anger? You know how I feel about people rudely dismissing me in the middle of a conversation. I abhor that and you *know* it."

"Cheyenne, it's late to be getting into this."

"Oh? Why? Because you think I should be tired? Yeah, I caught that too. What do you think you know that accounts for you acting like this?"

"Gee, I don't know. Why don't you enlighten me on why. Anything you want to share about tonight?" Tellum asked, leaning in her direction with both of his hands behind his back. His ice-cold stance was of a man she didn't recognize.

"No. I don't need to share anything with anyone."

"I know. You are your own woman, and you can do what you want. Including..."

She waited for the words that would include a name but that didn't happen. Tellum, instead stopped talking and held his lips tight.

"Including what? Ask me. I know what you think you saw. Go ahead and ask me."

"You talked to Melodi or was it someone else?"

"Melodi came storming into my villa with a story. I want to hear you ask me. I want to know what it is that you really think of me. I want you to take a few seconds and think about what you *believe* your eyes saw. Then, ask me. One thing you know about me is that I am *not* a liar. Whatever the question, I will answer truthfully, but don't you *ever* hang up on me like that again. I didn't deserve that. I was trying to talk to you. I would rather you not answer a call from me if you're mad before you hang up like that."

"I wasn't ready to hear it."

"You weren't ready to hear what? Ask me!"

When Tellum looked away, Cheyenne followed his eyes wherever he turned them. She knew she looked crazy moving her head all around. The last thing she cared about was her look at this moment.

"Cheyenne," he said slowly and a lot calmer.

Tellum got the message. He'd never seen her this angry before. He'd hit a nerve and that nerve showed up at one in the morning to read him from today until Sunday.

"Don't you *dare* Cheyenne me! How could you believe anything so untoward about me? Do you really think that after inviting me to your magnificent resort, that I would hook up with someone? Have you ever known me to hook-up with anyone other than you? You know that's not me. It wasn't me before I met you and it has not been after. If nothing else, you should have called me right away to make sure I was okay. It was *Reed*. Are you serious? Is that how little you think of me? Reed? Reed Howard! Are you insane? Is this what jealousy does to you? This is me. I'm not one of those fly-by-night women you have been known to entertain. This is me. You know me better than anyone else in the world. Is that what you think of me? I want to hear you say it to my face."

Tellum tried to move around her. He stopped when he realized she wasn't about to let him off the hook.

"I saw you dancing with him earlier."

"I've danced with him before. I danced with quite a few guys tonight. It was a *party*. Everybody was dancing. Are you mad at them all or is your anger reserved just for me? I was *dancing*, Tellum. You didn't invite me here to have a good time? I shouldn't enjoy the festivities?"

"Look, I'm sorry I hung up on you. That wasn't me and you didn't deserve it."

"Damn right I didn't"

"There is never a situation where that kind of behavior is acceptable. I was jealous; I can admit that. My manhood isn't in question because I was jealous. I haven't seen you in six months. When I do, you're dancing with Reed. He's been trying to get with you since you and I first started dating. Though he hasn't flirted openly with you while we were together, tonight, he was clearly making a play for you."

"So, what? Do you have any idea of how many men make a play for me on the regular? That's not ego, that's a fact. That's also something you know. What have you always said to me? I'll answer for you. There was never a day that you didn't tell me how beautiful I was; not one single day while we were together."

"You're beautiful, even now."

Cheyenne shook her index finger at him to push off his compliment.

"Not now, Tellum. Your timing sucks. So, you were upset about me dancing. I caught that in your eyes. I saw you watching me. I was trying to have fun; my appreciation for being here like everyone else. If you had asked me to dance, I would have danced with you too. You were too busy throwing a silent tantrum. Again, I have danced with Reed before. There was no humping, bumping or grinding with him or anyone else. I wouldn't allow a man that I'm dancing with to be all up on me. It was all innocent."

"It was Reed. He wants you."

"I don't care what he wants."

"I know how that feels," Tellum murmured slyly.

"I heard that. You asked, why I'm here at this hour? This is why. What are we doing? Why did you invite me if you're going to make assumptions that will make us both miserable in the process? If you have a question on the tip of your tongue, ask me."

Cheyenne almost died and went to heaven from an overabundance of lust. Tellum stuck his tongue out and slowly licked his lips. At the same time, his eyes roamed up and down her body. It was clear to her that his anger was wearing off.

"Damn."

"Stop it. I know your mind. I'm mad at you right now. Focus on that!"

He smiled and her heart melted. Damn, how she missed him. Why did he have to be so fine? For a split second, her eyes focused again on the fact that he was shirtless. His body was actually a little wet as if he'd just stepped out of the shower. Thinking of the many times they'd had shower sex, she shook her head furiously from side to side to regain focus. She needed to stay angry.

"I wasn't thinking anything."

"Ask me," she said again.

"No."

"Why? You think the answer will be a hurtful one?"

She knew the answer and so did he. She hated these kinds of games. They never fought when they were involved.

"No. I'm not going to ask because I already know the answer. I let my mind go there. Reed, in his narcissistic way tried to get under my skin and I know it."

"Yet, here we are. You didn't know the answer when I called? You didn't give me a chance to talk to you."

"I'm really sorry. I know that's not you. I just know him."

"Look, Reed and you have this battle going on around whose is bigger. I don't know about his, but I know yours is massive. I don't care what his is like. I never, ever plan to find out. I wouldn't do that to you. I wouldn't do it here on your resort. I wouldn't do it back home. Never, Tellum. Never, ever. Whatever Reed had you thinking, that's between the two of you. I don't want anyone to think of me in the way you did. The idea that you would think that cuts deep."

When Tellum moved in her direction, she stepped back. He raised his arms up in surrender. She remembered another time when he'd done that. It was back at her place the night she ended their relationship. He wanted to reach for her then and she wouldn't let him. That was happening again.

"I know. I'm sorry. Cheyenne, you can't blame me for being jealous. You know how much I love you. That hasn't changed. I invited you here because I want you to relax and enjoy yourself. I can also admit that I had an ulterior motive."

"Which was?"

"I wanted to see you. I wanted to know what life has been like for you over the past six months. Is my hanging up on you any ruder than you not taking my calls when I call you?"

She opened her mouth and closed it tight. He had her there. It was clear that they've both made childish mistakes. In her opinion, no response is better than a rude one. The two weren't the same, but she got it. Point made.

"I'm sorry about that. Yes, my behavior was rude as well. I apologize for that. But you thinking that I would, what, sleep with Reed? That hurts. How could you think I would do that?"

"Okay, I get that. Think about this. What if you had been walking by my bungalow after midnight and you saw a woman coming down the steps? What would you think? Am I so far removed from your heart that you wouldn't care? You wouldn't be even a little bit upset? I invite you here and then parade a woman in your face? I wouldn't do that."

"*Exactly*! That's all I'm saying. You wouldn't do that to me. I know you wouldn't. If you were already seeing someone else, you wouldn't have invited me. I wouldn't take this invite as an opportunity to get laid. If I were seeing someone, I would have declined your invitation. Neither of us is that heartless. Trust me, if I haven't done it since the last time we were together, I wouldn't have waited until now to do it."

"Wait, what?"

Tellum's left eyebrow raised with a lot of questions. She knew what she'd just revealed. She wasn't ready to discuss that yet.

"Another conversation for another time. Right now, I want to be sure you know that I wouldn't get with any man, especially Reed while here. I didn't come here for that. Beautiful place, by the way. I've only been here a day and it's been both amazing and already sprinkled with a little drama. When I called you, Melodi told me that she thought she encountered you seeing Reed coming from my villa. He was."

Before she could continue, Tellum moved from his position near the door to the glass wall of the larger-than-life shower. She heard his huge intake of breath. Like when he hung up on her, he didn't want to hear what was coming next.

"Cheyenne, we can't have this conversation."

"Yes, we can. You didn't let me finish on the phone. Please listen to me now."

She spoke without rage this time. They needed to have this conversation. They hadn't seen each other in months. There was no doubt that curiosity on both ends was living between them. Their love had been fast growing and deeply intense. There was enough jealousy of what they both could have been doing to cause the kind of friction that happened after he hung up on her.

Again, he huffed loudly and then nodded.

"I'm listening," he said.

"I did not invite him there. He showed up. I left the party early. I wanted to have some peace. You provided me with the perfect lodging. I mean, it's over the water. Melodi said he asked about me when he saw her and didn't see me. She told him I went back to my villa. She didn't tell him which one, but he found it anyway. I didn't even let him in the gate. If I'm really honest, I thought it was you. For a second, I was excited thinking that you had come to see me when I heard footsteps on the path. I know we didn't get a chance to talk earlier because you were busy. It's your resort. It's your pre-grand opening; your big launch. I didn't expect to get to spend any time with you. That's mainly because we aren't together. Also, again, this is your baby."

"That used to be you," he interrupted.

"What?"

"My baby."

The softness and overpowering love in his eyes warmed her. All the anger she felt flew out of the window. She understood his jealousy. He was right, if the shoe was on the

122

other foot and she'd seen a woman coming from his place at this hour, she would be just as angry. Seeing the softness for her in Tellum's eyes is how he was able to be the first guy that she slept with right after meeting him. Everything about him was magnetic, especially his eyes.

"I miss hearing you call me that," she admitted. "Let me finish, okay?"

"Absolutely."

"When I saw it wasn't you but Reed, I opened the gate, but again, I didn't let him in. He said he was checking on me because he thought I was ill. It was a lame excuse for him being there, but that's fine. I peeped that. He then asked me out. I said no. I let him know that under no circumstances, whether I had been your girlfriend or not, would I be interested in him. I wasn't mean about it. I simply put it out there for him that it wasn't going to happen either here or back at home. He tried that, lunch or dinner here or lunch or dinner back in Detroit. It was a no to all of that for me. He tried to play on my mind by trying to insinuate that you were a womanizer. He wanted me to believe that you dropped me because you wanted other women. I didn't fix that ideal for him because I don't care what he or anyone else thinks. I know you're not like that. At least you weren't when we were together. You can be and do anyone you want. He tried it though. He wanted me jealous enough that I would probably use him to make you jealous. I would never do that. He left when his ploy didn't work. That had to be when you saw him. He was there all of five minutes. I don't know what transpired between the two of you, but nothing happened on this end. Do you want to ask me?" she said, putting the question out to him again.

"No, Cheyenne. I had a few minutes of temporary insanity out of my love and desire for you. What transpired between Reed and I didn't take words. A gesture or two from me, but no words. He knew what he wanted me to think. My mind went there and I'm sorry. I do know you well enough to know that isn't you. He goaded me and I fell for it. That's it. That's my entire story. I will forever be jealous of any man who finds a place in your heart. I'm just pissed that it's not me anymore. Wait, let's go back. You wanted me to come see you? You thought it was me?"

Cheyenne nodded.

"I did."

Now, it was her turn to look away. She wanted to admit that the months from him were torture. Her life was a mess. She'd made a blunder. Leaving him had been her greatest mistake. Her mother was right. Melodi was right. Her own heart was right.

"When I saw him, outside of being angry, I wanted to be him. I was wide awake and, in my bungalow, because I was going through something since you arrived. Why are we torturing ourselves when we both know what we want? Life doesn't have to be like this," Tellum clarified.

Cheyenne didn't reply. He was right. She didn't know what to say. Should she admit she wanted him back after being so confident when she broke up with him? Would he trust her with his heart again? Could she trust herself with his heart again? Taking a break from such a heavy conversation, she took her only out to give her brain a breather; she changed the subject.

"I love what I see so far of your bungalow. You did an amazing job with your vision."

"Are you done ripping into me? If so, can we calm down enough for me to offer you a tour? I know it's late, but you are here. If not now, any time works for me. I'll be here for the next four days after today or actually, yesterday since it's after midnight."

That admission got her attention. She assumed he would be here the entire week like her.

"Four days? You're leaving early?"

"Four days, not including today – so, five days in total. I have a business meeting in Denver."

"Oh."

Cheyenne didn't want to show her disappointment. She didn't know what her expectation was of his time.

"Have dinner with me before I leave?"

"Yes," she blurted out before the last word left his mouth. The world stopped and then they laughed it off. The mood in the room shifted from one that was tension-filled to one of content. They were beyond what happened. She still had a few words for Reed. She didn't appreciate what he tried to do.

"A tour or is it too late?" he asked.

"Like you said, I'm here now. I'd love a tour."

"Okay, let's start downstairs."

When Tellum reached his hand out to her, she put hers in his. Her head said new beginning. With her lips, she remained silent. This moment was exactly what it needed to be without overthinking anything.

11

Tellum kept his eyes focused on Cheyenne as she took in the lower level. Each bungalow had its own design. This was his favorite of them all.

"The resort is adult-only. Each living space is designed for singles or couples. The larger bungalows can also be used for groups. We did some focus groups and there were a lot of responders who said they would like to have a large space where women could stay together during a girls' trip. This bungalow has two bedrooms down here each with a separate commode, but they do share the large vanity area, shower and tub."

"The bathroom is the size of a small apartment," Cheyenne admired.

"Each bedroom has a walkout to the wraparound pool. That's for those who don't want to venture out of their living space while they are here. There is a small kitchen with the bare minimum including a mini-fridge, microwave and coffee pot. No stoves because we don't want anyone cooking. Food can be ordered and delivered twenty-four hours a day. Our main kitchen is always open. The great room has the large screen television. Each room has one as well, just not as large as this seventy-five-inch one. There is a privacy fence around the wraparound pool that can be opened by remote control for those who want to be able to see the ocean."

"Everything is so nice and clean. Fresh flowers. Oh, by the way, thank you for my flowers. They were all so beautiful."

"Any and everything beautiful for a beautiful woman. You're welcome. Ready go up?"

"Yes."

Tellum led the way back up.

"Up here on this level are two more bedrooms; only one master suite. There are two bathrooms, the deck and a jacuzzi. The circular seating out here could also be used as an outside bed is a hit."

"This view is amazing. Look at the ocean," Cheyenne said stepping out onto the deck. "You can see everything from this high up."

"Apparently, you can see too much, as well."

Tellum couldn't apologize enough for making such a hasty and nasty assumption about her. If he had taken a second to think more about her and less about Reed, he would have known she wouldn't have hurt him in any way, even if he hadn't seen Reed.

"We're good?" she asked turning to him.

Tellum stood in the sliding glass door frame with his hands up gripping the top of it. Cheyenne leaned back against the railing with her elbows resting up on it and one foot up on the bottom base.

"We're good. I'd like for us to be perfect."

Her smoldering gaze spoke volumes. Seeing her in his place under the moonlight on this silent night couldn't be more perfect. She looked angelic.

"What does that look like?" she asked.

He was surprised. Cheyenne didn't shut him down and out the way she had the day they'd split up. Had something changed? Was she having a change of heart about their relationship or lack thereof? He didn't know, but he would remain hopeful.

Moving away from the doorway, he walked over to her. If she moved away from him, he would know how to spin the conversation to not make her uncomfortable.

"You spending the night with me," he said softly.

Her eyes searched his. He watched the throat where she took in a large gulp. She didn't say immediately say no. He hoped that was a good sign. She was thinking about it.

"Can I say something off this topic before I respond?" she asked.

"The floor is yours."

Tellum moved even closer. This time, he cocooned her by putting his hands on the gold bar behind her and held on to it. There wasn't much space between them. If he moved his head forward slightly, he could suck on her lips and tongue with his own, making them one the way he'd been longing to do for months. He had been dying inside for months without being able to kiss her.

"I can see what you would have seen from this vantage point. I'm sorry," she offered by way of apology.

"Baby, it's alright. I got it. We got it. I will say that Reed's going to get it as well as soon as I see him. I don't appreciate him trying to put that kind of image of you in my head or in anyone else's head. A man wouldn't do that; a male would. There is a difference."

"No confronting Reed. Let this go. You know what didn't happen. I know what didn't happen. Melodi reminded me of how much she hates him. I don't want to hate anyone, but I really dislike him."

"You are not alone. His father's company is good business for mine. If he doesn't deal with Reed, his son will one day run it in the ground."

"Promise me that you'll let this go. He's not worth the energy. This is your resort. Don't let him take you there in your space."

Tellum fought his inner demon that said he wanted to wipe the floor with Reed. Like any other time since they met, he couldn't deny Cheyenne anything.

"I promise. Now, my question?"

"Right. Spend the night with you. Just this one night?"

Tellum was ready to dance with joy. Was she giving him an option of more than tonight?

"I'll tell you what I'm thinking. No pressure. You know how much I want you. There is no mistaking that."

Before he could continue, his eyes followed Cheyenne's eyes as they ventured down his body to that part of him that he knew she could see hard and ready for what her body was yearning for. All the signs were there. She was braless, he knew that for sure. He could see her nipples hardening through her dress. Breasts he loved loving on. She still desired him. Her body language spoke it. Her eyes glowed with it.

"Yes, I know."

He leaned close to her left ear.

"You smell amazing. I see you still love lavender."

"You know, it's a really warm night."

Tellum chuckled close to her ear. She was nervous as if they weren't already familiar with each other in the most intimate kind of way.

"That may be true. The fact is, the heat you feel is radiating between us. You know how it is when we're this close together. Now, my idea? Want to hear it?" he whispered and took a chance with his next move. He lightly licked her earlobe. She shuddered. He'd hit gold.

"Yyyesss," she stuttered out.

"I think that we should just enjoy this time here on the island. I'm talking, you and me, and whatever we want to do together and to each other. If you want or need anything from me while you're here, all you have to do is give me a sign. You can call me, text me, email me, sky-write a message, morse code, I'm talking whatever it takes. If you want me, I'll be there. I already kill myself slowly with thoughts of you with someone else. I won't survive that here on the island. I know you said you wouldn't do that to me. I wouldn't do that to you either. There is a lot of respect between us. Can I ask you a very personal question? I promise I won't get upset over the answer. I know you won't lie to me."

Cheyenne looked up at him with concern. He was getting deep. He wanted their cards on the table. Besides, he had to know.

"I wouldn't lie about anything. Your question?"

"Have you had your desires met since we broke up? I'm not sure I want the answer, but still, here I am answering. This is a place where desires are to be set free. You know I created it with us in mind, yet, being apart, I didn't think we'd be here together. By together, I'm talking about in the same place and space. Of course, going further, I want more."

"Tell, I already told you that I haven't been interested in anyone. Therefore, I haven't been with anyone."

"In six months? I know you alluded to it a few minutes ago, but I wanted to be sure I heard what I thought I heard."

"Yes, you heard right. Is that hard to believe? I know it's different for men. I won't even ask you."

Tellum wanted her to know. He pressed his body lightly against hers. He moved his lips close to hers without touching.

"Ask me."

He meant it. There is nothing he wouldn't tell her. He was and always would be an open book.

He watched the show of emotions that crossed her face. He could tell the words were on the tip of her tongue. He wanted her to know.

"Why? Like you, do you think I haven't hurt myself with the images of you with other women? I know your appetite. I was on the other end of it for a long time; night after night; day after day. We had a healthy sex life. You have a strong hunger for it. I learned that early in our relationship. I was glad that my craving for you, matched your hunger for me."

"Cheyenne, stop it. For starters, if at any time you wanted me to love all on and in you, all you had to do was tell me."

"We were broken up."

"So? I know you don't do the casual thing, but we were beyond that, even if we weren't together anymore. I want to offer you me and my loving while you're here. Again, no pressure for anything beyond that if that's how you want it. I know how we left things. I hate it, but I love you more. I'm here for four days. Think of all that we could do to each other in that time, uninterrupted. No one has to know about this but me and you; well, and Melodi. I don't think much gets by her."

"That's true. I have no doubt that she's expecting us to tear at each other's clothes tonight."

"Oh, how I love the idea of that. I'm not wearing much, but feel free to snatch it off if you want. Do you?"

Tellum inhaled deeply. He could smell her arousal. It was mixing in nicely with his as it always has done.

"What? Do I want to rip off your silk pajama bottoms?"

"No and yes. Damn the visual I just had of that. Do you want to indulge while we're here?"

Tellum gave her an example of what could be in store for her. He leaned his face forward until they were a whisper away. He stuck his tongue out, keeping his eyes locked on hers, and licked slowly across her lips from one side to the other. He then made a pass back to the other side, hearing her breath hitch. He kept his tongue out right at her lips. Not surprisingly, Cheyenne moved her lips closer to his and quickly allowed her tongue to touch his in a move that had them both moaning.

Tellum felt drunk with need, with hunger. Nothing changed with their connection over the months.

"Should we?" she finally released the air she was holding to ask.

"First, ask me," he uttered.

"Tellum."

"Cheyenne? You know I would never lie to you. I would never do it to get you in bed. I know you're interested in the truth. There is no need for either of us to be mysterious about my life. You said this to me earlier. Now I'm saying it to you; ask me."

Cheyenne searched his face. He wouldn't look away. She needed to see what she needed to see. There would be no hiding anything; not if there was a chance to eventually get back together.

"Since we broke up, has there been anyone else?" she asked softly.

He could hear the hesitancy in her voice as if she wanted to know but not really. He didn't make her suffer long. The strain on her face was clear.

"No. Not a single person. I kept my belief locked onto the idea that one day, you would realize there isn't anyone else for either of us to love the way we love each other. I know I love sex. I enjoy making love to and with you. I don't want anyone else, Cheyenne. Maybe now isn't the right time to talk about that. I don't want things to get complicated. What's the least complicated route for us right now? I haven't touched another woman. I can't imagine doing so unless there was no hope for me and you. Enough time hadn't passed yet. I didn't want to come to you having to explain that in six months, I was already trying to find a replacement; even a sexual one. There isn't one."

Cheyenne nodded. He had no doubt she believed him. She could read him better than anyone.

"Six months? No one? You must be..."

She didn't finish. He knew what was coming next.

"Horny as *hell*? Damn right I am. Sweetness, you have no freaking idea. You're here in front of me looking like a miracle from a dream. You're sexy as hell. I desire you. I hunger for you and only you. The question is, what do you want from me?"

Tellum was about to continue his questioning her to see where her mind was. He wasn't left with room to do so. Her lips were on his in an instant. He enjoyed when she took control of getting from him what she wanted and needed.

"Yes," she sexily slurred against his lips, pulling back only giving him a second to think before she took his lips and possessed them a second time. He pulled her body flush against his as her arms went up around his neck.

"Damn," he murmured against her cheek.

They kissed with a fervor that existed only between them. He couldn't let himself believe that anyone else could be this connected on a level not visible to the eyes. Here he was with her in their own world. He loved seeing her just like this. Cheyenne was adrift in desire and pleasure as she moaned into his mouth with each pass of her tongue against his.

With Cheyenne's body pressed back against the railing, Tellum needed his hands all over her. That was the only way he knew that her kissing him again like he belonged to her was actually happening. His body was aching for her; her lips; her hands; her body.

He quickly became aware that they were standing outside on his balcony, but luckily, not many people could see them because of the trees. Still, if they were going to love, he would move them inside. First, he needed to get his fill of his hands on her skin. It had been too long.

He moved back from kissing her. He smiled when he saw the discourse on her face.

"What?" she questioned him quizzically.

"You are so damn beautiful. You are a vision of pure breath-taking enchantment."

Tellum allowed his hands to caress the skin of her arms. They were warm and silky. When she shivered, he understood. It wasn't due to the temperature because it was clammy and hot. He knew she was feeling the excitement of them being together like this again after so long. When he touched her, it felt anew. He leaned down and kissed one shoulder and then the other before sliding the arms of her dress down until her breasts were exposed for his perusal. He kept his eyes locked on hers while his head lowered to her chest. As her breathing increased, he planted a series of kisses in succession between her breasts. His head drifted to one nipple before quickly shifting to the other. His mouth lingered on the other when her moans encouraged him on. Cheyenne's body shifted from side to side. He knew that meant she wanted more.

"So beautiful," he expressed against her flesh. "I've missed this; I've missed you."

When her hips moved in a circular motion toward him, he moved his hands down her dress until he reached the end of it. With his mouth loving on her hardened tips, going from one side to the other, he slipped his hands up under her dress expecting to encounter some type of silky panty that he was anxious to remove from her body. When he encountered nothing, he smiled against her breast. Nipping at a nipple, tugging on it with his teeth, he knew what that move did to her body.

"Yes, yes," she groaned out again and again sending tantalizing vibes through his body.

"Cheyenne, baby – you came here with no panties on? Damn! That's hot as hell. You know what that does to me; the image of you with no barrier preventing me from getting inside of you."

Moving his hand around, he parted her legs and slipped his hand between them. Moisture coated his fingers sending his body into a frenzied need.

"Tellum, please," she begged. "It's been a long time. I need you," she uttered sexily.

He knew what that meant. He wanted to be inside of her as much as she wanted him too, but he needed something else that he missed.

Picking her up in his arms, he turned and laid her flat on the round shaped lounge chair on the deck. He loved that it was big enough to accommodate them both, including him with his height.

Pushing her dress up higher on her hip, he moved down until his head was exactly where he wanted it. He raised her legs up and over his shoulder, wasting no time in feasting on her wetness. Cheyenne's sharp cry of desire pierced the darkened sky. He didn't care who heard her. He'd missed tasting her. He wouldn't move or stop until he had his fill. He missed hearing her screams when an earth-shattering orgasm tore through her, piercing the air around them. This loving was long overdue.

He lapped at her slowly, at first. He covered his tongue and his lips with her wetness. Cheyenne's legs shook when he raised them even higher in the air. His long arms held them in place. He could see her head flopping back and forth with immense longing. He could feel the wind of her arms flapping about wildly trying to grip something. Her body flailed about haphazardly around and around. He gave her more and more, increasing the movement of his mouth and tongue working in sync. With his hand, he reached between his mouth and her womanhood and stroked her with expert precision. Knowing her body, he knew what it would do to her. As much as Cheyenne would try and ride out his loving without letting go, he didn't want that. After six months, he wanted all of her. He wanted that first release that would start of their night of loving.

When Cheyenne covered her mouth with her hand while her hips raised from the seat to get more from him, he gave her what her body had been missing. Pressing on the hardened nub that greeted him with a need that surpassed understanding, the combination of his finger and the pad of his tongue, he felt Cheyenne let go. He used the other hand to grip the curve of her hip to hold her in place. Her hips moved with him, urging him on. As long as her body cried out for him, he gave her all of him.

He felt her hands in his hair as she quietly called out his name over and over. As her hips slowed, he tampered down the rhythm of his finger and mouth.

"I've missed this," he slurred out, moving up her body. "You taste like peaches," he declared, locking their lips in a fiery kiss.

"I'm seeing stars. I'm not talking about the ones in the sky," she huffed out lovingly.

Tellum gave her a moment to catch her breath while he removed the dress from her body.

"Just like this. Anytime you want to come see me, feel free to do so just like this; no bra and no panties."

"I'm naked and you're not," she said breathlessly.

"I'm about to remedy that. We need to be inside. I have plans for outdoor lovemaking before I leave. I know how much we love making love with nature all around us."

"Mmm, on the beach?" she asked smiling at him from ear to ear.

"Yes, baby, on the beach. For now, I have other plans for this body."

Cheyenne reached for him. Tellum lifted her into his arms, leaving the dress on the seat. Getting them inside, he closed the balcony door and entered the darkened bedroom. He placed her flat on her stomach in a way that her entire body was on the bed from top to bottom. When she grabbed a pillow, placing it under her head with her hands flat against the headboard, he smiled knowing they were on the same page. Sexual positions were there thing. They tried a lot of different ones and loved them all. They had more positions than the Karma Sutra. Their loving was never, ever boring. It wasn't sex that drove them apart. On purpose, that part of their relationship was always perfect.

Getting as naked as she was, he refused to waste even a second of their time together.

"No music?" she asked.

"Unless you want it, my answer is no. The only sounds I want to hear are those that will come from me and especially from you. I need that tonight. It's been far too long since I've last heard the sounds of our making love."

Tellum climbed up on the bed and opened her legs a tad bit, but not fully. He only needed a little room for what he had in mind.

First, he let his hands roam across her back and up to her neck. He massaged her deeply there, then her arms, feeling her relaxing under his touch. With her arms up above her head and her head turned to the side, eyes closed, he moved his hands down to let his fingers run across the sides of her breasts.

"Your hands are so magical," she said groggily.

He knew she was still feeling the impact of her last orgasm. He was excited to give her even more of them throughout the night.

Cheyenne rolled her hips under him.

"Enjoy, baby," he encouraged.

Moving his hands up and down her back, he relaxed the flesh he encountered, reacquainting himself with the feel of her. When his hands reached the flesh of her ample behind, he let them linger there. Lowering his head, he licked and then kissed one cheek after the other.

Cheyenne giggled.

"You love my behind," she laughed.

"You have a perfect, natural ass and I love it; you already know."

"I love this position," Cheyenne sexily crooned.

"I know. I want to be sure this night is memorable."

Moving his body so that he was lengthwise on top of hers. He slid his hips from side to side, moving them in slow motion against her, letting her feel how extremely hard he was for her.

"Look back at me, sweetheart," he said tenderly.

When Cheyenne lifted her head slightly and looked over her shoulder at him, she did exactly what he knew she would do. He watched her eyes drift down to where he was preparing to join their bodies together.

"Whew, stop teasing me," she expressed impatiently.

"You know I love making love to you with your sexy behind between us. I love how it jiggles when I pump in and out of you from this position. Ready for me?"

Cheyenne nodded her head, her eyes locked on their bodies.

Tellum held his hard, straining penis in his hand as he guided it between her legs. He already knew she was hot, wet and ready for him. He watched her eyes light up with delight as he slid inside of her a little bit at a time. Even when they would make love every night, he still needed to allow her body time to adjust to his size, especially when he was as hard as he was with veins in his shaft appearing as if they were about to pop.

Holding onto her hips, he moved slowly out until only the tip of himself remained inside of her. Cheyenne parted her legs a little more. He moved a little faster. He loved her like this; a way that they both enjoyed and derived much pleasure from. Moving so that his body once again covered hers completely, he quickened his motion. The bed rocked under them. Cheyenne moved along with him. The room was filled with the sounds of their loving. Their combined pheromones caressed his nostrils, sending his own body into a tizzy of need for more.

As he moved inside of her, he softly spoke into her ear, telling her of all the things he wanted to do to her in the days they had left. He let her know how much he missed being with her like this; how much is body longed and hungered for her. Her moans drove him on feverishly as he pumped away, surging into her on a beat that could only be heard by their hearts.

Cheyenne's hips moved erratically; his own drove him on harder and faster. She slammed her hands flat against the headboard as her body gave into the pleasure that seared through her. Her body moved about brilliantly and elegantly. When he thought he was riding her, she was really riding him. Her mating with him pushed him to the brink to follow her into a blissful explosion like the one she was having.

Tellum tried to hold on but couldn't. Knowing they had all night, he exploded inside of her so powerfully that he reached up and placed his hands on top of hers on the headboard. His hips possessed her body with perfect care. Being inside of her hit all of his zones. He rode out his release feeling an intense itch up and down his spine. Her pleasure pushed forward. He was reaching his peak with lovingly, powerful strokes. They cried out together. The embers of desire were stoked and blazing hot like fire. The world around his head crashed again and again with groping oneness, sending his love for Cheyenne on a new level.

As their loving slowed, Cheyenne's thrusts back to him continued to meet his thrusts forward. Tellum collapsed on his elbows to not put all of his weight on her body. He needed a moment to catch his breath. Everything around them quieted. He heard her suck in a deep breath of air as he kissed her back from one shoulder and then across to the other.

"My hunger for you can't be tamed, baby. I don't think many people love as deeply as we do. Please don't make me go back to a life without being able to love you; not like this with our bodies or our hearts. I need you."

Cheyenne joined their fingers together and relaxed her body under him. Tellum placed his head on her back and stayed there. He needed to stay in this moment. He said a silent thanks that she had come to him. He didn't care the reason. He only cared that she was here.

"I won't. I promise you I will never do that again. I will never again choose anything or anyone that doesn't include us. I love you."

He nodded against her back. He didn't need words. He only wanted her words to live in the air.

12

Tellum woke with the sunlight in his eyes. Cheyenne was right beside him, asleep on her stomach. He smiled when he saw her head buried in the pillow. He wasn't sure of the time, but knew that they had been asleep for a while after making love for a fourth time just before daylight. His body was partially covering hers; his leg thrown across her legs. His was sticking out on the other side of the comforter.

Reaching behind him, his hand searched for his phone. He checked the time, and it was after ten in the morning. He couldn't remember the last time he'd slept in this late. He was thankful that he'd put his phone on silent before they fell asleep. He'd missed several calls from both of his brothers and a few other people. None were important. Nothing was more important than the uninterrupted time he was able to spend with Cheyenne. He intended to carve out more time just for her while he was here. He already hated that he was leaving a few days before her when what he wanted to do was stay in paradise with his love for as long as she was here. That wasn't to be. In the midst of all of this bliss, he still needed to get business done.

He scrolled through texts from Callum about a meeting he was missing. He recalled that they agreed to a meeting early in the morning to allow them to each have time to relax and enjoy the island. He hadn't planned on missing the meeting, but after the night he and Cheyenne had together, he was surprised he wasn't on oxygen. His lady love had turned to him several times and as usual, he obliged her desire for him and his for her. He made her a promise that while they were on the island, if she wanted or needed him, especially to stoke the fire inside of her, he would give her his attention.

Taking his phone, he moved out of the bed and as naked as a jaybird, the way he always slept, he walked into the bathroom and shut the door. He dialed Callum before his brother called again. The phone rang a few times before he answered.

"What's up?" he asked when Callum finally answered.

"Daylight is. Where the hell are you? Did you forget we had a meeting this morning? Also, Shelton Sullivan is flying in this morning. He's coming with his lady love to hang out a few days before she flies home. He's going to meet us in Denver. Did you forget we all have friends who are here? Your best buds are looking for you. We're supposed to meet up to play pool and hit a few cigars."

"Damn. I forgot about Shelton. I mean, I didn't, but I did. I've been a little tied up. I'll be there shortly. I hope this isn't a long meeting. I need some sleep. Something tells me this pool and cigar time will span most of the day," he laughed.

"You got that right. How often are the three of us taking some time to chill together? Add in all the guys and you know it's a party. Before you show up, is your mood better?"

Tellum thought about Cheyenne and grinned like a kid who just raided the candy jar.

"Man, I'm better than I've ever been; that's a fact. You have no idea."

"All I know is whatever or whomever is making you smile with that goofy grin I know you're sporting, it better be Cheyenne. I'm never accepting another woman for you that isn't her. If it's someone else, stay in your room and don't come here. I may have to have Byrum join me in beating you down. You know Cheyenne is here. After last night, I knew you would be grumpy. I'm hoping that mood didn't lead you to bed some random chick."

Tellum held his phone away and shook his head.

"Really? Who do you think your brother is? I'm never going to be mad enough at Cheyenne or jealous enough of her with anyone else to be disrespectful in her face with another woman."

"But you are with a woman?" Callum asked.

"Yes, I am."

"So, you're with Cheyenne?"

"Yes. Since last night. She's sleeping which is why I'm in the bathroom whispering on the phone. You ever known me to whisper like this?"

Tellum laughed at himself.

"Ah, that's why you didn't answer the phone or return my texts this morning. Does this mean you're back together?"

"I don't know what it means at the moment. For now, we're enjoying each other's company."

"Does that mean last night when she was dancing with Reed and other men, sending you into a downward spiral was for nothing?"

"It was. You know how I feel about her. You also know how I am when it comes to Reed. I have to tell you and Byrum about that later on. He tried me last night. For now, I'll be there as fast as I can. Cheyenne will probably sleep for a while longer. I'll grab a quick shower and meet you in my office? Is that where we're meeting? I forgot."

"Brain cells. You're missing a few this morning. Get it together, bro!" Callum joked.

"Whatever."

"Yes, your office. Byrum and I are already here. Shelton will touch down in about four hours. He'll want to settle in and relax. We'll talk about a time for pool when you get here. And hey, whatever this is with you and Cheyenne, I'm happy for you. Watching you without her for these months has been brutal."

"Bro, I was living it. You have no idea what that brutality was like for me. Is Lisa-Marie around? I don't think she's flying out until tomorrow."

"Yeah, she's here. When I got to your office, she was moving and shaking. She gets stuff done."

"That's why I will pay her just about anything to make sure she stays around. I need her to set up one of the cabanas for me and Cheyenne for tomorrow night. She'll know what I want – the whole lover's package."

"Oh, yeah? I see you wooing your woman back. Good for you. Look, get off the phone and get here. The meeting won't be long. Byrum wanted to touch base on what we thought of last night. I'll let Lisa-Marie know you need to connect with her. I wouldn't want you to have a whispered conversation with her too!"

"Shut up! I'm moving. See you in a bit."

Ending the call, Tellum went back into the bedroom and rejoined Cheyenne in bed. He hated to wake her, but he didn't want to leave without letting her know.

"Baby?" he said close to her ear.

"Hmm?"

Tellum chortled. Cheyenne responded but not one part of her body moved.

"I need to run to a meeting with my brothers. I'm going to grab a shower and head out. Are you good?"

"Yes."

Her one word came out muffled under the pillow. He kissed her on the back.

"Are you sore anywhere?"

He knew their loving had gotten powerful, especially that last round with her on top. The way she rode him, he would have thought that she was on top of an actual horse. He recalled hearing her call him her stallion.

He watched her wiggle her hips a little and then stilled.

"A little," she garbled out.

"When you get up, take a hot bath, baby. Do you need anything from your room before I leave?"

"No. I'll call Melodi. She'll check in later for breakfast. She can bring me some stuff."

"Breakfast? Uh, baby, it's after ten in the morning. I think you're going to miss breakfast with her. I'm thinking you'll probably be in time for a late lunch."

"Ten? In the morning?"

"Yes. We've been asleep since about six."

He snuggled up to her body, tossing the blanket across his hips, rubbing his body against her.

"Stop that or you'll miss your meeting."

"Those knuckleheads won't miss me."

A lingering kiss on her shoulder stirred her further awake.

"We made love all night. Do you realize that? I lost count of the number of orgasms I had. My body remembers though."

"Too many to count, I do know that. Very enjoyable I will say. Remember my offer?"

"I do."

"Are we on for that?"

"Right now? No. I need more sleep."

"I know, baby."

"I mean, I didn't get to taste you as much as I wanted to last night," Cheyenne admitted and made a kissing sound.

"None of that either. Sleep. Do you want me to call or text Melodi for you? I bet she's been calling you this morning like my brothers were. Where's your phone?" he asked.

Cheyenne, still didn't move, but pointed to the table near the sliding glass door.

"I think there," she said.

"I see it. Do you want it?"

"No. Can you call Melodi and let her know I'm fine. I'm going back to sleep. I'll call her later. If it's ten, I've already missed our spa appointment. Tell her I'll meet her for zip lining at three."

"You really are sleepy."

Tellum hopped up from the bed and grabbed her phone.

When he tried to hand it to her to unlock it, without even opening her eyes, she knew.

"You know the code."

"It's the same?"

"Yes."

Unlocking her phone, he dialed Melodi.

"Girl, where are you? Are you still buried under your man?" Tellum couldn't hold in his amusement.

"You're hilarious. It's Tellum. Cheyenne is asleep. She's not going to make breakfast or the spa appointment y'all have. She said to let you know she'll see you for the zip lining excursion. You cool?"

"Am I cool? I'm perfect. That works for me. As long as she's happy. She is happy, right?"

"Ecstatic, just like me."

"That's good to hear. I thought I heard what sounded like a banshee in heat hollering in the sky last night. I assume that was her."

"Oh, if you heard that, it was probably me. Can you bring some of that girlie smelling stuff for her to take a hot bath when she gets up? You can leave it at the door and she'll get it."

"Bruh, what did you do to my girl? Can she even walk this morning? Damn, Tellum."

"Hey, you should ask me if I can walk this morning. The answer would be barely," he kidded. "I need to run out to a meeting. I'm going to have something delivered for her to eat when she's ready. She doesn't have any clothes with her. You got that covered?"

"I always have my sister's back. I got it covered. Go ahead to your meeting. I hope this means the two of you settled any issues as a result of the shenanigans of you know who."

"We good. Him? If I hadn't promised her I wouldn't hurt him, he would be meeting some concrete later."

"Well, I didn't make a promise. I have a few choice words for him. He tried to put a stain on my girl's character. That slimy snake is the worst of the worst. I'm good with checking someone like him when I encounter them. His whole attempt to get with her has been pissing me off. She's always turned him down, but he's a persistent bastard."

"Melodi, trust me – he has nothing coming. He's not a factor when it comes to her or me. I peeped his game. I'm fully aware. I don't recommend that he keep trying me. Thanks for being you. Cheyenne has the best friend in the world."

"Thanks, Tellum. The best friend and the best man in the world. She's a lucky girl, just like you and I are. I'll leave some stuff for her in a bag at the door. Let her know it's there. If she wants to skip out on ziplining, I understand. We're going with a group, so I'll be in good company. I want this time for her with you. Both of you need it. Try not to wear her out too much. Walking is something I don't want to have to teach her to do again," Melodi snickered.

"I've got six months to make up for not having her. I'm not making any promises. You should be telling that to her. I'll give her your message. Catch you later?"

"Definitely. Tell that fine Callum I said hello. If I didn't have Stephen, I would ride that cowboy."

Tellum laughed so loud, he had to cover his mouth when Cheyenne opened her eyes and tilted her head his way. He winked at her and she closed her eyes again before pulling the blanket up and over her head.

Placing her phone on the table next to the bed so that she could reach it, Tellum went back around and joined her in bed.

"What are your plans for tomorrow night? I know you probably have plans with Melodi for the live show tonight. I think most people are going to try and make it to our version of Coachella. There are some big artists performing; some of the biggest in R&B and rap."

"Yeah, we're going to that. Tomorrow night I don't have any plans."

"You do now. We're having a special night of dinner and dessert on the beach. I'm going to plan it all out and have my assistant put it into play."

"All night?" she asked.

"Yes. All night with me on the beach. It'll be very private, safe and secure. Just me and you, a firepit, curtained bed, soft music and loving all night if we choose. How about that?"

Cheyenne turned her head in his direction.

"I love all of that. Loving and sleeping under the stars. I can't wait. Does that mean I won't see you tonight at all?" she asked, yawning to the point that her whole body joined in on it.

"Remember my offer? If you want me, I'll be here, meet you in your villa or anywhere else you want. I have a friend flying in shortly. I was going to make an appearance at the show tonight. Over all of that, you are my priority. I'm all yours whenever."

"I like the sound of that. Have fun with your friend. I'll text you when I get up to meet Melodi."

"She's leaving some stuff for you for a bath and a change of clothes at the door. When you get up, check for it. Food will be delivered. You know where to find that. The chute for that is right at the door. Coffee, juice, a western omelet and some fresh fruit?"

"And some crispy bacon on the side."

"Bacon it is."

Tellum pulled the cover from her body, allowing his eyes to take in her nakedness. He did what he always loved doing. He kissed her behind, going between both cheeks.

"I'm telling you that you should stop right now if you plan on making it to your meeting."

"Don't tempt me woman. I love you," he said covering her back up. "I'm jumping in the shower. I promise to let you get back to sleep."

"I love you," she said.

13

The concert was in full swing. Guests were singing and dancing as the brothers finally stepped away from their prime position off the side of the main stage. As performers came and went, many expressed their love for the amenities while declaring how they couldn't wait to bring their partners back during a time when they could enjoy the resort for vacation and not work. Byrum walked behind Tellum and Callum. He assumed Callum was hustling to get a late-night flight out to Denver. He would be the first to kick off a meeting all three of them would be at in a few days. He should have left earlier, but it was rare for the three of them to be able to relax together without work being the purpose. Tellum, he was sure, was heading for his bungalow to get some rest. He couldn't count the number of times his brother had yawned throughout the day. This was, after all, a time when he was supposed to be focusing on relaxation only. No doubt, he was also making his way to Cheyenne.

Earlier, they got the chance to hang out and chill with friends after they had all finally arrived. The group of them got together over pool, darts and cigars at the brand-new pool hall that had been a new addition to the resort. The popular hangout spot consisted of fourteen pool tables, twenty dart boards, five chess tables and of course, everyone's favorite, fifteen poker tables.

As they eventually smoked their cigars and chilled out on the deck, Byrum's best friends, Mason Jackson, an accountant running his own firm and Noah McDonald, a college professor at an HBCU, caught him up with what they'd been up to since they had a chance to last get together a few months ago.

Also in their group were a few of Tellum's friends, Omari Clark, a district court judge from Chicago and Tommy Johnson, his best friend who ran a sports management company. A friend and a business associate to all of them, Shelton, who was closer to Tellum, hadn't come to the concert tonight. He decided that tonight was the perfect time for him and McKenna to stay in and enjoy their bungalow.

Callum had invited several of his close friends which included his best friend since elementary school, Finn Adams, a local Detroit club owner and Luke Perry, a well-known Chef out of Atlanta. Together, they relaxed and put work behind them. Inviting them all to the VIP area at the concert was their way of keeping the bond of brotherhood they'd developed strong. Slowly, each guy started making their way back to their rooms to either spend the rest of the evening with their women or to actually get some rest. That was something not many of them actually took much time away from work to do.

Making his way out of the concert and unlike his brothers, Byrum had some work he needed to look over even at this late hour. The next resort opening, *Silent Whisper*, would fall on him. Though the brothers worked together on all of the resorts, this next one was his baby just as this resort was Tellum's project. This week, he was hoping Tellum would step away from worrying about the resort or anything else work related. He'd been so busy over the past year trying to get this place to the level of perfection that he wanted that vacation had been the last thing on his mind. They all agreed that until he left the resort to join Callum in Denver, he would handle all work-related issues, allowing Tellum to have some down time. He was happy he could give Tellum a break, especially now that it appeared he was well on his way to getting his love back. The minute the idea of Tellum getting his heart back came to mind, he looked ahead of him to see Reed coming in their direction. His eyes caught Reed and Tellum the moment they saw each other. Things didn't look like they were going to go well when Tellum made a slight turn in Reed's direction. Byrum didn't rush ahead when Omari pulled Tellum in a different direction. That encounter could have been a bad one for Reed. When it came to Cheyenne, Tellum didn't play. After he told them all what Reed tried to do, keeping the men apart was on his radar. He, on the other hand, had no problem with pulling Reed up and being aggressive if need be.

Before Reed could get too far, Byrum walked over and caught up with him. He patted him on the back and held him by the shoulder to keep him there.

"Let me chat with you for a few ticks," Byrum said.

No one came for either of his brothers without getting a piece of his mind.

He walked the path away from the concert with Reed. He needed them to be able to talk where the music wouldn't drown out what he had to say. When they were far enough away, he stopped walking. Reed turned to him and crossed his arms across his chest.

"Great concert. You all knocked things out of the park with this opening. I've heard nothing but rave reviews from everyone. I have to admit, I had my doubts, but this resort is absolutely five-star. You did a great job," Reed asserted.

"Tellum," Byrum said.

"What?"

"Tellum. You are mistakenly complimenting the wrong brother. It's Tellum who gets the most credit for this place. This was his baby. Each of us has taken on the lead responsibility for each of the resorts we're opening. This was mainly all him. You wouldn't give him the credit though, right? Listen, I don't want a battle to come to fruition between you and my brother."

When Reed's eyes widened as if he was clueless to where this conversation was coming from, Byrum's anger started to come to the surface. He hated when Reed played innocent. He'd known him for a lot of years. That was his go-to response when things got heated for some reason.

"There isn't anything untoward going on with Tellum."

"Oh? That's not what I heard."

"Really? What have you heard."

"Don't play with me, Reed. I know you too well. I know you have your eyes set on Cheyenne. That's well known with those in my circle. You and I have been cordial for a lot of years. I don't know what this thing is between the two of you and I don't care. I will say, do me a favor and don't come for him."

"Byrum, I don't know what you've heard but nothing is going on. I haven't come for Tellum. I understand he and Cheyenne aren't together anymore. I get that she used to date Tellum, but all is fair in..."

"Don't go there. I'm telling you, do *not* go there. You know how much my brother loves her. Even if they are not together, for you to make a play for her here on this resort that my brother owns, is low even for you. You've done some dirty things that I am well aware of. Your reputation precedes you. I'm going to say this in the kindest way possible; do...not...come...for...my...brother! He is aware of what you tried to make him believe about you and Cheyenne. That's some kiddie, childish, high school mess."

"What are you talking about?"

Byrum had finally lost patience. He looked away, inhaled and then focused all of his attention on making sure Reed got the message.

"I know you tried to make Tellum think something happened with you and Cheyenne last night. Before you try to deny it, I already know it's true. I spoke to Tellum about it. Melodi said she realized what she had walked up on when she saw you. She talked to Cheyenne who then went to talk to Tellum. She knew he had to be upset. Yes, they may not be a couple, but the love is still very much there. This thing you have for always trying to get one up on my brother is getting old. Now, I can't say that we are the best of friends, but we're good. We always have been. You and Tellum, not so much. In every instance, I will always side with my brother; with both of my brothers. I don't care the situation or the person on the other side, I will always side with them."

Reed shifted on his feet.

"Byrum, look..."

"Save it. I'm telling you, don't press your luck here. Tellum is the most diplomatic of the three of us. He has the biggest heart. He gives people the benefit of the doubt. Callum is the wildest one of us. He lives life on the edge. He's also the smartest of the three of us. He has a keen ear and eye that benefits us in the business world. Now, me? I'm the enforcer. I will go from zero to sixty against a fool in no time at all when it comes to my family; to those I love. That includes Cheyenne. She's like a sister to me. I don't want to see her hurt. I also don't want anyone to put the idea in anyone's head that she's some kind of woman who would invite a man into her space for cheap, quick sex. You tried to do that. You tried to make Tellum think that. It's taken everything in him to not slay you. You would be no match for him, and you know it. Stop pressing his buttons."

Reed tried to stop him.

"Look, Byrum..."

"I'm not finished. I want to be clear about something. You need to hear this. Tellum isn't the one you need to worry about. That would be me, Reed. I'm warning you, with a smile, to pull back on this thing you have about my brother. I don't know if it's jealousy, admiration or what. Pull it back. I will reach out and touch you in the worse way and welcome a law suit. I would hurt any and every one for my brothers. I'm the one of the three of us that just doesn't give a damn. I will protect my family with my life. Don't make me come for you. Our families do great business together. I'm looking forward to continuing that partnership. I want to be clear about something very important. I will back out on any and all partnerships with your family's airline. Me coming for you physically, you won't want that. You don't have to try and explain anything to me. I'm telling you, pull it back now before there is no opportunity for you to do so. I only give one warning and this is it. Now, I'm heading back to the concert to enjoy myself. I know you're leaving in two days. I hope you can continue to enjoy your stay here and have a safe flight back home. When it comes to Tellum, back off. You got it?"

Byrum watched Reed's body give in as his shoulders slumped.

"Yeah, I hear you. I meant no harm," Reed explained.

"Oh, you did mean hard. I get it. Like I said, this is your only warning."

"Noted," Reed said.

With that, Byrum put out his hand for Reed to shake When he took it, Byrum held onto it. He then tightened his grip, pulling the man closer to him. He could see the pain in Reed's face as it resonated from his hand and up his body to his brain. Byrum knew how tight the grip was.

"Walk away, Reed," he said before turning him loose. Without looking back at the man, Byrum turned and headed back to the arena. He hadn't meant to threaten Reed, but when it came to his brothers, there isn't a hurdle he wouldn't flatten for both of them.

With an extra pep in his step, he walked with pride, shaking off the encounter with Reed. As he got close to the arena, he spotted his assistant, Keiko heading away from it with two other members of their team. He pressed for her to find more time for enjoyment. He didn't want her totally focused on work. Back at home, she had enough to deal with when it came to a horrible ex-husband and a five-year old son, Tru. He knew that she rarely got time to herself like this.

He admired the way her long black hair fell straight down around her shoulders and down her back. She was a natural beauty who came from an African American father and Japanese mother. He'd never told another soul, but to him, there wasn't another woman as lovely as her.

"Byrum? You're missing the show," she said when he reached her.

"I know. I had to step away for a few minutes. Are you leaving already?"

"Oh, we are having a late dinner in the Italian restaurant. I'm also hoping to winddown early. I've been having a good time."

"I'm glad you're enjoying yourself. I was hoping you would. How's Tru? I bet he's missing his mom."

"He is. I talked to him earlier. My parents flew in from Boston to spend this time with him at my place. He said that he was having a real good time with his Paw-Paw."

Byrum knew that she was going through a tough time with her ex-husband. He hadn't been eavesdropping, but he'd overheard her end of several of their phone conversations where she'd gotten pretty heated. She deserved better treatment from a man than what he'd witnessed so far.

"I won't hold you ladies up. Let me know if you need anything," he said.

As they walked away, he tried to not look back at Keiko. When he could no longer resist not getting a last look at her, he turned only to find that she had also turned to look his way. With a quick, slight wave, and a beautiful smile, she turned a corner and was out of sight.

He had to get it together.

"No way," he said to himself.

"No, you can't," the imaginary devil on his left shoulder said.

**

Tellum was heading back to his bungalow, exhausted after a long day. He still hadn't had a chance to catch up on sleep after being busy all day. He had hoped to get back to Cheyenne for some quality time. They'd texted throughout the day. She was having fun, so he didn't want to interrupt her time. She hadn't given him a signal, so he assumed she would hopefully make time for him the next day. He wasn't too disappointed in not being with her tonight knowing that they were spending the night together on the beach the next night. He was looking forward to that.

Racing up the steps to finally get in bed, he opened the door, turned on the light and stood stoic, amazed at the sight before him. He hadn't missed out on seeing Cheyenne after all. She was sitting up in his bed watching television.

"You're here!" he shouted excitedly, shutting and locking the door behind him. He flipped a switch on the wall that illuminated a red light outside of his door. That meant he was not to be disturbed.

"Yes. Is that okay?"

When she looked at him as if she wasn't sure that she should be in his bed, he doused that by racing to the bed and pulling her up out of it and into his arms. With her legs crossed behind his back, he kissed her with intoxicating zest. When her lips parted for his entry, he breathed a sigh of relief and uttered sweet words of thanks that she'd just made his night. He expected the surge of hot desire that flooded his body and his soul.

"Did you get your answer?" he asked when the kiss stopped. He still held her close.

"Yes, and I'm glad. I didn't know if you remembered you gave me the passcode to get in. I know you're tired and wanted to get some sleep."

"Well, I will sleep better having you here with me. You should be asleep too. If I remember, you sent me a text that you had finally gotten out of bed around one, just in time to eat and run to meet Melodi. How was ziplining?"

"Amazing! I love the feeling of flying through the air. It definitely woke me up. The look down was beautiful. The concert tonight was good too. I saw you on the side of the stage. Melodi and I had great seats."

"Did she leave with you?"

"Yeah. She said she was actually tired and just wanted to relax. Part of her coming with me was not just to be hanging out the whole time, but to also relax and do nothing. She was looking forward to doing that tonight."

"Good for her," he said, setting Cheyenne back on the bed.

"Do you want anything? I ordered some fresh fruit and a couple of salads. There are also some small bottles of wine on ice. I didn't know how tired or hungry you would be when you came back."

"No, I'm good. I just want to get a shower and cuddle up in bed with you."

"That sounds like a perfect plan. I started to go to my room, but I really wanted to be here with you."

"Baby, I will always want you with me. Never doubt that, okay?"

She nodded. He winked and headed in to take his shower.

"Can we sleep in tomorrow? Do you have a meeting or anything in the morning?" she called out to him.

Tellum came back into the bedroom and removed his clothes.

"We can sleep in as late as you want. For my last few days, I don't have any meetings or anything else business related.

That's the great part of having a powerful team in place who know how to handle things without being tightly managed. I know some bosses like to micromanage every aspect of the work their staff does, but not me or my brothers. We hired people because of their talent. We trust that they know what they're doing. They'll let us know if they need us. Otherwise, I step back. I'm all yours."

"Tomorrow night still on?"

"Whew, baby, you have no idea how on tomorrow night will be. We're going to be surrounded by, do-not-disturb, invisible signage. It'll be me, you and nature."

He waited as words escaped both of them. He didn't look away. There was a look on Cheyenne's face that said she had more to say. He waited.

"I'm glad I came here this week. I know I've said it and so have you, but I need to say it again. I have missed you like crazy. I was empty without you. I can't believe that I didn't have the faith in us that you had. You never wavered, did you? All that wasted time could have been avoided."

Tellum heard the pain in her voice. She was living through regret. No more, he thought.

"Let it go, baby. We are here. We don't know the future, but I do know I want you in mine. We promised we would do this while we're here. We will talk about more another time. I don't want anything bringing your spirits down. I don't want any regrets, no misgivings and no qualms. We will figure this out. Okay? If you want us, I'm not leaving. For now, let's just live in this moment. At the end of this week, there is no end to us. You being here with me, smiling and happy, the only option is us. I'm in if you are. Are you?"

"Yes."

"That's all that matters. Mistakes can be fixed. I think the time apart has shown us both that together is where we want to be. If there are hurdles, we'll leap over them together. Team Tellum and Cheyenne?"

Cheyenne wiped her eyes and gave him a thumbs up. He headed back into the shower and left her to her thoughts. Guilt was in every word she spoke. He was going to make it his job to remove all of that. The only outcome was to fill all that guilt with love.

14

Cheyenne had never felt more beautiful than she did at this very moment. Seeing herself in the mirror and knowing that the big smile was because a few months ago, she never thought she'd be here again, at least not with the man she couldn't wait to spend a quiet evening with. Knowing Tellum, she was preparing for a romantic night that dreams of women everywhere were made of when it came to unconditional love from a man who was worthy of their hearts. If there was anything she knew about Tellum, it was how romantic he could be.

She admired herself in the golden yellow form fitting dress that she chose for the night. Her curves were popping the way she loved. She loved showing off what she was blessed with. The moment she saw the dress in the small boutique that she and Melodi visited before the trip, she knew she had to get it because she knew how much Tellum would like it on her. Even though she didn't know that they would reconnect, she still had him in mind knowing what his reaction would be to seeing her in it.

Running her hands up and down her body from her hips to her neck, she imagined her hands being replaced by Tellum's.

"You're late," Melodi said entering the room after ending her call. She had received an urgent call that there was an issue with her gym that had quickly been taken care of. She still reached out to Stephen and her assistant for an update.

"I'm not late. Tellum isn't even here yet."

"It doesn't matter what side you turn to, you look beautiful. In fact, how is it that you are the one that has this killer body, yet I'm the one who owns a gym? Are you ready?"

Cheyenne turned and sat down on the bed. She was pairing a sexy pair of metallic gold wedge heels with her dress, quickly strapping them around her ankles.

"I am more than ready. I know I seem like some woman just going out on her first date but in so many ways, it really feels like one," she explained with excitement.

"It's been a long-time relationship-wise with him, but you've been together for the past couple of days. My texts throughout the day today were to make sure you were allowing him time to breathe. I did run into him when I was leaving the gym a little while ago. He said you were asleep."

"There was no sex at all today, not even last night. He came in from the concert, took a shower and the television watched us sleep. We ordered breakfast in this morning. He did take a couple of calls. Lunch was delivered later. One of his friends, who was only here for a day, was leaving. He wanted to see him off. He told me he ran into you on his way back just in time for lunch. All I can say is, if you have a chance, order the fried shrimp and ribeye steak. We had that with some delicious cheesy cauliflower and salad. We napped a lot because tonight, there will be no sleeping. I don't want to miss a minute of our time together. Tonight, will be one of the most magical nights of my life. This is our time. It was hard leaving him earlier but I wanted extra time to get ready for tonight."

"Don't mess this up," Melodi warned in the voice of someone who truly cares about the happiness of a best friend.

Cheyenne nodded. She knew.

"I won't."

"You better not. Stephen and I miss our double date nights."

"I've missed that too. Tellum and I were talking about that."

"Let's get back to it then. I have something to tell you."

Cheyenne turned and tilted her head to the side.

"You're pregnant?" she questioned.

"Girl! Are you insane? Of course not. I can barely take care of myself let alone a baby. No, it's nothing like that. And don't put that in the atmosphere either or I'll wish it on you!"

"You can if you want to. I wouldn't be mad."

The calm way in which she responded took them both by surprised. She shook herself up hearing the words come out of her own mouth.

"What? Stop it, Cheyenne. Now you're playing with me."

"I'm not, and I am at the same time. I'm just saying, I would never be mad about having Tellum's baby. I'm not going to do that, of course. One day, I want to have a lot of babies with him."

"See? For a minute, you weren't even thinking of coming this week. It's a good thing he sent that invitation."

"As soon as I saw him again, I knew it was going to be hard leaving here and not being with him. I'm not talking about intimately or being here at the resort with him either. I'm speaking about earning his love again."

"Girl, that man never stopped loving you and you know it."

"I know, but I think his trust in me was shattered a little. I need to get that back. He has to be able to trust that I will never walk away from him again because I won't."

"No matter what?"

Cheyenne knew the meaning behind those words. There was an entire life back in Detroit. It was destroyed once by her father, but never again. She deserved her own happiness just as he sought out and had for himself with her mother.

"You said it; no matter what. Now, do not switch the subject to me. What did you want to tell me."

"Stephen is flying in tomorrow."

"What? Really?"

"Yes, really. I know there aren't a lot of days left, but I was missing him something terrible. Seeing you happy with Tellum again had me thinking about sharing a piece of this paradise with my own man."

"I'm happy for you. I know you've been missing him. You've been trying to hide it. I get it, though. Love surpasses distance without a doubt. Still, there is nothing like being in a place like this with the one you love the most."

"Like you?"

"Exactly like me. When does he arrive?"

"I'm not sure. He said he would call me. Here is the best part. Are you ready?"

Cheyenne tapped her foot intolerantly.

"Just spill it, girl!"

"Tellum made it happen. When I saw him earlier, we talked about Stephen. It would be hard to get a last-minute flight here. He offered to make the arrangements. I called

Stephen to see if he could make it here if Tellum got arrangements. He laughed and told me he was already heading home to pack."

"Nice."

"Within an hour of running into your man, he had made my day."

"Well, he is perfect that way. Stephen is going to love it here, especially when he sees your bungalow."

"Don't expect to see too much of me for the remaining days. I plan to have that man handcuffed to that big ass bed. I wonder if there is a store at the mall that sells those fur kind?"

"Uh, oh – there goes that kinky mind of yours. Don't tell me about it. I'll pray for Stephen though. That brother has no idea what's in store for him."

"Oh, you mean like Tellum tonight?"

"Every single time is like the first time. There is a never-ending passion between us."

Before she could continue, the buzzer to the gate of her bungalow rang.

"That must be Tellum," Melodi said getting up and racing out first.

Cheyenne didn't move.

"If it is, he's early."

"Oh, it's not him," Melodi yelled back.

Cheyenne turned and smiled when Keiko, Byrum's assistant, walked in ahead of Melodi. In her arms, she held, what Cheyenne assumed, was the gift basket for Tellum that she ordered.

"Keiko! What are you doing delivering baskets?" she questioned.

"This is an important request," Keiko answered.

"When I saw you yesterday and inquired about getting something for Tellum, I wasn't asking that you actually bring it to me," she explained.

"I know. I had the team pull this together in record time for you after we spoke. I wanted to be sure it arrived and had everything in it that you wanted."

"What's this?" Melodi asked after Keiko handed it to Cheyenne.

"It's huge! It's a basket full of a lot of Tellum's favorite things. I noticed in the shop here on the resort that it contained a lot of each brother's favorite things. I wanted to get him something special. Tellum is always giving me amazing gifts. I don't try to compete with his style of gift giving. No one compares to him. Doing something nice for him was a priority for me today. I stopped by the concierge desk with a list of the things I saw that I wanted to get him. They told me that Keiko mentioned I would be stopping by."

"I sure did. I hope you like it."

"This looks amazing! I see the cologne he loves, the items he uses for his shower regiment and so much more. I think there are about twenty or so items in here including candy and island mementos. I love it! Thanks so much. I can't wait to give it to him in the morning."

"I'm glad you like it. You look amazing. I trust you're meeting up with Tellum tonight?" Keiko asked.

"I am. He should be here soon."

"How is the resort treating you?" Keiko asked, looking at both ladies.

"All I have to say is, if the other two resorts that the Blackstone brothers are opening are anything like this one, I'm going to go broker."

"She's right. From the moment I stepped on the property, I've been amazed every step of the way. From the amenities to the food and then the entertainment, this is all top-shelf. They really did it up. I've been to their other locations and though they are all nice, nothing compares to this one," Cheyenne noted.

"That's because this project was led by your man!" Melodi shouted.

"Wait until you see what Byrum is doing with the next opening. It's almost like the brothers are trying to one-up each other," Keiko said.

"I bet he has you and the rest of his team working overtime," Cheyenne said.

"That he does, but I don't mind. I love being a part of Byrum's amazing vision. I'm happy to see that you and Tellum are working on things. That makes me happy. I know Byrum is ecstatic!"

"Oh?" Cheyenne asked.

After they broke up, neither of Tellum's brothers said much by way of being upset over the breakup. She'd run into both of them at least once afterward. They didn't talk about Tellum. Mostly, they asked how she was doing in general.

"He considers you the sister they never had. He once told me that you were as perfect for Tellum as a woman could be. We all know about the Blackstone brothers when it comes to women," Keiko elucidated.

"No one is as wild as Callum, though. And Byrum, your boss, he's smooth with his. You don't hear much about his love life," Melodi said, adding her opinion. "I bet you know all of the secrets, right?" she asked Keiko.

"If I do, I'm taking them to the grave. Like Tellum, he's a good guy. One day, when he's ready, some woman is going to be the luckiest in the world besides Cheyenne."

Cheyenne looked to Melodi who just happen to be looking her way. They shared an unspoken thought; Keiko's words were more than just an employee who admires her boss. There was something in the way she always spoke of Byrum. If she were to think really hard about it, there was always something in the way Byrum spoke highly of Keiko as well. She let it go. She'd met her not long after meeting Tellum during one of her early visits to his office. Besides being gorgeous with her exotic looks, she remembers Tellum saying how much of an asset she was to the company. Keiko was known for keeping every aspect of Byrum's business life in order. There was often a look in her eyes that said there was a personal stake as well. She decided not to pry.

"Byrum hasn't been seen publicly with any beauties in almost a year. That's surprising considering how the good-looks gene is strong in those brothers," Melodi said.

Cheyenne didn't miss that Keiko didn't respond and actually seemed a little uncomfortable. She let that slide also.

The buzzer at the gate went off again.

"I do believe that is who I have been waiting on," Cheyenne said and moved ahead of Melodi to the gate. "Don't even try it!" she warned her best friend who stopped in her tracks and sat back on the bed.

"I'm going to head out. Enjoy your night out. Let me know if there is anything else the resort can do to be of assistance," Keiko said.

"You are amazing!" Cheyenne said as the two of them walked out together.

"Tellum," Keiko said, greeting him.

"Hey there! Good to see you. I'm glad you were able to make it. Byrum mentioned he thought you may have had an issue with your son. I'm glad it worked out since you're here," Tellum said.

"It did. I worked hard to make something happen so that I could come. Well, I'm heading to a girls' night out with a few friends. Have fun you two!"

Keiko waved back as she walked off.

Cheyenne turned to Tellum and tried to greet him with a hello when he kissed her senseless before she could get a word out. She melted into the kiss and into his arms. Her night was already starting out on a high, steamy note.

"Wow!" she said when he let her up for air.

"I've been thinking about that kiss as I walked here. Hello," he finally said.

"Hello to you too. I love how you say hello before you say hello," she said.

"And these are for you."

From behind his back, Tellum produced a large bouquet of white roses. Oh, how she loves flowers.

"These are so beautiful! Thank you."

"Anything for you. I saw them and thought of you. Are you ready for our night on the beach?"

"I am. Are you sure I shouldn't bring anything at all?"

"Just you, that gorgeous smile and an open mind. You look amazing. This dress says you know me so well," Tellum decreed confidently.

"You are my prince charming. I'm ready. Let me send Melodi on her way. Oh, and thanks for bringing Stephen to the resort. She told me you have a hand in that."

"Not a problem. I could tell she was missing him. This place will do that to someone in love."

"Brother-in-law!" Melodi shouted and pulled Tellum into a tight hug.

"Melodi!" Cheyenne yelled in a chastising, yet teasing way. Her calling Tellum her brother-in-law was strange. She looked to Tellum who wasn't fazed at all.

"You still call me that?" he asked.

"I never stopped. I don't know about you and my bestie here, but this day was bound to happen. A love like what the two of you shared had to come back around to the two of you being here together like this. I'm out! I've actually been invited to join Keiko and her friends for their girls' night out. Have fun and keep the volume down," Melodi joked and walked off.

"That woman!" Cheyenne said.

Tellum laughed behind her. She turned to him with her hands on her hips.

"Funny?" she asked.

"You act like you just met Melodi. She loves dishing the shock factor as she leaves a room. She's not wrong, though. In the heat of the moment, the volume can get pretty ear-piercing."

"Okay, okay. I'm not the only one of us who gets the loudest."

"True. Then how about we make our way to paradise, volume up and all," Tellum offered.

"I'm all yours."

15

Tellum was just as surprised at the beach setup as Cheyenne was once they arrived and saw the bright lights and romantic cabana along with the firepit. Even though he'd planned out everything with the resort event planner, he didn't expect the magnificence that was in front of them as they walked between the two security booths at the entrance. They were escorted, hand-in-hand, to their private, dreamy oasis. Behind them was the ten-foot privacy fence the protected whatever their night would be from prying eyes. His original plan was the have six-foot privacy fences around each cabana. He was glad that he'd changed his mind knowing how important it was to allow guests to be as free as they wanted without having to worry about being watched. He watched with happy eyes as Cheyenne moved ahead of him to take in all that had been prepared.

In front of them were bright white lights draped all around the fence that wasn't just behind them but on each side of their cabana.

Further ahead of them, a short walk from the cabana nearer to the firepit was a table set up for them to have dinner. It was covered in a red tablecloth with a setting for two in gold.

There was a serving tray with a food over steamers. To the side there was something bubbly chilling on ice.

"Amazing!" Cheyenne acknowledged. "This is so nice," she added.

"I take it you like what you see?" Tellum asked.

"My favorite part? The beach. Look at how serene and completely calm the water is. There is a full moon that appears to touch the ocean. The stars are bright tonight. Nothing can beat this night. Nothing will ever compare to what you've put together for us."

"I needed a magical moment with you."

"You did that. I love it! How did you come up with this?"

"Cheyenne, did you forget that when I created all of this, I did so with you and I in mind? My only thought was around how much I love you and what a perfect Shangri-la, our heaven on earth, would look like."

"I wasn't sure what I would see here. The cabanas are perfect with the large round bed, privacy curtains that can be pulled all around the bed. The skylight opening in the top that allows us to see the beautiful sky. We're spending the whole night here?" Cheyenne asked.

"I'm here with you for as long as you want. If it's all night, I'm set for that."

"But I didn't bring anything. I would have had a sexy nightie with some delectable underwear like I know you love."

"Baby, I have all of that and more. We're going to start with a massage for you, even before we eat. I have everything we need inside the cabana from towels to oils to extra sheets. We're going to dance, sit by the fire, have dinner and since we are spending the night, we can do whatever we want to do."

"What's for dinner later?"

"Lobster drizzled in a special butter sauce that my mother shared with the resort chef. I think she plans to put out a cookbook one day. There is honey butter bread, collard greens, roasted potatoes, crab cakes, broiled and not fried like we both prefer and to start off with before dinner is a magnificent Greek salad with all of the olives you can stand. I know how much you love them."

"You know me when it comes to my olives."

"We also have dessert," he said.

"Dessert? All this and dessert? You did think of everything. What are we having?"

"A simple display of four different kinds of cake slices."

"Cake! Yes. I know I don't need it but when I'm on vacation, healthy eating goes out the window. I do love cake. Wait, did you say massage?" she asked.

"That I did."

"I can definitely use that. Your hands working on this body is all I need."

Tellum walked toward her and took her hand, walking them toward the cabana which was already set up for them.

"Then let's get started, shall we?"

Tellum gloated when Cheyenne saw the oils, candles, speakers with soft, romantic music playing and most of all, the bed was ready for her. All she needed to do was undress. He wanted that to be a job for two.

"Do you trust me?" he asked walking up behind her and whispering in her ear.

"Of course. I trust you more than anything," Cheyenne responded to him without hesitation.

"You trust that I will keep you safe and our time here together private?"

"Tellum, I trust you implicitly."

"I just want to be sure. I have plans for us tonight that will be uninhibited. I want us to be free to love as we always do."

Tellum reached to the side of the bed and pulled out a large gift box, wrapped in pink and white sparkly paper.

"What's this?" she asked. "You told me not to bring anything. I had a gift for you that I left back in my room."

"I know I did. I appreciate that. I'm sure I will love whatever it is."

"Can I take a look inside?" she asked.

Before he even answered, Cheyenne sat on the side of the round cabana bed and ripped the paper off.

"Woman, the way you are tearing at that box is hilarious!" Tellum kidded.

"You know I love a wrapped gift box. That's mainly because I love the idea of tearing into it."

While Cheyenne pulled out more lotions, body oils, a sexy black night and satin pajamas for him, Tellum pulled the curtains together to give them more privacy.

"You like?" he asked.

"I love. Is this oil strawberry?" she asked taking the top off the smell it.

"Of course. There is also a vanilla rub because I know you love that too. Come here."

Cheyenne stood and walked into his arms. Tellum turned her so that her back was to him. He kissed her neck from behind while he slid her dress down her arms. As it layered at her hips, his lips covered her back until he reached the top of her behind. Pulling the dress completely from her body, he captured the snap of her strapless bra between his teeth and in a second it fell to the floor in front of them. Cheyenne gayly laughed out loud.

"The way you do that with just your teeth is wild!"

"You smell wonderful."

Cheyenne turned to him with just her thong and heels still in place. Before he could protest that he wasn't done, her intent was in the way she was looking at him. He stood still and let her have her way.

"So do you. Besides that, you look amazing. I wanted to say that because right now, I want you naked."

"Baby, that's not how a massage works, at least not that I'm aware of. Is there something you want to tell me?"

"Tellum, do not try me with that. If I'm having things my way tonight, I prefer my massage therapist be naked as a jay bird. You know the saying."

He threw his hands up in surrender.

"It's your world, sweetheart."

With their eyes connected, Cheyenne removed his clothes, taking special interest in his arousal straining toward her.

"This will be a short massage if you don't stop teasing me like this."

She nodded at the focus of her attention.

"Teasing will be the name of the game tonight. Now that I'm naked, I need to get you out of this thong and up on the bed. Place your head at the foot of the bed. I have a large towel to cover your body. I want to do like any other massager would do. Though I will say, please don't ever go to get a massage from a man. If you want one, I'm your man."

"Never anyone else. You give great massages. I have no need for anyone else, ever."

Tellum's eyes took in Cheyenne sliding the thin material from her body. When she handed it to him, he placed it in the pocket of his pants.

"You know you're not getting this back."

She shook her head at him as she laid on the bed.

"You and my panties."

He leaned over and kissed her cheek.

"I still have every pair I've collected since we first met."

"You do?" she turned and questioned.

"No joke."

"You're weird Mr. Blackstone."

"Why? Because I love the sexy panties my woman wears? That's why I have always bought you the sexiest kind I can find."

"I know you love seeing me in them. I love wearing them for you."

"Forever?" he asked.

"And a day, yes."

"Okay, baby. Relax and let these hands do their job."

Tellum picked up a large towel and placed it across her back, covering her behind while leaving her back open. He reached for the strawberry oil and began massaging her shoulders.

"That feels good," she uttered quietly. "That smells good too."

Moving to the bed from his place on the side of it, Tellum straddled her body, lightly resting on her lower legs. He began humming while he worked to one of his favorite songs as it played for their pleasure, *She*, by Stokley."

For a good five minutes, they were in the moment. No talking, only feeling and music."

Feeling the need to replay the song, he spoke it and the song repeated itself. He sang out loud with it.

"She, is the queen of mine, perfectly designed, without even trying, her lips her eyes they drive me crazy..." he sang.

"How can a man with a voice as deep as yours sing that song so eloquently at a pitch that high? You missed your calling as a crooner."

"When it's about the woman I love, it just pours out of me. Only for you," he replied. "Are you relaxed?"

"More than I've ever been. You've given me massages before, but this one is beyond sensual."

"Baby, I want to be sure that you understand that as much as I love making love to you, this time with you isn't about sex. We moved beyond that a long time ago."

Cheyenne wanted to say more, but no words would come out once Tellum's finger stroked between her legs. Her hips shot up off of the bed. He caressed her back and legs to relax her.

"Your touch is one-of-a-kind. That's because of how we love. This feels magical. All if it, especially your hands and your fingers."

"Turn over, baby," Tellum whispered in her ear.

"What are you thinking about?"

"You are my love. You get that, right?"

Cheyenne leaned forward and kissed him. Their eyes remained open for the sweetness.

"Yes, I know."

Tellum smiled when Cheyenne's legs encircle his hips, pulling his body down on her until her breasts caressed his chest. Her lips captured his cheek and then down to his neck.

She moaned into his neck.

He let his hands slide down to caress her breasts. He enjoyed the feel of them in his hands. Their large size didn't allow his hands to fully encase them but feeling them stirred his body more.

Lifting his body slightly, Tellum moved one hand between them. He felt her wetness the minute he touched her womanhood. His lips found hers and the potency of their connection empowered and encouraged him. Cheyenne's hips moved in a slow circle. The dancer in her was evident in the way she moved.

He pressed his strong body into hers, his hips moving around with hers. They moved as one. The fiery kissed became one of great determination. It was clear they needed more. Cheyenne's lips curve into a smile. That was the moment he knew she felt him, long, hard and strong right at the entrance to her body. He didn't make them wait.

Lifting because he knew Cheyenne loved watching his body as he moved inside of her, he slid slowly inside. He growled when her hands caressed his shoulders before she moved them and dug her nails lightly into his back. That drove him to surge strong, yet still slow in and out of her body.

Reaching with both hands, he found her hands and locked their fingers together. Raising their hands up above her head, he used the open opportunity to apply kisses to every part of her skin that he could find. He started with her face, using the pad of his tongue to lick around to her ear. Her head turned slightly to the side to give him better access. He wasted no time giving her the attention he missed giving her throughout the months they were apart.

He took control of her lips once again, igniting an even hotter fire that shot desirously through his veins. Cheyenne gazed hungrily into his eyes allowing him to see that glassy, amorous intense yearning for him. She was clearly ready for it all.

Releasing her hands, he reached down and cupped her behind tightly in his grip. The move allowed him to bury himself deeper inside of her. Her cries of pleasure encased his entire being. If they were in a more private setting, her roars of pleasure would have bounced off of the walls.

"You feel incredible," he spoke against her lips.

If Cheyenne could have responded with words, she would have. Her body didn't allow for any words. Her hips moved franticly under him, pumping up as he pumped down with precise strokes. Cheyenne quaked against his body when her mouth formed an 'O'. Tellum kissed her, drowning her moans with his mouth, keeping the sounds and pleasures of their lovemaking between the two of them. She rode him hard from the bottom. Placing his hands at hips, he rose to his knees while lifting her hips higher. His body clenched as his own orgasm rose and shattered him into a million pieces. He stroked her more intently, his own head thrashing about.

One explosion after another hit him like the strong waves of a hurricane hitting the ocean water.

In the moments that followed, Tellum collapsed as he attempted to catch his breath. His body covered hers as they attempted, together, to return their breathing to normal.

When she flicked her tongue out across what he knew was his sweaty neck, he moved and gave her his lips. He needed that connection.

"We are so amazing together," she acknowledged.

"The intent is never sex," he offered against her lips.

"I know, baby. The intent is always love."

Tellum smiled.

"With a lot of lust laced throughout."

"Can we spend the night right here on the beach?"

"Tonight, this island is ours. This space is ours. We can sleep right here under the stars. We will make love as many times as we can stand. I want to eventually go to sleep and then wake up just like this."

"Whoa!" Cheyenne declared.

Tellum chuckled. He knew what that was for.

"I feel you coming to life inside of me."

"I can't help it."

"Over," Cheyenne said.

Tellum knew what that meant. Without hesitation, he turned them, without leaving the warm, softness of her body. Cheyenne was now on top. She reached behind them to the top of the bed, the opposite of where they were laying. Grabbing three of the four pillows on the bed, Tellum leaned up as she placed them behind him.

"Again?"

"Well, from what I can feel, you're in the mood again. When it comes to you, I'm always ready."

Cheyenne's body moving on top of him silenced all words. The only thing happening was love.

**

An hour later and they still hadn't eaten dinner. Cheyenne wasn't in a rush. They laid so that they could see the sky through the opening in the top of the cabana cover. The stars sparkled from one to the other as if they were creating the perfect romantic pattern just for them.

"How can life be this perfect?"

Cheyenne moved her body so that her head could rest on Tellum's bare chest.

He kissed her on the forehead. His arm held her tight.

"Because it's you and me."

There was more. She knew it. He didn't say it. Sitting up she faced him.

"What? I know your voice. There was more, but you stopped."

"I need to ask you something, but I don't want anything to mess up this perfect night."

"It won't. We promised that we would never tiptoe around each other. Whatever it is, just say it," she said and waited.

"Was there anything else about our relationship that made you unhappy? Or, was it really just answering the call from your father?"

"Of course not. It was all about giving in to him. I'm sorry I did that."

"Okay," he said quickly.

"Would you tell me if there was anything about our relationship that didn't make you happy?" she asked.

"I wasn't the one that ended us. I was and still am happy to be with you."

"I want all of you. I wish that I could go back to a point before things ended. I would like a chance to make a different choice. I cried a lot. I didn't sleep enough. I missed you so much that I think I could really feel my heart aching."

"Baby, you don't have to go back. We only need to go forward. The same issue will be there at home when we get back. What then?"

"I'm not worried about that. I'm worried about not waking up to you. I'm worried about not loving you like this. I'm worried about not hearing you tell me how much you love me every day. I'm worried about not saying the same thing to you. I'm worried that if I let you slip through my fingers again, there won't ever be another you. I want to live my life happy. That means with you."

"You have me. You have all of me. I will forever fight for us. I wish that I had fought earlier than this, but it's okay. We're here now. There will be no going back. Agreed?" he asked, kissing her lips sweetly.

"Agreed. Now, this night is still early. I feel powerful when I'm up here on top of you. You knew that which is why you rolled me on top again."

"Sexy, you are in total control. Let's get it!" he swooned against her lips just before Cheyenne rose up and joined their bodies again.

When her head dropped back and she set a slow, rhythmic pace for them, Tellum knew that from here on out, he was onboard for the forever ride of his life.

**

Reed couldn't see over the privacy fence that led to the cabana where he knew Tellum and Cheyenne were. Two hours later after he first walked in this direction, he found himself walking back to the path that led to the secure entrance. He was jealous. He freely admitted that to himself. Knowing that they were on the other side of the fence together pissed him off. He had hoped the end of them had actually been the end. That doesn't seem to be the case anymore.

Hours ago, he was planning another chance walk up to her villa in hopes of convincing her to have dinner with him even though he'd been warned to not even think about it by Byrum. He appreciated the friendship they shared, but his pull to

Cheyenne was strong. Perhaps it was because Tellum had her yet again.

He'd been in the shadows as Tellum walked with his arm full of flowers down the path to her. He followed him until he was out of sight. He waited behind a tree, knowing he looked ridiculously like a stalker. He hoped that the dark night hid his appearance.

Minutes later, the two of them left hand-in-hand and headed toward the beach. He knew he wouldn't be able to follow them in but his anger at seeing them together had him on their trail anyway. Before they reached the guard's station, he took out his phone and snapped a picture of them walking together.

"This will soon get interesting. I'm sure daddy dearest doesn't know about this latest turn of events. He will in a few minutes," he snidely remarked to himself.

Once they were out of sight, he sent his text message complete with the picture. If her father wanted his help with anything business related, he would have to sacrifice his daughter to get to it. He didn't care how he got Cheyenne as his own as long as he did. Her father was the perfect guinea pig. It could be a winning situation for them both if he played his cards right. If he had to deal with Byrum in the end, he would. By then, he would have had his taste of Cheyenne, just enough to throw it in Tellum's face. The man and his cocky confidence continued to get under his skin.

"Soon, Blackstone. Soon and very soon."

Turning away from the where he'd been lingering, he walked back to his own room in order to pack for his flight the next morning. He had a plan to finish putting in place.

16

Tellum exited the shower, knowing Cheyenne wouldn't be in the bedroom waiting for him. She had been quieter than usual when they woke earlier. As he held her in his arms and took in the sweet peachy scent of her hair from the late-night shower they took together, he tried to engage her in conversation. He stopped trying when he realized she wasn't in a talkative mood. She was more sullen than usual; especially compared to the last couple of days. He knew the reason why. He was leaving today to head to an important meeting in Denver.

After dressing quickly, he looked around to be sure he hadn't left anything after Cheyenne helped him pack before his shower and before she decided to go down to the lower level to watch television while he dressed.

Moving his luggage to the door after slipping on his favorite Jordan's, he took the steps two at a time to find her. She was cuddled up on the chaise lounge in front of the television. She was playing a game on her iPad, not even focusing on the television.

He stood still and took everything in about her from the way she sat cross-legged to how she'd pulled her hair up into a wild bun of braids on top of her head.

"You didn't join me in the shower?" he whispered in her ear, just before kissing the lobe.

"You know how that would have turned out. You have a fight to catch. You would have been late."

"I would say we could have had a quickie, but as much as we try to do that, it never happens. Once I'm inside of you, there is no rushing; ever!" he declared.

"You know how I get when you focus on my ears. You are running the risk of not getting out the door on time. I don't want anyone thinking it's my fault if you're late for your meeting. You already delayed your flight by an hour."

"That's because I'm struggling with leaving you here in paradise without me. Promise me that you'll come back with me soon."

"In a heartbeat. There is so much peace here. I could live here. From the ocean view to this bungalow and my villa, to the food, to all of the amenities – it's all perfect. I know I can do all of these things back at home, but here, I didn't think about work, not even one day. I didn't think about anything but this place, you and me."

There was silence.

"This time with you was more than I could have dreamed of."

"I bet one of your favorite times was driving those ATVs. You're a natural pro on those," she noted.

"I'm already thinking of buying one at home. You know, the city is thinking about building a park where ATV and dirt bike owners can ride legally. I'm in full support of that. Callum has already reached out to the mayor to offer our support with the project. It'll keep the streets and the kids safer."

Cheyenne turned her full body around and smiled up at him.

"You are so remarkable. I love how you think of others all the time. You are the most unselfish person I have ever met. It's one of the many reasons why I love you so much."

"Still?" he questioned.

"Always."

"Always?"

"Forever."

"Forever?

"Tellum? Why are you repeating my words?" she joked.

"Because I want to be sure we're on the same page. I love you, baby."

"I love you too."

"Even when we're back home?"

"Especially when we're back home. We need to talk about that, right?"

Tellum nodded. Before answering, he leaned down and picked her up into his arms. Taking her seat on the chair, he placed her sideways on his lap.

"Oh, yes, we definitely need to talk. I don't have time to do that if I'm going to get out of here on time."

"I can tell you're thinking clearly," she laughed.

"What?" he asked.

"You didn't straddle me across your lap like you usually do."

"That's because if I did, that would be easy access to, well, you know. I'm trying to keep clean thoughts before I end up cancelling my trip."

"No. Keep it clean. This business meeting is important. We can talk when you get back to Detroit. I'm going to miss you."

"You know I hate leaving you here. When I see my future, you are the constant that is there."

"That's all I needed to hear before you leave."

"Can you stop being sad now?" he asked.

Tellum's eyes followed hers when she tried to look away.

"I just; I hated where we were."

"I get that. We're not there anymore. We are here."

"I should have chosen you."

"Baby, it's not about choosing me. It's about choosing you. You and I will work our thing out. Your father is still an issue. He still dislikes my family. He will still want you to stay away from me. We can't hide our love when we're back at home. That will never work."

"I know. I will deal with that. I don't want you to worry about whether I'll go back to the dark side," she said facetiously.

"The dark side was a terrible place for you and me."

"You need to go."

Cheyenne attempted to move from his lap. Before she could, he pulled her back to him for one last, heart-racing, soul-stirring kiss. He then stood with her in his arms before placing her back on her feet.

"I'll call you when I land."

"How many days will you be in Denver?" she asked.

Tellum moved them to the stairs where they walked up together to the front door.

"Two days, three at the most. I'll be back on Saturday morning if all goes well. That's the current plan. I'll let you know if that changes. I need to stop by the office that morning but then I'm planning on going home for a long winter's nap."

"You've been busy, huh?"

"I've been doing a lot of traveling. I'm going to check in with Lisa-Marie and then I'm hoping to come see you. Does that work?"

"That's perfect."

Tellum kissed her again.

"Are you going to stay here in the bungalow? You can if you want to."

"I think I will. Now that you flew Stephen out here to see Melodi, I have a feeling she will be tied up, literally knowing her freaky behind. Thanks for doing that."

"No problem."

"I think I'll stay here."

"Don't stay cooped up in here. I still want you to get out and have fun with the time remaining. Don't be in here all sad because I had to leave. Be safe. Make sure you use the escort service if you are out late. Tellum and Callum are already in Denver. I'm the last to leave."

"Don't worry about me. I don't plan on going out at all and yes, that will be fun for me. I want to lay around and enjoy the peace and quiet. I bought a few books when Melodi and I went to the mall the other day. I want to do some reading, soak in the tub, swim and eat everything that will make me work overtime when I get back to shake the pounds off."

"Not too many. I love all of you in any way, shape or form. No matter what, just enjoy yourself without a care in the world. The real world will be waiting for you when you return."

Tellum picked up his luggage. Pulling Cheyenne close one last time, he kissed her and himself senseless before reaching for the door.

"I could walk with you to your car," she said, snuggling close to his side.

"You stay here and start your relaxation. I'm good. I'll stop in the main office before I leave. I love you."

"I love you more!" Cheyenne exclaimed as he opened the door and raced down the stairs. He waited until she closed the door behind him to walk off.

"Hey brother!"

Tellum turned and faced Melodi who was racing in his direction.

"Hey! Where's Stephen?" he asked.

"I put him fast asleep. I was coming to check on Cheyenne since I knew you were leaving today. I thought you would have taken off already. Thanks again for flying Stephen here."

"Both of you are welcome here anytime. It'll always be on me. Yesterday with the four of us hanging out again, it was good."

"It was. I wasn't sure we would see the two of you after your night on the beach."

"Cheyenne said she wanted to hang out at least one day. She knew I was leaving today, so yesterday was the only day we had free with me still being here. I would do anything to make her happy. Us having a fun day did that."

"I'm telling you, I like you more and more each day. So, things are good with you and my bestie?" she asked.

"I know you had a hand in talking her into coming. I thank you for that. Yes, things are great."

"Now or moving forward too?"

"Now and forever. I'll share more about that with you when we're back in Detroit."

"Uh, oh. Do I hear some fantastic news coming soon?"

"Maybe."

Tellum winked and walked off.

"I'll watch out for her until we leave. I'm assuming she'll be missing you so much that she won't want to leave the bungalow."

"She told me she wanted to relax, especially since Stephen is here with you. Yes, watch out for her."

"Tellum?"

When he started to walk away, he turned back.

"Yes?"

"Thanks for never giving up on her. The struggle will continue though. Know what I'm saying?" she asked.

"I know exactly what you mean."

"Captain Joe is something, huh?" Melodi asked.

"That he is. He has a strange kind of way of loving his daughter. If he doesn't watch it, he will lose her all together. I don't care much for him, but I don't want that either. He's still her father. I won't let him make her vulnerable to his foolishness anymore."

"I know that's right. She's worth the fight, right?"

"That and then some. See you back in Detroit."

Melodi waved at him as he hustled off. The quicker he could get his business in Denver over, the faster he can get back to Cheyenne since she'll be arriving back in Detroit before him. Melodi was right; they still had her father to contend with. This time, Cheyenne would not be doing it alone.

17

Tellum found himself unable to concentrate even though the view in front of him was the most serene he'd ever seen outside of the ocean view he'd left behind the day before. If it weren't for business reasons, he wouldn't touch the land in front of them that would, in a few years, be the home of the largest concert venue in the Denver area.

After leaving *Secret Whisper* and getting only a few hours of sleep after he landed and had dinner, he was up early with Byrum and Callum looking over the large parcel of land that they were only a few hours away from acquiring. The fact that it was only a few short miles away from their Denver resort, was the icing on the cake for them.

"If Tellum would stop daydreaming for a minute, perhaps he can answer that question?" Callum yelled.

Tellum turned toward his brother with his middle finger in the air. Not only did the three of them double over in laughter but so did the four assistants who stood behind them admiring the location.

"I know what or should I say who is on his mind. Did you even let her up for air the entire week?" Byrum asked.

"This is not the time to discuss my personal life. Though she's always on my mind, I wasn't thinking about Cheyenne. I was thinking about the amount of land we'll have. This is a major investment," Tellum said.

"From the meeting, Tonia will circle back with us all with takeaways. Shelton got what he needed. He's back at the resort reading over all of the financials. We'll connect in a few hours so that he can get out of here. Take a look around. This view will soon change, if we each give our thumbs up. I like what I see here and in the paperwork. The attorneys will have the final say," Byrum explained.

"Where is the owner of the land and his team? I thought they wanted to be here for our walkaround," Tellum said.

"They'll meet us back at the office at the resort. I wanted us to look at the property and not be biased because they were here with us," Bynum explained.

"We didn't get to see this much of the land the last time we were here. I'm impressed. I really like how flat it is. We won't have to incur the extra expense for the leveling, though we will need to get our people here to assess. What are we talking? Two years?" Tellum asked.

"Yes. We've looked over the schematics. Once the final contracts are signed, construction can begin in about a year and a half, two years would be the latest it would start. After that, the venue would be open and ready for business a year later. That's the timeline we're working with, building in the winter weather, of course. Denver and its snow are no joke. Still, the timeline is aggressive but we're used to that. I will make sure we add in time for anything that could cause a possible delay," Callum noted.

"That's a good idea. Our first free standing concert venue. I like this. This will lead to big things," Tellum said. "Look at the response we got to the concert venue at the resort. I'm seeing big things here."

"It will be big indeed," Byrum added.

"I want to get a closer look. It's good seeing it from this high vantage point. I want to actually walk around the perimeter. Since we came out in separate trucks, why don't the team go back and start making the calls that are needed," Callum suggested.

"Great idea. Guys, meet us back at the resort," Tellum suggested.

They moved as soon as the last word was spoken.

"I'll meet you both at the far end. I want to check the surrounding roads for getting in and out. The number of permits we will need keeps growing. We have no choice with that. What I don't want is gridlock on any of the main highways that lead here. I also want to be sure traffic won't be impacted at the resort due to concert traffic," Callum said.

"We'll meet you there in a few minutes," Tellum said.

He looked to Byrum with his, *I need to talk to you*, face. Byrum understood.

They waved to Callum as he got in his truck and pulled off behind the team that were already headed out.

"This location will be epic. The design those brothers from Pioneer have come up with are something out of this world. No one's ever seen anything so forward thinking when it comes to design. We can go from any kind of concert, to Broadway-like plays and even sports events," Byrum said.

Tellum stretched trying to shake the tiresome feeling from his body.

"I could use a few more hours of sleep," he said.

"Tellum? Did you hear what I said?"

When he looked like he was about to comment as if he were listening, Byrum put his hand up to stop him from speaking.

"What?" Tellum asked.

"What? What is going on with you? Are there issues with Cheyenne again that you didn't want to talk about in front of Callum? I know we share a lot with each other, but he likes to make fun of everything. I'm sensing something strange and strong happening with you. What gives?"

"I will say that I was being truthful when I said everything was good with Cheyenne. In fact, I think things are going to be better this time around."

"She's not just any woman though, right?"

"Damn right. She is THEE woman; the only woman for me."

"You worried about her father and what will happen when he finds that the two of you are seeing each other again?"

"I was until yesterday. When I left Cheyenne at the resort, I knew that she wasn't going to go back down that road with him again. I don't doubt that he will try to persuade her, but it won't work. We are moving ahead."

"Then what's going on?"

"It's the resort."

"What? Did something happen after I left? I haven't heard anything," Byrum said.

"Nothing like that. Listen, I want to run something by you. In my head, I swear what I'm about to say makes me sound soft. I've been struggling with that. What I know is my life is different. How I see my future is different."

"Okay, I'm open-minded. Let me hear it."

"The three of us have been all about the ladies and our lives as single men. We've spent a lot of time focusing on purchasing and opening resorts geared toward singles and couples."

"True. That's because, like you said, we're all single and saw the need for more spots for singles to hang out, especially when it comes to vacation spots. As we saw with *Secret Whisper*, the idea was the best we've ever had."

"I agree. My point is when I woke yesterday and saw Cheyenne sleeping, the life we will have together flashed across my eyes. I saw her wearing my ring and trusting me with taking care of us. I saw her pregnant with our kids knowing that she will be an amazing mother. Then I saw us taking trips with our kids because I've come to understand what Pop always meant when he said that once he and mom had us, he made sure he was a constant presence in our lives. Work became secondary. I love what we do, but now my focus has changed. I want to work towards focusing on us all having our own families one day. That means resorts that are family friendly. Sure, we can take our kids to vacation spots and resorts around the world, but I want them to grow and learn to appreciate these places that will have their names on them. I want to think about not just these resorts and vacation spots for singles and couples; let's expand our creativity. I want to consider securing or building family resorts. We saw a ton of them in the Dominican Republic. They get big business. I want to tap into that. Not at our current spots, but new ones. Be honest, you can't really see yourself single forever. We want families and kids. I want to have places we take them to that have our names on them. What do you think?"

Byrum hadn't thought about that.

"I think that's a great idea. I'm sure Callum will think so too."

"I don't sound all mushy and in love? You know how both of you like to clown me over this love thing."

"What, you think you're the only one of us with a soft side?"

"Now, it's my time to ask what are you talking about? Are you getting soft on me? What? Is there a woman? There *IS* a woman!" Tellum yelled.

"Man, can you be a little less excited? I mean, there is a woman, sort of but not really."

"What the hell does that mean? A woman has snagged your heart? Two of us have bit the dust? Who is it?"

"It's not like that. I'm not out here hungering for her or anything like that, but there is someone who has snuck up on me."

"Oh? Should I go through the long list of women from the past few months that I know of? Which one? I know, it's the boutique owner you dated. What's her name? Kendra or Kenya? Wait, it has to be Candace, that woman from that reality show that you've been hooking up with for a while. Man, there are just so many. I can't figure out which one of them has had a big enough impression to make you think that she could be more than a friend with benefit."

Byrum tried to interrupt but that turned out to be fruitless.

"Tell," he rushed out with frustration over the conversation that somehow switched to his personal life. He loved being an ear for his brothers, but hated to share anything about himself when it comes to women.

"Don't even think about shuffling this conversation. You have no problem being all up in my business here and there. And I know you're all up in Callum's on the regular. You see the validity of a family-oriented resort without me having to convince you. You were the staunchest of supporters for all things about single, sexy vacation spots. Without any push-back, you see the validity of a place that includes kids?"

"Hey, all I said was that it's a good idea."

"What aren't you saying? Who is she? I know who it is. It's that bank vice president, Marlow."

"Her name is Harlow and no, it's not her."

"We could stand here all day with me running off names. The list is unending or until Callum calls wondering where we are."

"Okay, okay. It's none of them."

"It's someone I know? You're in love with her? How is that possible and I don't know her."

"I didn't say anything about love. I just happened to like someone for more than just sex. In fact, I haven't slept with her."

"Oh, damn. Now I really need to know. There is a mysterious woman out here who has you thinking she could be more and you haven't been intimate with her yet? She must be some woman."

"It's complicated."

"Most times, it is. It doesn't have to be."

"This time, it does. There are repercussions that could tarnish her image. So much could be at stake. So much would be in jeopardy."

"Hey, I won't push you. If you ever need to talk, you know I'm here. If it's about love, I think I'm in expert now."

"Bro, who knew that this would be you. I'm really happy for you. You are getting it all. You deserve to be this happy. Let me warn you right now. Do not tell mom that you're thinking of a future with babies. She'll start buying baby clothes right now."

Byrum laughed but he meant it.

"You don't have to tell me twice."

"Have you told her that you and Cheyenne have patched things up?"

"No, not yet. It was a plug she put in my head that got me to invite Cheyenne to the island. Mom came to see me the week before I left for that trip to Atlanta. She blasted me for letting Cheyenne slip through my fingers without much of a fight. Did you know she was still going by the house to spend time with mom?"

"Oh, yeah. I stopped by a few times and they were there baking or planting flowers or something. You know how mom loves those small antique shops. I pulled up one day when they were getting out of Cheyenne's car. Those new lamps in the entryway came from a shop owned by one of Cheyenne's friends. Mom said they went shopping and out to lunch. I can't believe you didn't know."

"I would go by the house too. I never ran into her; not even once."

"I will say that on that particular day, you were in Montana on the Sullivan Ranch with Shelton. That was when you wanted to see the construction for the new racecar track. In fact, another time I went by there to pick up Pop for a round of golf, she was there then. You were in Miami at an NBA game."

Tellum nodded and Byrum knew why; they both did.

"Cheyenne would be there when she knew I would be out of town. I'm assuming mom would tell her when I was away."

"Having no daughters, she loves Cheyenne like one. They had gotten pretty close."

"Another reason why I fell in love with her. The connection between the two of them was genuine."

"Marriage and babies? Are you really thinking about that?"

"More now than ever. We still have some things to talk about and iron out. Life and love were amazing at the resort. We'll be back home to reality."

"Captain Joe?" Byrum asked.

"You got it."

"Are you sure he's not a factor?"

"You can't buy what we share."

Tellum grabbed his vibrating phone.

"Callum?" Byrum asked.

"You know it. He texted that he thought we'd be on the other side of the property by now."

"Can you ever imagine Callum finding Ms. Right?"

"Never!" they shouted together.

As if on cue, together they walked to the truck, Tellum in the driver's seat. They were still laughing when he pulled off.

"Callum is going to be that uncle who will spoil our kids. He's not a one-woman kind of man."

"Oh, I think with the right woman, every man can be. It's a matter of being open to it."

Byrum heard the words come out of his own mouth. He surprised himself. The last thing he ever wanted or expected was to find a connection with a woman, even one off-limits to him. He didn't know what he was going to do. His world could crumble all around him if he ever decided to act on his feelings. Pushing them back, he had to continue to fight his attraction to her. It wouldn't pan out well for either of them.

Byrum's phone rang. He looked down at the number. Though he knew it had to be about business, he still smiled when her number flashed across his phone. He moved it to voicemail. The less his brothers knew right now, the better he was. He couldn't explain how he was willing to risk it all for a woman who had no idea how he felt about her.

18

Cheyenne walked into her condo dragging her two suit cases and her overnight bag across the floor where she dropped them with a loud thud. The nighttime flight from the Dominican Republic was an exhausting one. She hadn't slept even an iota though everyone else on the flight had. Flying first class was quiet and uneventful, perfect for sleeping. Still, it eluded her. She could have used the rest. She smiled slightly realizing that even with the exhaustion, she wouldn't change a thing about the week other than missing time with Tellum on her last day. Other than some texts, they haven't had time for phone conversations. He had a lot to accomplish, so she gave him the space he needed. She had promised him that for her last day, she would focus on herself and her own self-care. She had done just that.

After kicking off her shoes, she looked through the mail that was piled up on the end of her dining room table. Her mother had looked after everything at her place while she was gone. Picking up a few pieces that she wanted to check out immediately, she walked into her kitchen and smiled. Her mother hadn't just dropped off the mail, she'd also cleaned up her kitchen.

Before she left, though it wasn't a mess, she hadn't put her dishes away like she usually does. After washing them, she set them out on the counter, leaving them to be put away when she returned home. Opening the dishwasher, her mother had also emptied that out and put those dishes away too.

A loud clap of thunder outside rattled her. She thought back to the bad weather-free week she'd just come off of. The day skies had been sunny all week with the nights being comfortably cool. Her mood of coming back to reality was not helped by the weather. She couldn't wait to get in bed and sleep all day the next day as well before heading back to the office on Tuesday. If it weren't for a few important meetings, she would work from home instead of finding herself in rush-hour traffic. Before she forgot, she grabbed her phone and dialed her mother's cell. She would have called the house phone, but she didn't want her father to answer. She'd been avoiding his attempts to reach her all week. She wasn't sure how much he knew about her week away. She told her mother that she was spending the week at the resort. She doubted if after the conversation they'd had, that her mother would tell her father much about it. Still, she wasn't in the mood for hearing him bark out orders to her after a peaceful week.

"Hey, mom!"

"Hey, sweetie. You're home?"

Cheyenne sat in the white and gold highchair at her white marble island and flipped through the mail.

"I am. I just walked in the door. Thanks for the mail and for the kitchen clean up. I keep telling you that you don't have to pick up behind me. I would have gotten around to it."

"I know, I know. I saw the dishes. I had some time on my hands. Also, there's a box on the chair in your family room.

Your aunt Glynnis sent it to you through me. I had lunch with her the other day while she was in town."

"Was she with Uncle Clarence?"

"No. I think that's done. She wanted me to hear about it first-hand. His philandering at his age has finally gotten to her. I can't believe she's going to walk away from forty years of marriage over a few women on the side," Ramona exclaimed.

"Momma, not all women are willing to put up with that. I'm surprised it took her this long to leave him. She's the only one of your sisters, like you, who are still married to men this long."

Cheyenne started to say more but caught herself. Her mother's silence on the other end was a tell-tale sign that she got the message. Captain Joe was like most other men; he couldn't seem to keep his zipper up either. She'd discovered her father's infidelity some years ago. There was no doubt that her mother knew, but she would never let her mother know that she knew unless she actually asked her. She hated that this was her father. Still, she wasn't surprised. Not much about him surprised her anymore. She had a week to picture him in a new light, his true light.

"Promise me that you will never, ever let a man make you his doormat. This is a much different generation than the one I came up in. The women my generation learned from accepted a lot from men. We had homes to take care of and children to raise. We needed to have the men to do that. Unlike you and the women of your generation, you can decide to have or not have. I love that for you. I love watching you make your way in the world. I know that you'll make a wonderful wife and mother someday. Most of all, I know that your life will be filled with trust and honesty because you'll expect and demand it. There are still a lot of women who are willingly living in bad situations that are far from perfect, but it doesn't ruffle the waters. At some point in life, some men and women just learn to tolerate each other through the good and the bad because that's all they know. You continue to be the powerhouse that you are. I already know that you'll never have to deal with men like your uncle Clarence or even like your father. It's okay to not say what I know you're thinking. You, will hopefully, have Tellum. In him, you would never have anything to worry about, especially a wandering man. Speaking of Tellum, did you get to see and talk to him while you were away? Did you have fun?"

"I did on both accounts. I had a lot of fun. Most of all, I had almost an entire week of being with Tellum. It was amazing!" she declared.

"Oh, I'm so happy to hear that. Does that mean that you're back together?"

"It is. Despite what I know Captain Joe wants me to do, I can't do it anymore. Tellum and I talked, we loved, and we reminded each other that our love is more powerful than anything and anyone. You didn't tell Captain Joe, did you?" "Of course not. If he finds out, it won't be from me. I haven't mentioned it to anyone. When your aunt asked about stopping by to see you, I told her that you went away with some friends for some much-needed downtime."

"Thanks, mom. What's in the box? Did she say?"

Cheyenne hopped up from the counter and walked through the living and dining rooms to the family room. In the middle of the soft pink sectional sat a large box wrapped in birthday paper."

"No, she didn't."

"It's birthday paper. My birthday over two months away."

"She knows. She said she was planning a trip with some friends around the time of your birthday. She wanted to get you something special."

Cheyenne ripped the paper and opened the box. Inside was a brand-new pink Birkin bag; one she'd been eyeing for a while.

"Wow! It's that big Birkin bag that I told you I saw on some show I was watching. How did she know I wanted this bag? You told her, huh?"

"It may have slipped out in a conversation. She asked me about something for your birthday. She wanted to know about anything you had your eye on. I casually mentioned a few things. She pushed me for a higher priced tag item and I mentioned the purse."

"Mom, do you know how expensive this is? Its five figures!"

"I know. She loves you; you know that. She wanted to do it. Besides, she reminded me that with the divorce that will be coming up soon, money won't be an issue for her. She's always loved splurging on you. Since she only had the three boys and no girl, you've always been that daughter she never had."

"She's got two daughters-in-law."

"True. No one can ever take your place in her life. Make sure you call and thank her for the bag. So, things went well with Tellum? I can't tell you how happy I am to hear that."

"Things were and are perfect. It still feels like a dream. He's still away on business. He'll be home tomorrow. We're going to spend the weekend having fun before it's back to work for me on Monday. How was your week?"

"Oddly quiet. Heads up that your father has been wondering where you went. He said he called you a few times and stopped by your place but hasn't been able to catch up with you. I'm sure he called your office, and they told him you were off for the week. I heard him grumbling to himself about how you hadn't said anything to him about being off. He tried to get information out of me. I told him like I told anyone else who asked, you went away with some of your girlfriends for some downtime. I let him know that you were fine. Then a few days ago, he came storming in here demanding that I reach out to you and have you call him. Ignoring him was the highlight of my week. Uh, yesterday, I had lunch with Tellum's mother."

Cheyenne paused. She knew they were cordial with each other but never expected to hear that they were hanging out.

"You did? Why?"

"She called and invited me to have lunch at the golf club where her husband plays. They have a membership. It was very nice. The food was amazing."

"Just like that? She out of the blue invited you to lunch? She knows that Tellum and I had broken up. Other than telling you today that we're back together, neither of us said anything to anyone else; at least I don't think he told her yet."

"She's under the assumption that you're still on the outs. We go to the same hair salon. I was leaving and she was coming in. I was there on a different day for the first time. My stylist had been off a few days and rescheduled me. That was Felicia's usual day. She invited me and I accepted. I had a wonderful time. She introduced me to a few of her friends. They do a lot of philanthropy work. Felicia asked if I would be interested in working with them. They work hard but also do a lot of socializing. She's a really nice woman. I see where Tellum gets his politeness from."

"She is an amazing woman. She raised an incredible son. Did you talk about us?"

"We did. I would never lie to you. We talked about how we both hoped that once the week was over, the two of you would return home in love and in relationship again. I can't wait until I can talk to her about how our wish has come true. Maybe he told her already?"

"I doubt it. He said he would do so when he returned. What should I do about Captain Joe? He will find out."

Cheyenne had thought about that on her flight. That was one of the reasons she couldn't rest enough to catch a nap before landing. She was imagining the storm that will come her way the minute he finds out.

"To be honest, I feel like he knows. I don't know how, but from his behavior of the past two days, something happened; something changed. He thinks you're being secretive. Just beware. You'll have to talk to him soon. Remember, I told you to live your life your way. I'm happy that you've finally figured out that your life is yours. I don't care what your father says, do you. Okay?"

"I hear you, mom."

"Have fun when Tellum comes home. Let's have dinner next week. I know you have a lot to catch up on at work."

"Doesn't matter at all. I will always have time for you. Let me know what evening works good for you. I'll make the time. Thanks for checking in on my place while I was gone."

"Anything for you. I hope you know that. I see your future and it all looks good. I'm here for you, I promise."

"You always have been. I love you."

"I love you too, precious. Have a good night."

Cheyenne picked up the bag and turned it in all directions. Her aunt has always treated her to the most amazing birthday gifts. Calling her first thing in the morning would be her priority.

Getting up she went into her bedroom and stood in the doorway. She glanced over at her bed. From where she stood, it looked empty. That's because it was. Even if she crawled up in it for a good night's sleep, which was her original plan, it would still feel empty. Her place seemed cold; it wasn't about the temperature.

She missed Tellum. She missed his smell. In fact, she knew exactly where she wanted to be. He wasn't there, but that didn't mean that everything that reminded her of him wouldn't be there. She wondered. Is it possible?

With determined strides, she walked into her closet, grabbed a pink and white duffle bag and filled it with some casual sleeping and leisure clothes. Not forgetting to toss in a few sexy items, she went back into her living room. Getting a few essentials from the luggage that she'd just sat on the floor, she slipped back into her shoes, grabbed her purse and after setting the alarm, she grabbed a special key that she was glad she still had from the drawer of the table by the door and left out. The only way she would know is if she would try.

19

Tellum settled back against the headboard of the bed in his suite preparing to rest up before his flight out in the morning. Thinking it was time to check to see if Cheyenne had arrived back home safely, his phone and iPad pinged at the same time. He read the message that told him one of his codes was being used to enter the garage at his condo. When he saw the code, he smiled. Not only was Cheyenne home, but she was at his place. He waited for what seemed an eternity before he got his next ping. This one alerted him that one of his passcodes was used to enter the elevator that led to his condo. Tellum smiled even brighter. A few minutes later, another ping signaling that the alarm code on his condo had been disarmed. Once the alarm was rearmed, he turned the cameras off inside and called her.

"Hello, beautiful."

He could feel Cheyenne's smile through the phone.

"Hi. I was thinking about you."

"I can tell."

"Oh? Right. What gave me away," she chuckled.

"The passcode at the garage."

"Is this okay?"

"Baby, it's more than okay."

"I was missing you. I know you're not here, but I wanted to be close to you. Are you sure it's okay that I'm here?"

"Will you be there when I get back tomorrow?"

"If you want me to be. That was my plan. I didn't think I could surprise you because this place is like a bank vault to get into. I must say, I was nervous all the way up to entering my code into your alarm system after my key worked in the door. Everything is still the same."

"You didn't expect that?"

"No. I was scared to death that the police would show up and charge me with breaking in if my old code didn't' work."

"Baby, that's crazy."

"I know. I was at my place talking to my mother. We were talking about you. I was home a few minutes before I decided to come here instead."

"She knows?"

"She does."

"Your father?"

"If he does, he didn't hear it from my mother and definitely not from me. My mother says he's been acting strange running all overlooking for me. The guard in the lobby of my building said my father had been by a few times. Something is up. I can't deal with him right now. I pulled up to the garage gate and stared at the box. After a car behind me honked two times, I realized I hadn't entered anything. I put those numbers and letters in so slow. Then the gate opened. I said a silent thank you. I pulled into the spot next to your truck. Your car wasn't there."

"I drove it to the airport. I usually take a car, but I felt like driving myself."

"Okay. Well, then, I entered my code to get into the elevator and that worked. I inserted my key and the elevator moved. Then I got to the door and again, my code key worked. You didn't change anything."

"No, I didn't. I kept hope that you would one day use your code and your key. Now that you have, never stop."

"I love being here. I love my place, but I really, really love yours."

"Good. This lets me know that our talks at the resort wasn't just island talk. We're doing this."

"No doubt about that on my end."

"Now that you're there, what does your evening look like?"

"Sleeping. I want to crawl into your big ass bed and sleep. I miss that bed."

"It always has been and will always be ours. You know that right?"

"Yes."

"Do you know what I'm saying?"

"I think so."

Tellum heard the uncertainty in her voice.

"Tell me," he shot back.

"No other woman has been in that bed with you since we started seeing each other; not even when we were apart."

"Correct. My life, my heart, my soul, my place and especially in my bed; it's yours."

"I love you," she said.

"I love you too."

"How did your meeting go?"

"Still going on, sort of. I'm waiting on a call from our money guy."

"Does that mean your deal is a go?"

"I'll know at a quick meeting in the morning before I fly home."

"I can't wait. I'll be right here when you get here. I'll be all rested up."

"In my bed?"

"Of course. I need you in it with me. I'm lonely. I spent a week of morning sex and screaming orgasms. I guess I'll have to take care of that myself in the morning, huh?" she laughed.

The mere image of Cheyenne pleasuring herself got a groan out of Tellum that he couldn't help but share with her ear; the sexy kind she loved. She was teasing him. Served him right for not being hot, hard and ready for her in the same bed first thing in the morning. One thing they had in common was their love for morning sex.

"Don't do that to me. Hold it tight and sexy for me until I get there. I know you have to be tired. Did you at least sleep on the plane?"

"Not a wink. I plan to sleep good tonight. I'm going to take a hot shower as soon as we get off the phone."

"Get yourself a glass of red wine. Your favorite is there in the wine collection."

"You are the best!" Cheyenne exclaimed.

Tellum beat himself on his chest with his free hand.

"I feel like roaring like the king of the jungle," he joked.

"Stop that. I can hear it through the phone!"

"Hey, you know how I do. I love when I can make you happy. It makes me feel like a king pleasing his queen. I'll take care of any other needs when I get home."

"Are we still going out tomorrow night? You won't be too tired?" she asked.

"I've been looking forward to going. I checked on our tickets. They are at the will-call window. We're all set. We'll do the play and then dinner. I'll be there by one in the afternoon. I need to stop by the office for about an hour after I land in the morning. Continue missing me until I get there."

"You have no idea how much I miss every part of you. Work will be crazy next week. Besides, I've also agreed to teach two classes at Melodi's gym next week."

"Have you thought anymore about what we talked about? Have you decided what you want to do?"

Tellum had high hopes that Cheyenne would let him help her live out her dreams. Though he knew she enjoyed her job, it wasn't the passion she really wanted to follow.

"I did think about it on the plane a little."

"Oh? What did you come up with?"

"I have a lot of savings. You already know my credit is perfect. I want to look into opening my own dance studio. I want to do it in the community where kids may not get a chance to take part in various dance techniques. That is my passion. It has been since high school."

"I know. If it hadn't been, you wouldn't have stuck this close to it all these years. You double-majored in undergrad, with one being dance. You love teaching your yoga and dance classes at the gym. If what you want is your own dance studio, I hope you'll let me help you if you need it. You spent years living the life you felt you were supposed to and not the one you wanted. The way you love dance, being a marketing executive is nice, but living out your passion is better; that's dance, baby."

"Tellum, are you sure?"

"Baby, don't do that. Don't react with a question as if you think I'm not sure about helping the lady I love. I would go to the ends of the earth for you. We talked about that for hours the day after our night on the beach. There are many properties around Detroit that I'm sure could be turned into the perfect studio. I know real estate; you know that. How about we take some time in the coming weeks to take a look at a few? No pressure at all. You can take a look and see while thinking about the possibilities."

"Melodi said the same thing to me on the flight back before she and Stephen slept like sleeping beauties. I admired her for not worrying about a corporate job. Instead, she went right for what she's always wanted to do."

"Well, now, you're ready for your own dream. Think on it. We'll talk when I get home."

"Thanks for not being upset that I'm here."

"That will never happen. If you never want to leave, I'm good with that too."

"I love the sound of it. Did I forget to thank you for my early morning text earlier today? I've missed those. Your love notes at various times throughout the day would put a smile on my face no matter what I was doing. It's been lonely without them. Some days I would check my phone to see if it was working right. I know I shouldn't have expected them. Still, I missed them."

Tellum had a secret. Now, was the perfect time to share.

"I never stopped writing them."

"What?"

"My love notes to you; I never stopped writing them."

"Really? You didn't send them?"

"I couldn't. It didn't feel the same though my heart still felt the same."

"What did you do with them?"

"Go into my office," he said.

"Your office?"

"Not the office building. The office in the condo. Go into it and look on the bookshelf to the left of the television on the wall."

He could hear her feet shuffling across the wood floors."

"Okay, I'm here. The box. You still have the box that I gave you with our name engraved on it."

"I do. Open it."

Tellum waited and then he heard it. He heard her large intake of breath. Then there was silence.

"Oh my. What are these?"

"I still wrote my love notes to you when I thought about you. I had hoped that one day, we'd be in a position for me to give them to you."

"Tellum, there must be over a hundred slips of paper in here."

He smiled hearing her move the papers around in the box.

"There are. Get your shower and your glass of wine. Climb up in bed and read until you fall asleep. You'll feel me close to you when you read them."

He heard her sniffle.

"I can't believe you did this and kept them for me."

"Don't cry, baby. I can't handle it from here."

"These are happy tears. I can't wait to get in bed and dive into them."

Cheyenne's phone pinged loud; he heard it.

"I'll let you go and get that or to get your shower. I'll text you when I land in the morning."

There was a long pause. Something was wrong.

"Uh oh."

Tellum sat up straight.

"What is it?"

"I just got a text from my father. I've been summoned to their house in the morning. He said he needs to talk to me about something important. This can't be good," she said.

"What do you need?"

"You know what, I'm good. I can handle him. In fact, I'm going to let him know that you and I are back together. He needs to know."

"If you need me, you call me. I'm here for you. I'm a phone call away if you need me. The alarm is on, so rest. Cameras are off on my end except for the ones in the hallway outside. You're good?"

"I'm better than good. See you tomorrow. Thanks for my notes. I still have all the other ones on my phone. Now, I want to print those out on notes like these so that I can keep them forever. You are so romantic."

"You bring out the best in me. I love you. Sleep well."

"I will. I love you."

Tellum stood from the bed and walked over to the large window that looked out over the Denver mountains. Now, more than ever, he needed to get to Cheyenne. Her father was able to come between them once before. He feared the man was on a war path to do it again. He wasn't too worried. Cheyenne had a new fight in her when it came to them. They weren't giving up or giving in again.

20

Dennis Blackstone knew where he could find his middle son on a Saturday, in his office. That was usually Tellum's first stop after being out of town. Exiting the elevator, he headed toward Tellum's office. Not surprisingly, his assistant was also here.

"Hi, Lisa-Marie."

"Hi, Mr. Blackstone. It's nice to see you."

"I see my son couldn't stay away. I thought he was cutting back on his weekend hours. He even has you here?"

"No, Pop. This is not my doing. I got here and she was already here."

"He's right, Mr. Blackstone. After spending a few days at *Secret Whisper*, I wanted to check up on things since I'm off until Wednesday."

"Ah, you were there too. Did you have a good time?" Dennis asked.

"I had a great time. I look forward to going back again very soon."

"Pop, stop holding Lisa-Marie up. I told her to get out of here. Our weekend team is here and can handle things. She's still officially on vacation."

"I'm leaving in a few minutes; I promise. I'm returning a few high priority emails. I know I could have done this from home. I wanted to be sure the office was still standing with most of us being at the resort the past week."

"Tellum is right. Go on and continue enjoying your time off. I'm going to go in here and bend my son's ear for a few minutes."

"How'd you find me?" Tellum asked the minute they were in his office.

"I just knew. How were things at the resort? You were there all of this time? What? Over a week?"

"No. I had a detour for business. Byrum and Callum were there too. Callum came back yesterday. Byrum traveled back with me today."

"Right. I forgot about that. You boys stay in the air. It's a good thing you have your own jet."

"True, very true."

"How did that go? Are you moving forward with everything?"

"We are. Everything looks good. I'm scheduling a meeting with all parties next week. Do you have time to join us for that? We still need to talk about you coming on board with us. You know we really want you to, but only if you're really interested. We also don't want to piss mom off. I know she has big plans for your retirement that I'm sure didn't include you going from working at GM to working with us."

"I'm in. I know we need to sit and talk about what that looks like. I'm putting in my retirement papers at the end of this month. Your mother won't be a problem. The idea of me working in business with my sons will be one of her proudest moments. Send me when and what time and I'll be here. This next move is exciting!"

"That's good to hear. The timing is perfect. Considering how much mom loves the Denver resort, we thought you could take a lead role in the acquisition and planning. She, will no doubt, look forward to traveling with you. We're excited to have you on board. Wait until you see the office Callum is having put together for you. We know you'll only be in it part-time. We still want to make a permanent space for you here. We have been looking forward to the day. You got us started. This is full circle as far as we're concerned."

"I'm excited about it too. Now, enough about business. Your mother mentioned that Cheyenne was at the resort."

Dennis leaned against the door frame and crossed his arms across his chest. He was thankful that he was the kind of father that his sons felt comfortable talking to him about anything including their relationships.

"She was. Without going into too much detail, we're back together. In fact, we're heading out for a date night tonight to a play and dinner."

"That's good to hear. Your mother was concerned."

"And you?"

"I never had a doubt. I know the son I raised. Unless Cheyenne took up dating one of your brothers, she would have a hard time finding a man as good as you," Dennis joked.

"I would be less two brothers if she did that."

Tellum was joking but serious at the same time. Dennis could see it in his flippant grin.

"Patience paid off, right? Just like in business. I told you boys that. Don't rush what is meant for you. All things come in time the way they are supposed to. I'm also glad to see you focusing on more than just work. Going to a play? You? I know you like them when you go to New York. You're not doing anything work related on a Saturday night; I'm impressed. Cheyenne has a great, positive impact on your life. You're learning to lean on the team you have in place. Your policy on staggered work schedules means your business never closes. There is always work being done. You and your brothers have recognized that some people need daytime hours for family and personal things and are free to work late evening hours on projects that don't require a lot of meetings. It's brilliant. You know that you don't have to be here around the clock. I don't want to see any of you running yourselves in the ground in the name of work. There is more to it. You've become successful pretty fast."

"Because of your help and faith in us," Tellum interrupted.

"True. That's because I have and will always have faith in you. If you ever need me, I'm right here. I want you to remember to take the time and enjoy the fruits of your hard labor. I want you to especially focus on your lady. Work is good. Business is great. Money and success are harmonious and can make you content. *Love?* Without even being there, I know that you and Cheyenne were able to slow your lives down enough at the resort to rediscover what your lives together mean to you. That can sustain your entire life. That's where happiness comes from. I made sure my sons saw me love on their mother all the time. I was a hard worker, but most of all, I made time for my wife and my sons. That was more important to me than anything else in the world. I would have gladly lived in a motorhome with the five of us on top of each other all day and night. The point is, being together was my goal."

"We always knew that. From an early age, I would see other kids who didn't have the kind of love from their father like you have always shown us. Most still don't know what it means to have unconditional love from a parent. You have been a great role model for us."

"What kind of life do you see yourself having with Cheyenne when it comes to long-term? I'm not trying to rush you into anything. I want to be sure you're appreciating what the two of you have and not just in the present. You remind me of your mother and me when we first fell in love. I knew from the moment I saw her that she would be my love for life. You once told me that was how it was when you met Cheyenne. Do you still feel that way? Your love for life?"

Tellum's head bobbed up and down fast and hard. Dennis thought it would fall off.

"Absolutely! I know you're not rushing anything. I see our life together one day sitting with our grandchildren in our family room watching their favorite movies," Tellum explained.

"I see that. Your mother and I look forward to being in the same position one day: again, no rush. You know I never miss a chance to give you boys my advice. I want to remind you to never stop making her a priority. She should be number one above everything else. The next resort or another business venture will always be there. Don't risk losing her by not paying attention to her now that you have her back. One day when you're married to her, and I know that's in your future, continue to date her every single day."

"I hear you, Pop. Mom once said that she loves how the two of you still date even all these years later."

"When y'all were little, we would put you to bed early. We couldn't go out to eat or to the movies because we had the three of you. She didn't like having other people looking after you. After the three of you were asleep, we would have picnics in the back yard. We would work on large jigsaw puzzles, something your mother still enjoys doing. What you saw in us is what has helped to mold all three of you into great, dependable men. You're not afraid to love openly. That's why Cheyenne fell in love with you. You don't have to be hard to be manly. You just have to love life and the people who are in it."

"I appreciate conversations like this, Pop. They keep me humble."

Dennis turned when Lisa-Marie walked up behind him.

"I'm sorry to interrupt," she said. "Tellum, you have a call on your private line."

"On a Saturday?" he questioned.

"It's not a work call. She says she tried calling your cellphone a few times and when you didn't answer, she tried you here. She sounds hurried like it's important."

"Is it Cheyenne?"

"No. She says her name is Ramona Reddick, Cheyenne's mother."

Tellum raced to the phone on his desk.

"Thanks."

Remembering he hadn't planned to be at the office long, his cell phone was in his backpack in the back seat of his car.

"Son. I'll leave you to it."

"No, Pop. You're good. Hello, Mrs. Reddick? Is Cheyenne, okay?"

"I'm sorry for calling you at the office. I wasn't sure you'd be there. I tried the emergency number Cheyenne gave me once for you after you started dating. I've never used it before. I kept going to voicemail. I needed to speak to you directly."

"Ms. Reddick? What's wrong?"

"It's Cheyenne. I need you to come and get her."

She was whispering. That was Tellum's first signal that something wasn't right.

"Cheyenne? Is she hurt?"

"No, no. I'm sorry if I sound mysterious. She's here at the house talking to her father. It's not going well. He knows that the two of you are back together. He's not happy about it. I don't want to remain quiet like I did before. Enough is enough. I don't want her going down this road again. She's supposed to be with you. I want you to come get her and never let her come back to this house again. I can explain more later. Can you please come? Please, Tellum?" she begged.

"I'm on my way."

Tellum hung up and reached for the jacket of his sweat suit.

"Son?" Dennis asked, drawing his attention.

Tellum moved around with a purpose while his mind spun in a million directions around what could be happening. The only thing he knew for sure was that he needed to leave.

"Something's going on at the Reddick house. Cheyenne's mother called. She sounded frightened. Apparently Cheyenne and her father are having an argument and her mother asked me to come and get Cheyenne. She's never done that before. It must be bad. He found out that Cheyenne and I are seeing each other again. I have to go."

Tellum rushed around his father and out of his office.

"Son, slow down."

"Pop, I can't. If you're about to tell me not to go, you're wasting your time."

"Tellum, stop moving and wait a damn minute. You know that man is out of his mind, especially when it comes to Cheyenne. You can't go trudging into that man's house."

"I can if Cheyenne is there. Her mother sent for me."

"What are you going to do?"

"I don't know but if I call you, that means it's pretty bad. You should have bail money ready. I gotta go, Pop. It'll be fine. I've got to go see about my lady."

21

Cheyenne couldn't believe she was having a déjà vu moment. She was in the midst of again being berated by her father. She stood in the kitchen while he paced around like a mad man, heated that she was back with Tellum.

After rising early this morning after a sound night of sleep in Tellum's bed, her father started blowing up her phone to be sure she'd gotten his texts and phone messages that she needed to come by the house. She replied with a text that she would be there. If she had known that he would be this toxic, she would have stay in bed and waited on Tellum to get home.

Her father had never been this angry at her before. He was on a whole new level of madness.

Where was her mother? Her car was in front of the house in the driveway. That meant she was here someplace. Was this another time where she wouldn't have her support in dealing with her father?

When she arrived and before she could ask if her mother was around, her father tore right into her screaming about defying him. She should have known this wasn't going to be a good visit. The tone of his voice messages and texts weren't pleasant.

"I don't understand why you can't do what I asked you to do. It's not like I'm asking you to do something impossible. Stay away from Tellum Blackstone! How *hard* could that be? There are a million men in this world, and you can't seem to stay away from the one family that is responsible for sending me into the poor house. How could you go behind my back and fraternize with the enemy?"

She listened to him rattle on. She stood her ground. She was happy that she'd found her own defense. No matter what, she was sticking to it this time.

"Enemy? Tellum is *not* the enemy. Any issues you have with Mr. Blackstone has nothing to do with Tellum or me. You can't dictate to me who I see?"

"Oh really? You think he's good for you? No one with tension with our family will ever be good enough for you. Now, I've set up a nice dinner here tomorrow night with a new business connect. He's someone you already know. I expect you here. I also expect you to give this young man a chance. He's told me how much he already cares about you. I am working on a new business proposal, and he thinks his family can help me get this off the ground. He's got money, power and prestige. Maybe not as much as the Blackstones, but he's good people."

Cheyenne shook her head in disbelief.

"Wait? You're pimping me out now in the name of business? Me? Your own daughter? Are you out of your mind?" she yelled.

"Don't you dare disrespect me with those words or that tone. Remember who you're talking to."

Cheyenne exhaled loudly. She didn't know what was going on.

"I don't know who I'm talking to. What are you doing? This can't be happening."

She threw her hands up in the air in disgust at the notion that her own father was using her this way for money.

"You will watch your tone. Now, forget about Tellum and make sure you're here by seven tomorrow evening for dinner. Reed will be here on time. You will be nice to him."

"Reed? Reed Howard? You're trying to set me up with a creep like Reed Howard?"

"That creep is going to get me back on track financially."

"How do you know Reed? What kind of twilight zone moment am I trapped in? Reed Howard? This is crazy. I'm not sitting down at any table with Reed. I'm certainly not interested in him."

"Well, you made that clear while you were out of the country. He told me about you and Tellum. He sent me a nice photo of the two of you together holding hands. Is that what you did? You had to leave the country to go behind my back. Have you been seeing him all along and lying to me about it? Reed came to see me yesterday to let me know what a great partnership our families would make with the two of you together."

"Maybe you shouldn't interfere in my personal life."

"Personal life? This is about my life and your legacy. I'm ruined if I can't sell this project. His family's airline could be the jumpstart that I need. He likes you. We agreed that you would make a great couple if you would stop hanging all over Tellum like you're desperate for male attention. There are tons of other fish in the sea."

"Fish in the sea? I'm in love with Tellum. This isn't some fly-by-night kind of thing. He's not a weigh station until someone else comes along. There is no one else for me. I let you talk me out of my relationship with him before. Not anymore. I know I can get another man. It has nothing to do with being desperate. I'm shocked you think so little of me that I can't tell when I'm in love with someone. I don't owe you and definitely not Reed Howard an explanation for anything. I'm not a child anymore. You can't control what I do."

"Like hell I can't. I made you. I paid for college, undergraduate and graduate school. No one else had a BMW at sixteen, but you did. I gave you the money for your condo so that you could afford the payments. What you have achieved, I have had a hand in. I have things I need you to do for me. In return for what I've been to you all your life, all I get is grief and dissention. This rebellious streak in you is something I can't deal with."

"Reed. It was Reed who told you about me and Tellum, huh? I'm not surprised at all."

"Why? Because your mother knew and didn't tell me? Yeah, I figured that out eventually too. I don't know why the two of you treat me like I haven't taken care of you all of your life. All I do, I do for you. I do know what's best for you even if you don't. Reed enlightened me."

"And what, I'm the consolation prize?"

"It's dinner, Cheyenne. He likes you. There's no harm. It's only dinner. The two of you may find you have things in common."

"Captain Joe, you're not hearing me. I am in love with Tellum. I will not allow you to get in my head again. I came here because you asked me to. If you think I'm going to walk away from Tellum a second time, you're sadly mistaken. I'm saying this with the utmost respect. I have my own life. It's not tied to your business decisions."

"Oh, yes, it is. You're going to help me do whatever I ask you to do. That's my final word on that."

"No, she's not."

Cheyenne turned around at the sound of her mother's voice behind her.

"Not now, Ramona. Go on back upstairs. This is between me and my daughter," Captain Joe declared boldly.

"Not this time, Joe. I mean it. Cheyenne is not doing anything you want her to do. Like I said, not this time."

Cheyenne started to speak, but her mother silenced her with one look. It wasn't often that she spoke up. Cheyenne gave her the space she needed and kept quiet. This was her mother's moment.

"Ramona, this isn't the time for you to be defiant. I thought you were at Ms. Shaffer's house? Weren't you going to the nursery together to pick out new flowers for your garden or something? I can handle this discussion with my daughter," he said.

"*Not. This. Time.* I mean it, Joe. Back off. Cheyenne is in love and she's happy. I won't let you play on her emotions of whether she should love you more than she should love Tellum. I watched what she went through in struggling to live up to your expectations before. She was happy. That's what we've always wanted for her. You start seeing dollar signs and nothing else matters other than money; not even your only daughter's happiness."

"I don't know what's gotten into the women in my life. All of a sudden, what I say requires an argument."

"Joe, I have sat back over the years and allowed you to run this house as the head of it. It took me a lot of years to realize I was willing to follow you without question. That wasn't the best idea. I know now that I haven't shown Cheyenne that her decisions in life, especially as a grown woman, should be about her happiness and not ours; especially not yours. Summoning her here like some child was more than I could stand. Cheyenne, I want you to turn around and go home. This isn't a place for you to be right now. Whatever scheme your father is about to cook up does not involve you."

Cheyenne started to walk away but her father's loud roar stopped her.

"Wait a damn minute! You are *not* in a position to make that call. This is between me and my daughter!" Captain Joe shouted.

Cheyenne grew nervous when her mother stepped around her and stood between her and her father. This was a new Ramona Reddick.

"First of all, lower your voice when you speak to me and our daughter. There is no need to shout or make demands. That will no longer work. For far too long I have allowed you to cause discourse in this house. Like a fool, I've gone along with it. That stops today. This is our daughter. She's not a pawn in some game of financial wealth for you. For months, her heart was broken, and you didn't care. You took satisfaction in what you thought was getting one over on the Blackstones. How? Why? Because you could? You used your own daughter. You took joy in her pain because you felt disrespected. I'm sick with myself for allowing you to do that without standing up for her. For that, I will forever be sorry to Cheyenne. She has a good man; a great man. He loves her. Do you know what that means? It means everything he feels for her is all love. There are no strings attached other than the smile he loves to see on her face. A daughter's first love is supposed to be her father. That's so that one day, when the right man comes along, she would know what real love feels like. She had that but didn't trust it because she didn't trust you. All this misery you're infusing in her life ends right now."

The ringing of her mother's cell phone halted all conversation.

"This is ridiculous. You both are acting like I'm asking you to commit a crime."

"Yes, please come in," Ramona said into her phone.

"Come in? Who? Come in where?" Captain Joe shouted.

"I told you Cheyenne is leaving."

"She's not going anywhere until I'm finished," he yelled louder.

"Yes, she is," Tellum said entering the kitchen.

"Who the hell invited you into my home. You can turn around a leave right now!"

"I invited him. This isn't just your home as long as my name is on it too. I asked him to come here," Ramona explained.

"Baby, are you alright?" Tellum asked Cheyenne.

Before she could find the words to respond, Cheyenne raced into Tellum's arms and held on for dear life.

"This is officially a circus," Captain Joe exclaimed.

"This place has been a circus for a lot of years. From your illegal business practices to your chicks on the side over the years. And before you try to deny that, yes, I know. Foolishly, I looked the other way, but not anymore. Your days of using me and your daughter are done. I called Tellum here to make sure Cheyenne leaves. Until you come to your senses, she won't be coming back here. I've had enough of you and your mess. She is our only child and the way you treat her is atrocious. I won't stand for it anymore. Tellum, please make sure Cheyenne gets to her car."

"Cheyenne, if you leave here..."

Captain Joe moved toward her. Cheyenne felt her body being moved until she was behind Tellum. He moved to a position in front of her.

"I respect you Mr. Reddick, but please don't make a move toward Cheyenne. Like Ms. Ramona said, Cheyenne is leaving with me. I won't speak on what I really feel because it would be inappropriate and disrespectful."

"Tellum, it's okay. At this point, nicety has gone out of the window. That happened the minute her father tried to hand her off to someone named Reed in exchange for a business deal," Ramona explained.

"He did what?" Tellum shouted.

"Baby, no. It's okay." Cheyenne patted Tellum's arm to calm him down. She knew what hearing Reed's name was doing to him. The situation was about to get out of control. She couldn't have that. "It was never going to happen. Don't get yourself worked up. He somehow connected with Reed who convinced him to bring me to dinner with them tomorrow night. Trust me, like I said, it was never going to happen. My father is desperate."

"Right, and desperate people make abysmal choices," Tellum said harshly, looking Captain Joe in the eyes.

Cheyenne put her hand in Tellum's. Her mother was right. It was time for her to leave; for them to leave. This was not a happy home.

"You can't speak to me like this in my own house. You can leave!" Captain Joe said to Tellum, pointing toward the front door.

"I'm leaving with Cheyenne."

"No, you're not."

"Yes, he is!" Cheyenne and her mother said together.

Tellum turned to leave, taking her hand. Before they got too far, Cheyenne turned to her mother.

"Mommy, come with me. You don't have to stay here," she said.

"Don't you worry one bit about me. I wasn't planning on staying. Tellum, you'll see two suitcases and two large overnight bags by the door. I've already placed three other bags in the trunk of my car. Please place these in there as well. I think my time here is done. I've lived through all I could. At this point, it's time I found my own peace. After all, I can't convince my daughter that she deserves all the peace in the world if I'm not willing to find it for myself. I'm done, Joe."

When Tellum was finally able to pull her hand enough for her to walk with him, Cheyenne took her mother's hand so that she was walking out with them at the same time. She looked back at her father who stood at the kitchen archway with his mouth hung open, glaring at them. Tellum picked up the luggage and they left. She was hurt that the idea of never coming back to the house now that her mother wasn't here was about to make her physically ill.

"Fine!" they heard Joe yell. "No man wants a defiant wife!"

"Don't respond, mommy. Just keep walking."

Tellum loaded up the trunk of her mother's white Mercedes sedan before shutting it closed.

"Come on, Ms. Ramona. I won't leave until you're in your car and pulling away," Tellum said.

"Mommy, where are you going?" Cheyenne asked, taking both of her mother's hands into her own and holding tight to them.

"Don't you worry about me. I can get a hotel room for now and figure it out later. One thing I am not is destitute. I feel free! For the first time in a lot of years, making that move to pack up a few suitcases was refreshingly freeing. I'll be fine. You go ahead and leave. Tellum, you will make sure she gets home, okay?"

"Yes, ma'am. I will."

"Mommy, come home with me. I have plenty of room. You love my place anyway. There is enough room for both of us. Stay with me for as long as you want. Please don't make me worry about you being someplace else. I wouldn't be able to sleep with you in some hotel. The idea of it is cold to me. You can take my room and I'll take the guest room. In fact, tonight, we can have a girls' night in."

"Nonsense. You already told me that you and Tellum have plans tonight."

"You can come with us. I'm sure he can get another ticket. You can even join us for dinner," Cheyenne pleaded.

"Ms. Ramona, Cheyenne is right. There is no need for you to go to a hotel. As for tonight, we would love for you to join us. We're going to see a hometown play about the beginning of the Motown sound."

"Listen to the two of you," Ramona smiled. "I will be fine not being a third wheel. I'll tell you what. I will take you up on our offer to stay at your place temporarily. I will make arrangements for myself soon. You have a life to live. You certainly don't need me hanging around. Go on with your plans. I'll settle in at your place and watch some television. This has been an over-exciting day. I could use some relaxation. You and Tellum go have a fun date night. I love that I can say that again."

"Are you sure? All I have to do is make a call to get you a ticket," Tellum noted.

"I'm sure. In fact, I think I'll get in bed early. I anticipate I'll sleep like a baby tonight. Cheyenne, if you weren't planning to come home tonight, don't alter your plans for me. I'm find. I know how you young people are. I'm not shielded from your love life. Go, have fun."

"Are you sure?" Cheyenne asked. "This has been a lot. In a span of minutes, you are moving out of the house. I'm sorry that this is so messy."

"It's been messy a long time. It wasn't until he tried to dictate your life again that I realized he became the monster I fed into for years. No more, though. Now, let me get in my car," Ramona said.

"Okay, but I'll meet you at my place," Cheyenne said.

"I will too. Thanks for calling me," Tellum said, pulling Ms. Ramona into a hug before she got in the car.

"When did you call him?" Cheyenne asked.

"The moment you arrived. I heard your father on the phone telling someone that he was sure you would be joining them for dinner. He also said something about making himself scarce before dinner was over. I didn't like the sound of that. When he thanked this person for telling him about you and Tellum being back together, I knew that enough was enough. I thought I would be sad, but I'm exhaling and smiling."

"I'm exhaling and smiling with you," Cheyenne said.

"That's all that matters to me," Ramona said.

"Me too," Tellum chimed in.

**

Ramona moved about Cheyenne's guest bedroom taking the clothes she'd brought with her and placed them in the dresser drawers. She carried other items into the large walk-in-closet to hang them up. When she turned, Cheyenne was standing in the doorway to the bedroom watching her.

"If you're going to stand there and stare, help me put some of these things away," Ramona said.

"Mommy, I wish you would take my room. I can stay in here."

"I agreed to stay here with you. What I won't do is push you out of your own room. Besides, I love this room. I helped decorate it. Remember that?" she asked.

"Yes, I do. I know you love this room. Listen, when we're done putting your things away, how about we order some food and watch some movies. You can then tell me about your decision to finally leave your home."

"Oh, I'm not leaving my home. I left your father's home. That place hasn't felt like mine in a very long time. I won't be under your hair for long. I have enough money to buy my own place, which is exactly what I plan to do."

"Really? You've thought this through? You're not just mad at him for the moment?"

Ramona moved to the bed and sat on the seat at the foot of it.

"Come sit next to me. We need to talk."

Once Cheyenne was seated next to her, she took her hand between both of hers.

"Yes, we do, especially since Tellum finally felt comfortable enough to go home. I told him that I'd like to reschedule our night out. I think you need me here," Cheyenne admitted.

"I spent a lot of years loving your father. That has not been the case in the past few years. Seeing you miserable for months was my undoing. I've been planning on leaving for a while. First, I wanted to be sure you were securely back in Tellum's arms. It's where you belong. Besides that, I needed you to see me be strong enough to stand up to him so that you would too. Instead, I watched you carry your own confidence. That made me proud and happy."

"Are you really sure about this? Captain Joe can be a monger. He's the hustler of all hustlers. He loves you, though. I know he loves me. He just has a horrible way of going about it."

"I'm sure I am not going back to your father. I just need a little time to figure out exactly what I plan to do. Now, as for tonight, there will be no food ordering or movie watching; at least not for you. I want you to pack your bag and go to Tellum. The two of you had plans that were derailed tonight because you wanted to look out for me. I get it. Trust me, I am fine. I'm going to be okay. I know it's too late for your date night out, but perhaps, there is still enough of the night left that you can have your quality time. I know how to order food. In fact, the best soul food place is a few blocks from here. I already know what I want. I have some movies I want to catch up on. You still have cable with all the channels, right?" she asked.

"Mommy?"

"Cheyenne, don't mommy me. I'm serious. I'm feeling good right now. I haven't breathed this easily in years. I'm going to take a hot bubble bath with some of that smelly stuff you love. I bet you still have tons of that too."

"I do in my hall linen closet. Use what you want."

"Good. After that, I'm going to have a glass of wine because I know you have a nice collection. I hope it's okay if I partake."

"What's mine is yours."

"See, good again. I'll then order me some food. I'll get comfortable on the couch and relax until I fall asleep. You go get yourself ready to head to Tellum's house. I know that's where you were planning to be tonight. Do not change your plans because I'm here."

"Stay as long as you want. My place is always your place. You have a key and the code."

"I do. Now, go be with your young man. I don't want anything messing up what you've been able to get back."

Cheyenne stood to her delight. Ramona stood with her and pulled her into a tight hug.

"Love that man like never before. Live your life like each day is your last with him. Don't let anything or anyone distract you from what is truly for you. That happens to be Tellum Blackstone. Now, get going. I have a bath to get to."

"You're sure. I mean, you're really sure?"

"Never been surer in my life."

Ramona pushed Cheyenne toward her own bedroom. When they were inside, she walked into Cheyenne's bedroom size walk-in closet and found an overnight bag. Handing it to her, she watched as Cheyenne started pulling items from her closet.

"I'll be back tomorrow morning."

"No, you won't. Do not make a fuss over me. I don't need a babysitter. In fact, I may not be here when you get home tomorrow. I have some friends that I've been avoiding for a while. I reached out earlier today and we're having lunch and a day at the nail salon. Promise me that you won't look back.

"I promise."

"Good. Do what you need to do. I'm going to run a bath."

"I'm happy you're here," Cheyenne said before Ramona left the room.

"So am I. I'm glad that I didn't waste any more time being in an unhappy place; in an unhappy marriage. I'm also glad that you're no longer in an unhappy place. Welcome back to love," Ramona said and then left the room. She practically danced to the guest bedroom feeling like today not only saved Cheyenne's love but saved her own happiness as well.

** **

Tellum sat down on the chair to watch a ball game from earlier in the day. After leaving Cheyenne's place where he hoped both women were settling in, his phone pinged with a text that his guest code had been entered into the entrance to the private garage. He smiled knowing that it had to be Cheyenne. She was here.

Switching the view on one of his four television screens in front of him to the view in the garage, he watched Cheyenne park her car in her usual space before getting out and retrieving her overnight bag from the trunk. The sight made his heart leap with joy. She was spending the night. Their plans for the evening were put on hold, but not cancelled. He was set to miss her tonight. She remedied that by showing up.

Minutes later, he heard his front door open and in walked the love of his life. She entered and winked.

"You're here! Hey, baby!"

He started to get up. Without using words, Cheyenne signaled for him to not move. His eyes followed her as she turned and walked with her bag in her hand toward the bedroom. Minutes later, she returned dressed only in one of his gray t-shirts. It looked more like a short dress on her. He continued talking to her, explaining how happy he was to see her. Still, she said nothing as she walked over to him. Her eyes never left his as she took the remote from his hand and turned off all four screens, plunging the room into darkness except for the moon that shone bright through the all-glass wall of windows. She silenced him with a finger to his lips. In a motion that set a world's record, Cheyenne reached inside of his gray sweat pants. The moment her fingers caressed him, there was no longer a need for the pants. That was the only clothing he put on after his shower once he arrived home.

She stroked him and kissed him. Her lips were demanding. Her potent desire for him was evident. His shown in how hard his body rose to attention the moment she touched him. It was at the moment when she rose up enough to give him room to embrace her behind in his hands that he knew there would be no words; none were needed. She needed to feel him. She needed to taste him. She needed to love him. He knew how she felt. They were always on the same page. After the day she had, he should have known that she needed to feel close to him; closer than ever before.

Guiding her where she needed him, he lowered Cheyenne over his manhood and slowly slid her down on him. The only sound in the room was of her expanded intake of breath at the pleasure that surged from his body to hers. Cheyenne danced up and down on him. He swirled his hips around and then matched her, thrust for thrust. With her hands braced on his shoulders, his mind was blown at the feel of the inside walls of her womanhood caressing him with her liquid essence. The muscles in his penis twitched with awareness. The sound of their loving flowed around and bounced off of the walls, creating a lustful serenade in his ears.

He saw her jaw tightening. He stroked the silky area with his lips and the pad of his tongue. She increased the pace, moving faster to a rhythm he easily followed. Her body tightened around his flesh. Still, they loved slow and methodically. He felt her release overtake her, triggering his own. They trembled and took the plunge into stimulating love as one.

Tellum cupped her body as they rode each other into nirvana. She continued to milk him for every pulse and surge into her body. When she slowed, he continued loving her, pulling her even closer into his body. His hands worked their way up and down her back underneath the shirt. This was a moment not meant for words.

They sat like this for an unmeasured amount of time. Cheyenne kissed his neck and sighed against him. It was clear that she reached the satisfaction she sought the moment she walked in the door.

"Baby, are you okay?" he spoke slowly and breathlessly.

"I am now," she replied into the side of his neck.

"You're here."

"I am."

"Thank you."

"For?" she asked, leaning back to allow him to see as much of her face as the moon outside would allow.

"For knowing that anytime you need me, I will be right here."

"I needed you tonight."

"I can tell."

"I wanted to be in your arms. This is the first night of being back in Detroit that I'm here with you holding me tight. I had to have this; I had to have you."

"You will forever have me. Did you eat?" he asked.

"No."

"Are you hungry? I can make you something."

"No. I want to sit right here just like this until I fall asleep. I'm tired," she mumbled.

Tellum turned them until they were in a laying position facing each other. With his back to the sofa, he reached in front of them and flipped the top of the large footrest, pulling out a blanket to cover them.

"I love you," he said against her lips

Cheyenne yawned and kissed him back.

"Like no other," she spoked after another yawn, this one bigger.

In seconds, she was asleep. Tellum held her. To him, this was the best feeling in the world.

22

Four months later

The celebratory atmosphere accompanied by thunderous cheering had the glass walls of the office conference room. Tellum wondered if the offices a floor below them could hear the vibrant, festive and unwavering happiness of the daytime staff having a good time. He was preparing to greet the team who worked the day shift, one of three shifts they offered to accommodate staff home life.

"Alright guys – settle down. I know you're excited but eventually, you all still have work to get back to," Tellum said in his attempt to curtail the excitement until after his speech.

"Nice tie, boss," Jacob, a long-time graphic design artist who works for them said.

Tellum looked down and flipped the tie out between his fingers before tucking it back into his suit jacket with what he knew was a massive stupid look on his face.

"Y'all know it was Cheyenne," Domingo, another team member boldly proclaim.

The entire room burst into laughter at his expense. Tellum happily laughed along with them.

"Yeah, yeah. Jokes this morning?" he jested.

"That's because we know she has amazing taste. Don't lie. Tell us the honest truth!" Keiko said.

His thoughts turned to his lady love who he was missing like crazy. A month ago, Cheyenne had made a life-changing decision to resign from her job. He encouraged her to take some time and work out her plan for this next, new phase of her life. She was thinking through the idea of opening her own dance studio. There was a lot to plan for. She needed time to herself to do that. Her plan began with taking a trip to her new favorite place in the world; *Secret Whisper*. Before she left, she'd given him a box with this very tie in it. She knew that he was going to have one of his powerful meetings with his team. She declared he needed a power tie to go along with the discussion. It was in various shades of purple. He chose one of his favorite charcoal grey suits to go along with it.

"Alright, you got me. It was a gift from Cheyenne. She wanted to commemorate this day. It's a big day, right?" he hollered and pumped both fists in the air.

Again, the room lit up with shouts and cheers.

"Big day, indeed!"

Tellum turned to yet another happy voice in the room and gave them all a thumbs up.

"Well, when we make a promise, we stick to it. I know we don't have enough chairs in here for everyone, but those who have a seat, take it and everyone else, get in and around this table where you can," Tellum encouraged. "It's been four months since the opening of *Secret Whisper* and we are booked solid for almost two years with reservations. Even with us going into the Christmas holiday season, the resort is packed. It's winter here in Detroit, but if anyone wants to know, it's warm and sunny at the resort," Tellum said, glowing with appreciation.

"Where did you find a cake almost the size of the table?" Lisa-Marie declared as she moved in to take the cover off of cake with the words, *Secret Whisper* in the center.

"The daughter of one of my mom's friends opened up a new bakery. I wanted to help get the word out. Make sure you take a business card and share the news about this new black-owned bakery right here in town. We look out for our own, right?" he asked.

"Yeah, we do and so do you!" Domingo yelled.

Everyone cheered again.

"My brothers and I hold to our promises. We told you that all of the hard work, late nights, early mornings and weekends that you put in to help us pull off the most amazing resort in the world would pay off. That starts in a big way today. There is no way we would be able to do all that was accomplished if it wasn't for the entire team. Now, I don't toss the word 'team' around loosely. I know that there are people who use that word because they have or are encouraged to do so. We actually are a team; I'm speaking of all of us. Every level of employee wins when you work hard for us. Where my brothers and I succeed, so do you. You're not here just to make the names on the building be successful. There is enough room for success for everyone. We aren't leaving anyone behind who wants to ride with us. A lot of you joined us at *Secret Whisper* for the grand opening. You even worked while you were there to help to make sure any issues remained seamless to our guests. I personally thank you for that sacrifice."

"Like you said, we are a team!" someone standing along the wall behind him yelled.

"And like a team, we celebrate our wins together. With that being said, I know a cake isn't the greatest thank you that

I could offer. It is how we do around here. This celebration is two-fold. We promised when we're successful financially with our business ventures, so are our team members; that's all of you. First up, bonuses for each of you will go out on Friday, that's tomorrow, just in time for the holiday. You'll see them in your bank accounts with your usual paychecks. Make sure you celebrate with your families because they made sacrifices too. Up next, Shelton Sullivan, one of my greatest friends and the man behind our financial growth is here for the next week. As promised, you each will be given your percentage of the profits from the resorts. It won't make you a millionaire overnight, but if you choose, Lisa-Marie can schedule a meeting with Shelton if you want his financial advice. The man is a master when it comes to money and how to make it grow for you. You've all heard about his family's ranch in Montana and how they've expanded to a billion-dollar corporation because of his wealth planning. See him or your own financial planner. I implore you to not waste any additional influx of money you'll receive as an employee here. This is your chance to make something big for yourselves, your families and your future."

"Lisa-Marie, I'm up first," someone yelled.

Others murmured the same sentiment.

"Relax everyone. The new office that was constructed at the far end on this floor is Shelton's new space. He'll use that whenever he's in town. It's across the hall from my father's new office. A few of you will be working with him directly whenever he is here. You already know who you are."

"I just need to know if any of his sexy brothers are going to be paying us a visit too. How are they breeding those hot guys on that Sullivan Ranch in Montana?" a woman yelled from the crowd.

Tellum shook his head at the single women around the room who were giving each other a thumbs up in agreement.

"I already told y'all that Shelton and his brothers are all either married or engaged. Keep it business," he quipped.

"We'll try. He sure can wear a suit," someone else said.

"Enjoy this cake and other refreshments that will be set up in here shortly. The delivery is on its way, right, Lisa-Marie?"

"Yes. Ten minutes out. I told them noon. There is a full spread of three types of chicken, lamb chops, braised ribs, four types of salads, southern dishes, sides and a few other desserts."

"Thanks. See, we really celebrate here. Let's not forget that Domingo, Casey, Keiko, Drake, Rosa, Tristan, Mara and Brian are all leaving us by the end of the year to take on responsibilities at one of our resorts. They've asked to be relocated to places they've always wanted to live and we've honored those requests. We look forward to our continued working relationships with them in their new positions. They can each bring you up to date on where they're going. I'm happy for them and all of you. Remember, we are open to those who would like new surroundings as we grow and expand. Your loyalty to this company is unmatched. My door is always open. That goes for Byrum and Callum as well. We will be bringing on new team members in the coming months. Continue to welcome them with open arms as you have always done. There's a reason why we have a low turnover rate. It's because of how you embrace and celebrate new team members."

"We got you, boss!"

Tellum looked up and saw Lisa-Marie and Keiko exit the room.

"Tellum, about our free week a year at any of the resorts. When can we take advantage of that?" Denison, another team member asked.

"Right. Yes, all team members get one free week a year at any of the resorts with travel included. You will have to book that through the executive assistant who overseas communication for each of the resorts. In the case of *Secret Whisper*, that would be Lisa-Marie and her three special assistants. Start with the special assistants first before reaching to the executive assistants. You all know who they are. If not, check the directory. You can put in your requests at any time. This does include all of the resorts, not just the new ones. Keep in mind, you can't all go at the same time. There is still a tiered priority to requesting vacation that is based on department and your time in the company. If there are issues, again, work them out with the communication teams. My brothers and I are staying out of that. Any more questions anyone?"

"Thanks, Tellum!"

Cheers and applauds around the room humbled him. He loved being able to say they believe in never leaving anyone behind as the world opens up for them. His eyes caught Lisa-Marie as she and Keiko re-entered.

"Food is here," she noted and then signaled to him that she needed to talk to him. Walking through the team who gave him pats on the back as he walked by, he stepped out into the hall.

"What's up?" he asked.

"Uh, you have a visitor in the lobby."

"Okay, you know how to vent my appointments."

"It's not a scheduled appointment. Security has him waiting to see if you'll let him up. I didn't want to make the decision due to your history."

Tellum rubbed his chin.

"I'm intrigued," he said.

"It's Cheyenne's father, Mr. Joseph Reddick."

"What? He's here? Why?"

"I don't know but he's been waiting for about thirty-minutes. He showed up right when you gathered everyone in the conference room. I didn't want to interrupt the meeting. I asked that they let him know to either wait until you were done or schedule a meeting. He opted to wait. They said he's been patiently sitting on a bench in the lobby."

"He's here to see me. This can't be good."

"I can tell them that he's not welcome and to ask him to leave," she offered.

"No, don't do that. He's here for a reason. I don't have a problem hearing him out. Can you have him escorted to my office. I have to make a quick call. I'll use Callum's office for that since he won't be here. He's on a business trip to Los Angeles. Stay in my office with him until I arrive. He can't be trusted."

Lisa-Marie nodded.

"Yes, I'm aware. I'll take care of it right away."

"And, do not let the team overwhelm you with requests for their week at *Secret Whisper*. You have your own assistants for a reason, right?"

"You got it. I'm not called the enforcer for nothing," she joked and then rushed off.

"Cheyenne's father is here to see me?" Tellum questioned himself as he headed to Callum's office.

23

Byrum raced up the steps to his parents' house wondering why he didn't see Tellum's car in the driveway. They had both been summoned to the house by their father who told them that while he was out of town wrapping up some business meetings in his new position as chief marketing officer for their company, they needed to stop by the house to help their mother change her office around. Byrum wondered why their father didn't just hire their usual interior designer to bring her team over to help their mother, but he didn't question it. He did what he was told.

Using his key to enter the house, his mother was coming down the long-spiraled staircase to greet him.

"You're late," she declared.

"Mom, really? If I'm late, then what is Tellum? I don't see his car."

"He's accountable for him. You're accountable for you. I'm glad you're here, late and all," she quipped. "Besides, he did call. He said a meeting with the team that Callum was supposed to do, he is doing it in his place. He said you knew about it."

"I did. Last I heard it was Callum's turn. I'm having the same meeting with our evening team members."

Byrum pulled her into a tight hug, lifting her slightly from the floor.

"Tellum mentioned something about that when he called to say he wouldn't be here."

"You're looking extra beautiful today. If I didn't know how much you loved dad, I would think you had a secret male suitor while he was away."

"Don't joke like that. You know I've got a million male suitors but none are as amazing as your father. I guess I'll keep him around a little longer," she shot back and strolled off after he put her down.

"You missed your career in comedy. What smells so good?" he asked following her into the kitchen.

"Meatball and sausage lasagna, your favorite."

"Only my favorite? I think we all love that recipe."

"Isn't Tellum flying to the resort this week?" Felicia asked.

"Cheyenne is at *Secret Whisper*. He's joining her for the week between Christmas and New Year's."

Byrum opened the oven door and inhaled the amazing aroma.

"Close the oven door. It's got about another half hour."

"Are those collard greens in the pot on the stove before I lift the top?"

"Yes, and don't you dare."

"I won't. I did come hungry."

"How long can you stay?"

"Until it's time for me to go home. That's hours and hours away. If you need anything else done besides moving stuff around in your home office, let me know. I'm free as a bird tonight."

"Really? Where is Layla? You should have brought her with you. In fact, I'm still waiting for you to invite her for dinner."

Byrum moved to the large kitchen table and sat down. A bowl of grapes appeared in front of him. He loved how his mother knew what he wanted and needed even before he did. He popped a few in his mouth.

"She won't be coming to dinner. I don't want to send the wrong message," he explained.

"The wrong message? What might that be? That you like her?"

"Mom, you know me. It's not the kind of like where you bring someone home to meet the family."

"Let's go into my office," she said.

Byrum stood and followed her knowing that the conversation was far from over. This was a usual topic when they were alone.

"Are we about to have that chat about my personal life again?"

"You're the oldest. I expected more commitment from you by now, but I'm not judging. I'm just asking."

"When I find the right woman, I promise you that I'll invite her to family dinner."

"Who would have thought that of the three of you, Tellum would be the first to fall in love. I mean, he's the one who I never thought would commit to one woman. Instead, you seem to be obsessed with not slowing down. You boys have your company and it's doing great. You know, the good Lord didn't bless me with any daughters. Until Cheyenne, came along, I thought my world would forever consist of my four perfect men. I'm so glad they've worked things out."

"You know they're living together?" he asked.

"Yes. Tellum told me about that. He explained to me what happened. I also know that Cheyenne's mother is living in her condo after leaving her husband. I'm sad that things didn't work out for them but I get it. So much has been going on. I wasn't happy to hear that you pulled up on Reed. You know better. What happened? Your father wouldn't tell me everything. He only said it was one of those moments where he had to call you by your full name, first, middle and last name. What did you do?"

Byrum leaned against the front edge of the desk and lowered his head.

"I know. I'm sorry. I warned him. I warned Reed to not come for Tellum or Cheyenne. He didn't listen. We had a meeting with the airline a few months back. That was after Tellum told me how Reed tried to barter with Cheyenne's father for her attention. That was a trashy move. During the meeting, Pop was with us, Reed has this look on his face as if we didn't know what he did. When the meeting was over, Reed walked up to me as if nothing had happened. He reached out to shake my hand and I lost it. I grabbed him by the throat and slammed him against the wall and held him there."

"Byrum! You are six-foot-seven. Reed is what, barely six-foot?"

"Give or take an inch he is. I think he wears lifts," he joked.

"Not a joking moment," Felicia reminded him.

Byrum removed the cunning smirk from his face.

"I know. Sorry again."

"His father saw all of this too?"

"He did. You know how angry Tellum was behind that. That weekend, he stayed in with Cheyenne. That Monday morning, he asked me to meet him at the gym. He went after that boxing bag like a maniac. He explained to me that Cheyenne's father was willing to give her to Reed in exchange for a business deal. Trash, mom. Reed is trash. So is her father, respectfully stated, of course."

"I'll give you that one. Her father doesn't garner respect in this situation."

"Reed's father asked what was going on after Pop called my name and told me to drop him. Reed assumed his father would take his side, but he didn't. He suspended Reed from the company right there on the spot because I was ready to break our partnership with them. Tellum was trying to go at Reed too, but dad was closer to him and held him back. Mr. Reed apologized for the behavior of his son. He promised an apology to Cheyenne and gave one to Tellum while we were there. I lost my cool for a second. I tried to stay out of it. I could see the restraint on Tellum's face."

"Don't tell your father I said this, but he deserved it. Don't do it again. I know your father taught the three of you to look out for each other. Just be careful that you don't end up in jail doing that."

"Well, if I do, keep bail money handy. Cheyenne is to be protected at all costs. That's how we do for family. Other than her mother and Tellum, she doesn't have a lot of people looking out for her. I'm already happy for the lucky woman who'll snag your heart. She won't ever have to worry about being protected and loved. No prospects other than notches?"

Byrum coughed.

"Notches? Where in the world did you learn that word?"

"You'd be surprised at what women talk about at the hair salon."

"No prospects mom," he lied. "And just so that we are clear on this, we are never talking about notches of any kind."

"Okay, deal. Do you like the furniture Tellum bought me? It's even prettier than I dreamed it would be. Now that I have it, I want things moved around a bit so that the sofa is along the window."

Byrum nodded and got to work moving the table in front of the sofa out of the way along with the rug it sat on. He kept quiet about the one and only prospect of a woman he'd fallen in love with but couldn't tell anyone about. He would move heaven and hell for her, something no one knew about, not even the woman in question. Surprising himself, he hadn't even told his brothers. He found it hard to believe that he'd fallen for someone who was clearly off-limits. He wasn't even sure she knew considering they saw each other around the office every day. He didn't know how to explain falling for her to anyone else. He was still struggling with the impact her mere presence had on his life.

"This all looks great."

"Now, after you move the sofa, there is a large wall mirror in the garage that's still in the box. Can you bring that in? I don't want it up on the wall. I'm thinking settling it in a corner. Say, do you think Tellum and Cheyenne are close to making a big move in their life? You know, like marriage or anything?"

Byrum cut his eyes her way. Though he smiled, she knew his look.

"Mom, I know you're not asking me information about Tellum's life?"

She waved him off.

"I know. I thought I would try. You three are so secretive."

"She is perfect for him. One day they will make beautiful babies," he offered.

"From your lips to...you know the rest. Anyway, grab my mirror. I may change my mind about which corner to put it in. By the time you get back and set that up, it'll be time to eat. Thanks for coming by to help."

"I wouldn't be anywhere else. I'll be right back."

Byrum hustled off thinking about the day Tellum shared that he'd fallen in love with Cheyenne. Those were the last words he ever expected to hear his brother say. Those were also words that scared him. Love and relationship weren't where he saw his life going. That was until... He needed to uncomplicate his life. Where his heart was going, he needed to break away from that direction. Nothing good could come from that. Perhaps the answer was to forget about her. Instead, he reached for his phone and dialed a female friend whom he could count on to not have him in his feelings unless it was a physical feeling.

"Shawna? Hey, luv. What are you up to tonight?"

"Well, I was hoping I would hear from you. It's been too long. I'm free as a bird tonight. What's on your agenda?"

Byrum grinned like a cheshire cat.

"You," he said.

"Well, you know the address."

"I'll see you in a few hours then. I'll bring some dinner and wine. I would offer to bring desert but since that's going to be you for me and me for you, maybe not?" he joked.

"How about something with chocolate. I can think of a few uses for that."

"Damn! You and hot chocolate. Keep it sexy. I'll see you later."

"Sure thing."

Hanging up, he grabbed the large box and carried it inside the house. After his call to Shawna, one of his friends-with-benefits, he was feeling regret. Heart be damned! He had to shake it off. There was no better way to do that than to let Shawna give him one of her famous, erotic lap dances. He was ready.

"Byrum?"

"On my way, mom."

"Good because the food is ready. I'm starving."

Hoisting the mirror up over his head, he was ready for a new focus when it came to women.

24

Cheyenne exited the tub and wrapped the large navy towel around her body. With the braids that she'd recently had in now out, her natural hair began to curl as soon as the cool air hit her wet hair. She'd just taken the longest soak in the history of baths. There was something about the tub in the *Secret Whisper* bungalow that made her want to stay in it forever. The only thing missing from the experience was Tellum. She smiled remembering that he would be joining her soon for a few days of loving bliss. In the few days that she'd already been here alone, she still had not left the confines of her favorite space. The best idea Tellum had come up with was to encourage her to take some time away alone for a few days after leaving the security of her job for what she hoped would soon be greener pastures.

Her desire to leave a career in marketing and replace it with her dream of opening and owning a dance studio had lived in the back of her mind for a few years. She was now ready to make moves that were for her and no one else. Because of that mindset, she woke up each day with a zest for what was next. The first big move in her life over the past few months was moving in with Tellum. Without her father's interference, they began planning for a future together. For the first time in her life, she started feeling like she could actually have all that she wanted and not just what she was told she could have. She was learning to live freer and it felt good. There was, however, one aspect of her life that was still in shambles; her relationship with her father. She struggled with the heinous way in which he tried to improve his own life while trashing hers. Still, he was her father and there were times when she missed the closeness they once shared. Her phone rang and she smiled knowing who it would be. She was expecting his call.

"Hey, baby!" she jubilantly spoke into her phone.

"Hi, daughter of mine."

"Mommy! I thought you were Tellum. I was expecting his call."

"Oh, I caught that by that sultry greeting. How are you doing? Is your time away helping you focus?"

Cheyenne walked out onto the balcony and made herself comfortable on the round seating, curling her legs up under her body.

"I'm doing great. Yes, this time has helped a lot. I'm working on a business plan. I've even looked at a few locations that are available that would make a great dance studio. I can't wait to take you around to look at them when I get back."

"Sounds good. Don't spend your time away focused on work. You're also there to relax."

"I'm doing that. I'll do that even better once Tellum arrives. How are you making out? When are we going to talk about the condo?"

A month ago, Cheyenne tried to have a conversation with her mother about her living in the condo permanently. With her living with Tellum and no plans to return to her place, she knew how much her mother loved it. She'd offered it to her but her mother was fighting her offer of transferring the mortgage over to her."

"I can't take your place with an offer of just handing it over. You have equity in this place. I don't want you to lose that. I know Tellum is well off and the last thing you need to worry about is money."

"You know that's not me. Even with his wealth, I want my own. You know it, and he knows it too. I just know that you love the condo. You're comfortable there. It's a safe place and it's central to everything. How about if I sell it to you? That is if you want to stay there. Tell me what you want to do."

"I do love it here. I love that it's not far from you and Tellum. I'm central to friends and other family. This is just enough space for me."

"What about the house? What are you going to do about that? Has Captain Joe reached out?"

"Honey, he reaches out all the time."

"Still begging you to come back?"

"Yes. The answer is and will always be no. I can forgive what he did to you but I can't forget enough to ever take him back. We are cordial enough to discuss finances. He knows I've always had my own money and my own accounts. We discussed the divorce, and he told me he would give me whatever I wanted, though he wants me. With that off of the table, he's been sending me money monthly. I've also noticed some pretty big deposits into my bank account. He may be a cad, but he has always taken care of me and you. In the past, the price of him doing that has been too high."

"You're in a good place?"

"Cheyenne, honey, I am in a wonderful place. Don't you worry about me. If I'm being honest, I would love to stay in the condo. I won't let you hand it off to me for free. Not even to just take the payments over. You won't let me give you rent, though I've put that away in a special account for you. We'll use it one day when you and Tellum get married."

"Mom, stop it. We haven't talked about getting married."

"I'm not saying it's going to happen tomorrow. You're living together. That's a big step. I'm hoping marriage and a few babies will come out of all that shacking up. That's a topic for another time. Let's talk when you get back about the condo. If you're sure you're not having any second thoughts about living with Tellum, I would love to stay here."

"Being with him has been and will be perfect. There will be no turning back. He loves having me there and I love being there. Before I left to come here, he surprised me with turning one of the extra bedrooms into my very own walk-in closet. My clothes and shoes were taking over our closet. I'm good with where things are. I just want to be sure you're good. You were married to Captain Joe for a long time. This is a new normal for you."

"And for you too. I'm not just talking about Tellum. Have you been in contact with your father at all?"

"A little. He calls a lot but I've only taken a few of his calls. He wants to sit down and talk over dinner. I'm not ready. I have had some brief chats with him. It's a slow build with him. I'm working at letting go of the control he had over me. He wanted to ruin my love life. For a while, he had. I do miss the good parts of our relationship."

"He's not perfect; I should know. I know that he really loves you. He lost himself for a while and became someone that even he didn't recognize. He is your father. You can have or not have a relationship with him. If you want one, then have one. It doesn't matter if it's a slow build or not. You be in control and not him. When does Tellum arrive?"

"Either tonight or tomorrow. He's been talking to me a lot about Captain Joe. After all that he's done against Tellum, especially that mess with Reed, he is still in his corner when it comes to me. He doesn't want me to completely give up on my father being someone I can connect with. He doesn't want years to go by with me full of regret."

"See? That's why I love Tellum for you. He could easily push you in a direction away from your father and he would have just cause. He's right. I don't things will be perfect but like me, the only mother you will have, he is the only father you will have. Whatever you choose to do, I'm with you all the way. As for me and him, we will coexist in this world as ex-spouses. It's different with a parent and a child. You think about it. I want you to think long and hard about what we're talking about. His punishment has been being without his daughter for these past few months. He never expected that. I've talked to him. I know he's hurting. I know he's sorry. If you have it in you to try again, don't miss the chance to do that."

"I hear you. I promise you I will think about it. For the next few days, all I want to think about is being in this amazing place with Tellum. What's for me back home will be there when I get there. Let's go out for dinner when I get back so we can talk about the condo. Feel free to already consider it yours. It's a matter of paperwork. That will be easy. I'm glad you love it."

"I'm glad you offered it to me. I went from living at home with my parents to marrying your father and moving in with him. It's a whole new world living on my own. There are times I miss being with someone. That doesn't make me want to go back or even look back. I can't wait to see what's ahead for me just like I am about what's in your future. Have fun. Hug Tellum for me. We'll talk when you get home. Love you, little one."

"Love you too."

Cheyenne ended the call just as her phone rang again. Her mother must have forgotten something.

"Hi beautiful!" Tellum said.

"Oh, hi."

"Oh, hi? That's all I get?" he laughed.

"Of course not. I thought you were my mother calling back. I just hung up from her. You know I'm always excited when I talk to you. I've been waiting for your call. I just got out of the shower and was on the phone relaxing on the balcony. How are you?" she asked.

"I'm wonderful now that I'm talking to you."

"What are you doing? Are you in the office?" she asked.

"I am. I just finished telling the team all the good news I mentioned to you. The power tie you gave me was a major hit. Some of them even brought up the fact that they knew the tie was your idea. I'm a boss when it comes to my attire. I guess your ties really make me. Never stop getting them for me. How is the resort? Are you enjoying yourself? I hope you're getting lots of pampering in."

Cheyenne huffed her disappointment in herself.

"Not exactly," she admitted.

"No! Why not? You didn't even go?" he questioned.

"I didn't. I couldn't leave the room. I have been so relaxed. I've been reading and studying up on running a business, especially a studio. I took your advice and looked at other large dance studios around the country to get ideas of what I want. The woman from Shelton Sullivans team and I have met by phone twice since I've been here. She's been educating me on finances and the best route to take. Thank you for that connection. I had no idea that there was so much money out there available in the form of grants for women of color to start businesses. I am floored at how uncomplicated it is to open and start a small business. Since it's also woman owned, the flood gates have been opening like crazy. I can't wait until you get here to tell you about it. I know you set up the spa appointments for me. Can we do the couple's package when you get here? I want to do them with you. I miss you."

"I miss you too, sweetness. I can't wait to get to you."

"I went shopping before I got here for something sexy and hot pink just for you. It doesn't cover much of my body, but I know how much you like it like that," she giggled.

"You know how I feel about that behind of yours."

"Mmm, mmm – it's missing your kisses. I talked to my mother today."

"Okay, first of all, horrible conversation transition from your behind and my kisses, to talking about your mother," Tellum laughed.

Cheyenne doubled over in laughter.

"That was crazy. I don't know what I was thinking. I need you here with me so much that I'm talking crazy!" she joked.

"Soon. I'll be there soon. I saw your mother last night. I went out to grab dinner to eat while I looked over some reports. I ran into her and two other ladies as they were leaving the restaurant. I followed her home to be sure she got in okay. You know she loves the condo. Even though her plan was to stay in it temporarily, I think she wants to keep it. What do you think?" he asked.

"I think she will. I was just talking to her about that. I think I've convinced her that it's her place now. It's in a safe area. The security is good at that location. It's also well lit. Because I won't take rent from her, she's been putting the money in a savings account. If nothing else, if she wants to buy it, I want her to be able to do so. I want to sell it to her for the lowest price that the bank will allow. Her and my dad are separated and not divorced. She told me something that was shocking."

"Oh?" Tellum queried.

"She said that my dad has been sending her quite a bit of money since she left. He told her he understands. Though he wants her back, he knows that she's done with him. Thankfully, he doesn't plan to keep anything from her when it comes to the finances. My mom has been with him from day one and he owes her. He told her he would give her whatever she wants."

"I don't think money will be a big problem for her. My mother asked me if I thought your mother might want a job at the charity she runs. Seems like they've become friends. I know your mother has been doing some volunteer work. My mom wants to consider putting her on the payroll. She could really use the help of someone she trusts. I think she would love it. Do you want to introduce the idea to her?" he asked.

Cheyenne danced in place.

"You're lying? Are you serious? My mother would love that. Working in a field where she can help others is right up my mom's alley. I'll talk to her about it when we get back home."

"It's over, huh?" Tellum asked her.

She nodded as if he was in the room with her. She was sad, but also happy that her mother was free. She understood that feeling.

"Yes, she's done. He tried hard to get her back over the past few months, but she was stern in her desire to have her freedom."

"That's understandable. I lot has taken place."

"It has. It was a long time coming. Knowing that she knew he has been seeing other women and still didn't leave is a lot. No woman deserves that. Why hurt someone like that when all you have to do is end things. Divorce is terrible but that kind of disrespect, in my opinion, is unforgiveable."

"I agree. We have a love that I hope you know you'll never have to worry about something like that with me. I have eyes only for you. We had drama that came from the outside early in our relationship. Now we know how to get through anything. Maybe we needed to go this route in order to be as happy in love as we are. I'm telling you, there is something about that resort that is magical when it comes to love starting up and love being rekindled. It's in the air there. The best part is that we didn't lose any of what we shared once we returned home. It's like, wherever we go, we still hear the secret whispers of love."

"That's it! You named this resort perfectly. You know with my degree in marketing, I think you need a campaign with a slogan about how secret whispers speaks to unconditional love. Can you hurry up and get here? I know you have business to take care of. I need to feel your touch," Cheyenne slurred out sexily.

"I'm coming straight there from the airport after I leave here. My calendar is clear for the next few days. I am all yours."

"Three days alone, right? No work?"

"Work only for the first few hours after I arrive. It will be pretty late tonight when I arrive. I want to get it out of the way. There were a few updates made that I want to inspect. After that, I am all yours. My team knows that I am not to be disturbed for any reason."

"What about Callum and Byrum? Are you telling me that they'll let you be for a few days?"

"Callum loves that he'll be in charge. He'll have a lot going on and won't have time to worry about me being out of the country. As for Byrum, there is something going on with him. I can't quite put my finger on it. I'm trying to give him space, but whatever it is, it's weighing heavy. Keiko will check in on him, I'm sure."

"Is she still moving to the *Silent Whisper* resort? In a brief conversation, she mentioned there were some issues with her son's father. She wasn't sure she was going to be able to get his sign off on her moving their son to an island in the Mediterranean. I know that's been a pained point for her."

"Byrum mentioned that. He's taking a full team with him for the next year while the work is being done. He is choosing to oversee that himself."

"That's major for him. He's actually moving away from Detroit for a year. It's a good thing you and Callum are increasing the management staff. You're going to need it. I know you're going to miss him when he leaves."

"I am. The difference in that location and Secret Whisper is about the amount of work that has to be done. He'll fly back and forth home, but for at least a year, his home base will be at *Silent Whisper*. He's been preparing for it for a while now. I know he wants Keiko to be a part of his team there. Last I heard, she was working it out. I think to start off, her son will remain in the states. After that, I'm not sure what will happen. Byrum will help where he can. She's going ahead of him in a few months."

"I don't know how you keep up with everything the way you do."

"That's because Lisa-Marie is a godsend when it comes to keeping my work life in order."

"I love that. Now, get here to me so that I can keep your personal and love life in order."

"I promise, I am on my way. I need to head into a meeting unless you need me on this call longer. My time is always yours first and foremost."

"I love you. I'm good. I just wanted to hear your voice. This is enough to tie me over until you arrive. There is a line dance party tonight that I plan to go to. You may get here before I get back. Text me when you land?"

"I will. Also, go ahead and book whatever you want for us from couples' massages to excursions. I'm open to it all as long as we're together."

"I'm going to do that as soon as we hang up. I'll order some food for later tonight. I know you'll be starving by the time you get here."

"Baby, that isn't where my hunger is. I hunger for you most of all."

"I know and I love it.

25

Tellum ended the call and kicked himself for holding back from Cheyenne that the meeting that he spoke of was with her father. He'd come into Callum's office to call her. He was going to mention his surprise visitor but decided to wait to hear what the man had to say. If it turned out to be a bad encounter, he didn't want Cheyenne worried or upset. It's been months since he's seen him. No doubt, he was leery of why he was here today.

As he left Callum's office, waving at Callum's assistant, Jamal Casey, he headed toward his office. He needed to get himself ready for this conversation.

As he walked through the executive wing hallway, he wondered how much communication Cheyenne had with her father. He tried to bring it up with her a few times. They talked briefly with him telling her that whatever she chose, he was with her. He encouraged her to think hard before completely cutting her father off. It wasn't that the man was worthy of her affection after what he tried to pull. It was more about him knowing that he couldn't go through life without his parents. He didn't want her to experience that. He gave her the space and the grace to work through her relationship with her father, especially if they were ever going to have one again. All he could do was be there for her in any way she needed.

Arriving at his office, he smiled at Lisa-Marie who was standing guard at the entrance to his office, keeping a close eye on his guest.

"Thanks, Lisa-Marie," he said as she exited the office and closed the door behind herself. Cheyenne's father was sitting on the sofa across from his desk. Tellum walked toward him.

"Mr. Reddick," he said.

"Captain Joe," he corrected.

Tellum stood his ground. He was one of the few people who would not continue the crazy moniker the man adopted that made no sense.

"Mr. Reddick," he countered.

When he nodded, Tellum knew they understood each other.

"Can we agree on Joe. I don't want to be too formal. After all, you are the man who loves my daughter. That makes us almost family."

"Not really, but okay. Joe it is. What can I do for you?" Tellum asked, taking the seat behind his desk. He signaled for Joe to join him by sitting in one of the two chairs in front of the desk. Once they were both seated, Tellum loosened his tie and waited for Joe to explain his visit. For a few seconds, neither of them said a word.

"Sorry. Right, I guess I should go first since I showed up here unannounced and uninvited. I'm sure you would like to know why," he finally said.

"Inquiring minds and all that good stuff. Yes. I am intrigued considering your ideal of me isn't a good one."

"How is Cheyenne?" Joe asked.

"She's wonderful. She's out of the country at the moment. She needed some quiet time at the resort."

"Oh, that's nice. I tried calling her yesterday and I haven't heard back yet."

"Give her a little time. She's taking some time to focus on her."

"Her mother told me about quitting her job. I didn't know she was unhappy doing that work. It pays extremely well."

"Wealth isn't the key to everyone's happiness. Cheyenne focuses on love and devotion. Career is not at the top of her list. Her career was at the top of your list," he asserted.

Tellum wasn't trying to hit the man below the belt. Being estranged from his wife and daughter was enough of a beating.

"I suppose it was. I'm glad she's happy. I understand that she's moved in with you."

"No."

"No? I thought that's what her mother said."

"The idea is correct, but the assessment of the situation is incorrect. Cheyenne and I live together in the condo we share. She's didn't move in with me. The moment we decided to live together, I had her name added to the mortgage, though I would never dream of her spending a dime on anything. I will take care of all of our expenses."

"You did that? Added her name to your place?"

"No, I added her name to *our* place. I needed her to know and feel like the house was ours and not just mine. Women should have that kind of security. Did you come here to ask me how Cheyenne is doing?"

"Only because I haven't heard from her. Now, I get it. She's away. We have spoken a few times. Still pretty chilly between us. I expect that. For a few weeks, she wouldn't take any of my calls. I miss my daughter. I know it's hard to believe after what I've done. I am atoning for that. It may not seem like it but I do love her. I have taken that love for granted for too long. I want to stop that. I really miss her. I came here hoping you could help me build a better bridge."

"Really? How can I do that? Cheyenne is her own woman."

"I know that. I also know that you love her. I know you want the best for her. You have a wonderful relationship with your parents. Believe me, I get that. That's a broken part of my relationship with my daughter that I'd like to repair."

"I can't fix this for you, Joe."

"I know you can't. You shouldn't. I have to do that. I'm only asking that you help me with what I need to do. I don't want to push her when she's not ready. I just want to know if and when the opportunity for me to do so presents itself."

"That's a hard one. You really hurt her. I mean, not just with the antics with Reed, but she finally realized that for her entire life, you have wielded and unhealthy control over her life and her decisions. I love her the way she is and for who she is. There are no conditions attached to my love. Yours came with all kinds of things that you convinced her to live up to. It got so bad that you tried to take away her love for me just because you and my father have a thing. The extent that you went to in order to reign your control is not something a loving father would do. I hope you understand why she is still hesitant."

Joe shook his head up and down. Tellum was surprised at the calmness that was radiating from the man. He was used to him being loud and boisterous. That's not who was sitting across from him.

"I understand. I only want a chance to redeem myself. I want to do it by any rules she wants. I've done enough to hurt her and like you said, control her. I don't want any of that anymore. I want to be a part of my daughter's life. I know it will take a lot for her to forgive me. I expect that. I am hoping and even praying that there is a little wiggle room in her heart left that I may be able to fit in. I'm coming to you because I have to admit that you know my daughter better than me. I've spent so many years chasing money that I forgot that my daughter may have needed me to just be her father. I slept on that for a long time. These past few months without her have been hell. I may not deserve for her to accept me back into her life, but I'm begging that she thinks about giving me a chance."

"I hope you and Cheyenne can fix things. Everyone needs their parents in their life. Even through toxic tolerance, which is what I believe has been going on in your life with her, there is room for love and forgiveness. Oftentimes, people let go, give up and throw in the towel, even when it comes to family. I don't believe in that. I believe we are given the families that we have for a reason. We are expected to figure it out and work it out; through the good, the bad and very ugly. Yours is definitely the latter."

"Thank you, Tellum. I know you don't have to do anything after what I've put you and your family through. I don't deserve your grace right now. I do appreciate it. I am truly sorry for the things I've said and done. I spoke to your father last week. I apologized to him for what I've said to and about him and your family. I know the things that I've done are why he turned down my deal. In spite of all of that, he agreed to point me to some people who can help me, though he can't directly. I want to be sure my business ventures are legitimate with no strings attached. I see why Cheyenne loves your family. Losing my connection with her made me stand up and take responsibility for the things I've done. I'm truly sorry to you. Anything I can do that you can think of that could help me mend things, I'm open to it all. I just want to be a part of her life again. I want to be respectful of the pace she wants to set if she allows it."

Tellum stood and turned to look out of the window. He didn't have to think long and hard. He knew that if there were any redeeming qualities in her father and they were enough for Cheyenne to work through with him, he would stand with her all the way. Joe was looking for an inlet. He had one. There was something that he was planning that only his brothers and Lisa-Marie knew about.

Turning back to him, Tellum walked over to the door that led to his private bathroom. On the wall just inside the door but before the actual bathroom, he put in a code and a panel on the wall opened to reveal a safe built into it. He put in another code along with his fingerprint and the safe opened. Withdrawing a small black box, he carried it back with him to his desk. Sliding the box across his desk to Joe, he eyed the man and waited. He signaled for permission for him to open it and waited for his response.

"Wow! Is this for Cheyenne? I've never seen such a beautiful diamond ring before. This is a complement to her without a doubt. And the sapphires that surround the diamond? Blue. That is her favorite color. This is gorgeous," Joe exclaimed.

"Thank you. Cheyenne's birthday is coming up. I am planning to propose to her at a party I'm setting up for her at *Secret Whisper*. She knows we're celebrating her birthday there, but she doesn't know that I'm inviting family and friends on my side and hers, to join us. I have two things that I want to discuss with you since you're here. First, because you're her father, I do believe in asking your permission to ask Cheyenne to marry me. I know things are wonky right now, but still, my parents raised me right."

"You've got that. You've got that a hundred times over. Yes!" Joe shouted.

Tellum chuckled.

"Thank you. Also, I think it would be great for you to be there when I ask her. I don't know if she'll be happy or not about that. I will say that I do know her. I believe having you there with everyone else and letting the world know that you said yes to me getting her hand in marriage, would be the best day of her life. I'm doing it the weekend of her actual birthday. I don't know what things will look like for the two of you in that time frame. I will say that I will help in any way that I can."

Tellum was taken back when Joe reached into his pocket, pulled out a handkerchief, something he didn't realize men still carried and used, and wiped his eyes. He was shedding tears of joy.

"I can't thank you enough for this honor, first of asking me if you could marry my daughter and then to invite me to her birthday celebration. You offer the kind of grace that is rare in people these days. After what I've done, you are still reaching out to me even though you owe me nothing."

Joe stood and extended his hand and Tellum took it immediately. He still didn't care much for him, but he was Cheyenne's father. He loved her and therefore, he would work on letting go and moving forward.

"I know she's hurting over the discourse in your relationship. Helping to make her whole is my priority. It needs to be yours too," he noted.

"That it is. Well, I won't take up too much more of your time. Here is my card. When you're ready to share the details of the event, let me know so that I can make travel arrangements."

"You won't have to worry about that. My assistant is planning arrangements for everyone at my expense. You're her father. The most important part is you make things right with her. You have some time before then to work on it. It will be a slow-moving train. I will encourage her from my end. I'm sure you would love to be asked by her to walk her down the aisle. It's up to you to get to that point with her."

"I will do that. Thanks for everything, Tellum."

"No problem, Joe. You can see Lisa-Marie on your way out. You can provide the business card to her. I'm sending her a message right now."

Joe waved as he exited. When he did and closed the office door behind him, Tellum exhaled as if he'd been holding his breath in the hold time. That was interesting, he thought.

Turning the ring box back around, he stared at it and smiled. He was going to solidify his future with Cheyenne in the most perfect place, *Secret Whisper*. It's where they rekindled and rediscovered what love is.

26

Cheyenne's Birthday Celebration at
Secret Whisper

Tellum and Byrum walked toward the event hall where Cheyenne's birthday party was in full swing. The event planner and her team who work full time for the resort looked his way. He signaled to her that he was ready. Now was the time to really get things started. With Byrum and Callum as his wingmen, he was ready to celebrate not only Cheyenne's birthday but their lives together.

His gaze flowed around the resort main event center, which was transformed into a festive birthday celebration in one of Cheyenne's favorite colors, shades of blue. He was happy that his entire family was in attendance. There were even distant relatives he hadn't seen in years. Also present were all of Cheyenne's friends and family. Her mother, who had arrived days earlier to help with the decorating, was keeping her eye on him. She knew what was coming up next. She even knew about their secret guest who had arrived earlier in the day.

Over the past few weeks after his conversation with her father, Cheyenne had informed him that the two of them had been communicating more. She asked his opinion about whether he felt her father was being genuine in his desire to be a real father; to change from who he was as a man she disliked, but still loved as her father. She wanted to believe he was. In response, Tellum sat her down and asked her how she felt about everything. She explained that her heart was telling her that her father was really trying. She had never experienced the Captain Joe that she has been talking with lately. When her father called him and asked if he should still come to the party, thinking only of Cheyenne, he told him yes.

Walking to the center of the room in the midst of the festivities, Tellum felt anxiety overwhelm him, but in a good way.

"It's time," Byrum leaned over and spoke.

Taking the microphone from Callum, Tellum moved to the center of the room, taking Cheyenne by the hand. She looked happy and assumed he was going to make a toast to her. He knew all of her looks. He couldn't wait to see a new one.

With family and friends gathered around, the DJ stopped the music. The overhead lights were dimmed. All around them, on cue, sparkling white lights lit up the room with a romantic glow. He stood with one arm holding Cheyenne close to him.

"Good evening, everyone! I hope you're having a great time celebrating this amazing woman who stands by my side."

The room filled with whistles and cheers.

"Yeah!"

Tellum turned to where Callum had yelled the loudest over the crowd.

"For anyone who doesn't know, that was my brother."

The crowd cheered louder for him.

"I'm the handsome one, is what he left out!" Callum added.

"Not on your life!" Cheyenne quickly countered in the midst of the laughter from everyone.

"My baby said it and so it must be true. It's me; I'm the handsome one. I'm also the luckiest one. Tonight, this room has been transformed into a winter-wonderland even though we're at a resort in the middle of one of the hottest days of the year here. Still, if you know Cheyenne, you know her favorite time of year is the winter season. I wanted her birthday to be magical. I wanted it to be filled with love and adoration. Cheyenne entered my life at the perfect time. It wasn't until we met that I felt deep down what had been missing from my life. This woman loves me unconditionally. I can say that without a shadow of a doubt. That means her love is pure; it's real. I feel it every single day. There is no one that I would ever want to walk through this life with other than her."

Tellum turned so that he and Cheyenne were facing each other.

"Love!" someone in the crowd shouted out.

"Yeah!" Callum yelled again.

"Now, I want everyone to hear this, so the entire room will go on mute," he said and looked around. There wasn't a sound heard amongst the crowd.

He saw the amazement on Cheyenne's face, especially when she looked to her left and her mother moved closer to them on Tellum's right. When her head looked to his left, he knew why. His parents had moved into place on his left. He took both of Cheyenne's hands into his and smiled. He had to pause. He knew what was coming and needed a moment to gather himself.

"We're right here, son," his father said softly.

"Cheyenne, not one day has gone by when I have not been thankful for your presence in my life. I want you to know that I've done something."

"What?" she stammered out, looking around a room full of big, bright smiles from everyone in the crowd. "What did you do?" she asked, turning back to him.

Cheyenne's hands tensed up in his. He caressed them to ease her anxiety.

"I wanted to make tonight as perfect as I could in a place where we rediscovered perfection in our love. I know how much you love being here with and without me, but mostly, yes, with me. I want to seal this place and our love for a lifetime. The moves I want to make in life would be nothing without you being there every step of the way to share it with me. Recently, your father and I had the best conversation."

He heard her gasp at what he knew was a vision of him and her father having a conversation that he would say was good.

"You did?" she asked.

When she spoke so that only he could hear, he leaned in close so that she could hear his response.

"Yes, baby, we did." He then stood and spoke into the microphone again. "We came to an understanding that I love you and nothing or no one will ever change that. It's important for our love to continue to grow and blossom that we have all love surrounding us. I revealed something to him during that conversation. I told him that I wanted to spend the rest of my life loving you, spoiling you, showering you and giving you the world on a silver platter."

Taking her hand from his, Tellum reached into the inside of his suit jacket and pulled out a sparkling platinum ring box. In response, he looked up and this time on cue for everyone, the crowd pulled out sunglasses and put them on. Cheyenne looked around the crowd and saw everyone, like a wave at a sports event, put their glasses on before she turned her eyes back to him. In them, he saw, not just love, but unshed tears.

"Tellum, what are you doing?" she whispered.

Cheyenne's lips trembled before his eyes.

"I'm making sure the world knows how much I love you. Now, before I open this box, there is something I need to do. You see, I'm an old-fashioned kind of girl. I can't help it. It's how my parents molded and shaped me as a man. I believe that in order for me to declare my undying and unwavering love for you for a lifetime, I need your father to give us his blessing. So, at this time, I want to ask Mr. Joseph Reddick and Ms. Ramona Reddick, if they would give their blessing for me to ask their daughter to marry me."

Tellum looked up and from behind him came her father. When he walked up and took Cheyenne's hand into his, no expected what came next, not even him. First, she looked down to where her father's hand was now joined with hers. He exhaled when with joy when Cheyenne gripped her father's hand tight in hers. Her head rose slowly up and to the side until her eyes finally landed on the man that she'd been estranged from. Though they had been doing better with having contact, he knew she was surprised that he was here at the resort.

"Captain Joe?" she uttered as tears raced down her face.

"Daddy," he said.

"Whaaat?" Cheyenne shakily spoke.

"Daddy," Captain Joe repeated. "My name is daddy or dad. Whichever works best for you. I don't know what I was thinking having you call me anything but one of those. Is that okay?" he asked.

Tellum waited and without warning, Cheyenne cried so hard as her father pulled her into a tight hug.

"I know. It's alright. I know and I'm sorry for everything. I need you to reserve some of these tears once Tellum is finished. Now, he asked me a question and I want to answer."

Cheyenne's mother and father stood on either side of her. Tellum wiped her tears. Her mother took her hand first, placing it underneath Cheyenne's, palm open. Her father then took Tellum's hand and placed it on top of Cheyenne's, palm open as well. Her father placed his own hand, palm open on top of theirs, making a tier of support.

"Sir," Tellum said, handing him the microphone.

"As you all can see, my daughter is surprised to see me here. There isn't a place I would rather be than right here at this very moment. When Tellum told me what he was planning, he said to me, that even though we have had a rocky road connecting, all my fault, he wanted me to be here for this proposal. I accepted not only his offer, but also his kinship when I knew he didn't have to do that. Family means the world to him. I know that he would move heaven and hell for my daughter. The way he loves her is how any man would want a man to love and cherish his daughter. Today, I stand here with Cheyenne's mother, and we give our resounding yes to their forever kind of love. I thank him for building a bridge that has helped start the healing process for so many rough patches. I join all of our hands today and I welcome Tellum's parents to join us with their hands here as well."

Tellum's mother moved and put her hand on the bottom under Cheyenne's mother's hand. His father moved into place and put his hand on top.

"Thank you," Tellum said. He felt his own tears welling up in his eyes at the image before him. He wanted nothing more than for them all to be one. They didn't have to be the best of friends, but they would be family. There was no stopping that. How they joined together as one was up to them all. He opened the door with a welcoming spirit because that's what Blackstones do.

"This tier of hands signify we are one family. We love and support Cheyenne and Tellum's love and happiness. Our hands joined as one means we will forever stand as a family, surrounding them with our love and support. Today, we say yes to the tux and the dress, and we welcome Tellum into our family the same way that the Blackstones have always welcomed Cheyenne," Joe said.

Their parents removed their hands and stepped away. Tellum lowered to one knee. He opened the box to take out the five-carat, cushion cut, platinum diamond engagement ring. Placing the box in his pocket, he took Cheyenne's hand in his. In his other hand he held the ring.

"Cheyenne, would you do me the honor of making me a better man by agreeing to not only stand by my side, but bless me by saying yes to becoming my wife?"

"Yes!!!" she shouted.

Tellum thought there would be a pause. He didn't know why. When he didn't move to slide the ring on her finger, he heard Callum yell from somewhere behind him."

"Bro? Today? Did you hear her? We all did. She said yes!"

"That damn, Callum," Tellum said.

He slid the ring down Cheyenne's finger. It was a perfect fit. Thanks to her mother and her best friend Melodi, he knew it would be flawlessness on her hands. He stood and pulled Cheyenne into his arms.

"I love you," she exclaimed.

"I love you more, baby."

He kissed her. His plan had been to make it a quick kiss knowing they would be in a large crowd of people. That didn't happen. The minute their lips met, he made sure his lips resonated what was in his heart. The kiss continued as he blocked out the noise around them. That is until, as expected, Callum had something to say.

"Save it for the wedding and the wedding night!"

Everyone laughed together as he placed Cheyenne back down on her feet with their lips still locked.

"Ladies and gentleman," Melodi spoke into a microphone as she joined them in the middle of the floor, "please welcome R&B artist, and one of Cheyenne's favorite singers, Mr. Johnny Gill!"

Tellum took Cheyenne's hand in his as she screamed and jumped up and down as the singer moved to center stage. As he congratulated them on their engagement and thanked Tellum for the invite, he went right into singing, *"My, My, My"*.

Tellum pulled Cheyenne into his arms and they swayed together.

"I can't believe you did all of this," she said. "You not only got one of my favorite singers here, but you brought my father here. I don't know if I could love you more. It's not possible. I just love you with every part of me."

"Forever and ever, baby. The hunger will ever die," Tellum exclaimed.

Epilogue

"Tonight, was perfect, don't you think?" Felicia asked as she and Dennis danced at the edge of the dance floor.

"Beyond perfect, my love. Looks like you got your wish. Tellum has settled down with Cheyenne," he replied.

"I have the same wish for all of my sons."

"Besides giving you daughters?"

"Yes. Besides that. I want them to each find the kind of love you and I have had since the moment we met. I knew that was the case for Tellum the moment he brought her home. I've seen him bring women to events as his plus one and other places, but Cheyenne was different. I saw the way he looked at her. That's when I knew. Ramona told me she knew it the same with Tellum when she first met him. We knew they were meant to be."

Dennis stopped dancing and looked at her questionably. Felicia knew she'd said the wrong thing. If anyone knew her, her husband did.

"What did you and Ramona do?"

"What?" she acted with expertise as if she was clueless to where his question was coming from.

"Felicia Blackstone! Don't you try that innocence with me. I know you. I also know how you feel about Cheyenne. Even after she broke up with our son, she still came around to see you often. You stayed close with her. I don't know how Ramona plays into this, but I know there is a connection. I saw the look she gave you when we arrived. You know as a Leo, I don't miss anything. You also know that if I'm asking, I already know the answer because my mind is already calculating what probably happened," Dennis said.

Felicia was caught. It wasn't often she could pull one over on him.

"We honestly didn't do much other than make sure both kids knew that they belonged together. We left it up to them to figure it out. As you can see, it worked. One down, two to go," she declared.

"What are you up to? Who's next, Callum? Byrum? You know our sons can pick their own women."

"I'm not picking women for them. You know me better than that. I don't have to go to that length."

"I wouldn't put it past you though," Dennis laughed.

"I will say that just as you have a calculating mind, I do as well. I predict that Byrum is next."

Felicia didn't appreciate how hard he was laughing. She knew saying that Byrum was next was a stretch. She knew what she knew.

"I'm sorry, sweetheart. For a second there, I thought you said Byrum. My ears are playing tricks on me."

"Stop it, Dennis. Remember this moment. I did say Byrum, and I meant it. Hmph, you need to stop getting your comic relief over this."

"Babe, you have to admit that Byrum falling in love with a woman is preposterous. He would be the last on anyone's list of men ready for commitment. Wait, that's not true – Callum, would be last, but Byrum is right at the bottom of that list of about five thousand men. Byrum? Are you serious? You and I both remember what happened to him four years ago. No one knows his truth but me and you. He never even told Callum or Tellum what happened. His heart will never be the same again. I know my son. I don't think he will ever find himself that vulnerable again. As much as I want things to be different with him, that kind of hurt lasts a lifetime; especially for him. He doesn't love easy. He did and unfortunately, he will never be the same again."

"I know what you're thinking. I do not agree. That was a devastating time for him. I know it's been a few years. He's still hurting over that. We can't fix that for him. I believe there is a woman who can help heal his broken heart. It will mend," she admitted.

"Oh? This is Byrum you're talking about. Losing her was almost the death of our oldest son. He's never gotten over that."

"It was a secret love that shouldn't have been kept a secret. I'm sad for him about that first and foremost. For it to end the way it did hurt him even more. Thankfully, he had work to dive into and change the trajectory of his thinking. I thought like you did for a long time. I assumed he would be one of those, forever kind of bachelors," Felicia admitted.

"What has changed? He's the oldest and least interested in settling down; at least not anymore. Tellum I could see because he may have entertained a bevy of ladies over the years, but he has the biggest heart. He only needed to find a woman who would appreciate that part of him without using him for his good looks, stature and financial stability. Byrum though, not even close to that. He's the hardest when it comes to anyone winning his heart ever again. He loves being a bachelor. He has proclaimed on more than one account that love and marriage was for suckers; his words, not mine."

Felicia stopped dancing and crossed her arms around herself in frustration. She expected him to stand by her on this. She knew her sons as well as he did. She also knew something he didn't know.

"Laugh now," she gloated. Felicia never doubted herself.

"I love you and how you love, love, but not Byrum. I think you need to settle for the fact that he'll be a bachelor forever. He loves his freedom."

"That may be the case, but I know different. Trust me."

"Really? How do you know this?"

Felicia turned Dennis around until he was standing in front of her.

"Look at your son," she said pointing at Byrum.

He stood at the bar sipping on a drink but not really.

"I see him."

"Look at where his eyes are."

She smiled knowing that in the next few seconds, Dennis would see what she saw.

"Who? The woman talking to his assistant, Keiko?"

Felicia laughed to herself this time.

"Oh, no. That's not the woman his eyes are on."

"Who?"

She felt Dennis' body stiffen and knew that he had figured it out.

"No way. No way!" he repeated, this time louder.

"Yes way."

"But..."

"Exactly."

"How do you know? What do you know?"

"I know that our son may not be in love, but he's well on his way. The signs are never obvious because of the implications of what it would appear to be to the staff. Like you, I pick up on everything. Our son has fallen for his assistant. The problem is, he doesn't know how to handle that. In his head, he feels it's inappropriate. In his heart, he's found the woman who could possibly complete him."

"Her. What do you think about what she's feeling and thinking?"

"What's happening is a two-way street. She's just as smitten as he is. Both are fighting it. Neither know how to avoid there being an office scandal."

"Well, then, that's the end of that."

Felicia turned Dennis back around to face her.

"I doubt that. I think it will be a rocky road, but in the end, mark my words when I say, the day will come when I can say two down and one to go. I'll also add, I like her for him."

"I don't know a lot about her."

Felicia did. What she knew, she liked. Keiko has a turbulent life dealing with an ex-husband that could be detrimental to Byrum's patience when it came to getting and having a woman he adores. She only hopes that Byrum would focus on having more patience than he's known to have. To her, his forever was right in front of him.

"I know all I need to know. Just remember that I told you so."

Dennis pulled her back close.

"Okay, enough of getting involved in our kids' lives. What do you say you and I slip out of this party and start a party of our own. Our son put us up in that amazing bungalow. We can order room service and enjoy peace and quiet for days without having to see another person. I've got plans for you."

He kissed her lips sweetly and Felicia shivered at the thought. Even after all of their years together, he still had the ability to make her swoon.

"Days? Aren't we leaving tomorrow? Don't you have a meeting?"

"Absolutely not. I did, but not now. We're going to stay at least five more days, maybe six, secluded away from the world. We can focus only on us. We don't get to do that often enough," he explained.

"Dennis, what did you do?"

"I'm making sure that with all this romancing you're planning for our sons, that you don't forget that I can still romance my wife."

"I only brought enough clothes for three days," she said.

He kissed her lips again, this time lingering there a little longer.

"If you need clothes, I'm not kissing you right."

She giggled and got the message.

"I'm ready when you are. See, this is what I'm talking about for our sons. They don't know what they're missing out on."

"If they're anything like their old man, they'll find out soon enough."

Before they could get too far, Byrum walked up on them.

"Hey, where are the two of you going?"

Dennis spoke up first.

"Son, that's a loaded question. Are you sure you want an answer? If I respond, you won't be able to forget the image it will plant in your head."

"Uh, never mind. Go do whatever it is you're about to do that I don't want to know anything about – ever! I'm flying out tomorrow to Silent Whisper. I'll be there for a few months. I'll be working out of the office there. We have a lot to do and we decided that someone needed to be more hands on with this resort. Since this one is my baby, it's me."

"Oh? Have you decided which staff will be joining you?" Felicia asked.

Without Byrum seeing, Felicia felt Dennis pinch her on the behind. He knew where she was trying to lead the conversation and that was his sign that he wanted her to let it go.

"Some but not all," he said.

"Is Keiko going?"

Byrum turned his head when just as they were talking, Keiko walked by them.

"Byrum?" she questioned trying to get his attention back. She poked Dennis who swatted her hand away before Byrum saw them.

"Huh?"

"She sure is beautiful," Felicia said.

"Yeah," Byrum said and then caught himself. "Um, yeah, okay. Have fun. I need to speak with Keiko about something."

"Call me when you land," Felicia said to Byrum's back as he ran off.

He didn't respond. Dennis took her hand and they walked off.

"I think you're right, babe," Dennis admitted.

"Told you. And so, it begins. I'm going to be silent for now. If Keiko is going to join him when he moves to the island in the Mediterranean, that's when life will come full circle for him. I love the name of that resort, *Silent Whisper*. I think our son has been silent for too long. That place will be exactly what they both need when it comes to a new start. Byrum needs that in order to forget about the hurt of his past. Keiko is the answer. I hope he discovers it before it's too late."

"Wife of mine, it's never too late for love. It happened for him once. You have convinced me that it could happen for him again. Let's hope that Silent Whisper works it's magic like Secret Whisper did for Tellum and Cheyenne," Dennis said.

"I'm with you on that one hundred percent. The time is now for Byrum."

Enjoy a look inside of the next installment of the Island Embers series, Desire for You, available February 15, 2025. Get ready for Byrum's story. Are you ready?

The wedding reception for Tellum and Cheyenne Blackstone was in full swing. An exquisite menu accompanied by live music and an even livelier crowd of two hundred guests, Byrum was having the time of his life. On a warm June day, months after his brother proposed to the love of his life, their closest family members and friends were gathered for the event of the year in downtown Detroit. The wedding had taken place over an hour ago in the same venue, keeping guests from having to travel from one location to another for the wedding and then the reception. Thankfully, both occurred at a five-star hotel that accommodated everyone to spend at least one night at the hotel.

Byrum leaned back in his chair at the head table where he sat next to Tellum on one side and on the other was one of Cheyenne's friends, who was one of two maids-of-honor. The other, her best friend Melodi, sat on the other side of Callum who sat next to Cheyenne. The rest of the wedding party were seated at three tables near the head table. He was still floored that Tellum and Cheyenne had ten groomsmen, not including him and Callum, and the same number of bridesmaids. This was one of the biggest wedding's he had ever been to or a part of. He shouldn't be surprised that his brother and his bride would go all out on their big day. Their love was as big and magnificent as the event was.

The food had been served, the cake had been cut and most of what kept him at the reception had surpassed. He was ready to head out to a space that was just him. He needed a night to relax and get his thoughts in check. For now, there is no place he would rather be than right here as Tellum's right-hand man. Then he thought about it and realized there was one place that would appease him a little more. His eyes cut to a table on the far left of the dance floor. For three months, he'd self-tortured himself by being close to a woman that he couldn't have, though she was all he wanted. Trying to avoid anyone seeing him ogling her, he lifted his drink to his mouth and sipped it slowly. He was hoping to hide where his eyes were focused. They were locked in on Keiko Lee, his executive assistant.

A few months back, he and his team had settled into their company provided accommodations on the island in the Mediterranean that would be the home of their next resort, Silent Whisper. It hadn't always been his plan to make the island his home, but with so much work to be done and with this resort being his baby, he made the sacrifice to move to the island pretty much full-time. He made trips back to Detroit and other locations for business purposes, but most of his time was spent on the island. He didn't realize how much he needed a break from Detroit until he did. Not only was he on the island, but so was Keiko with her exotic looks. She was an incredibly beautiful woman who heritage came from her African American father and Asian mother.

Keiko was five-foot-nine with the longest, sexiest legs in the history of women. She had long, thick black as coal hair that cascaded down her back. Her full lips had a permanent look of being thoroughly kissed. Gorgeous black as midnight eyes had a magnetism that made him want to stare into them without the need to ever look away. He did when he thought others may see his obvious, startling attraction to her; his insatiable desire for her. Coming home for the wedding, he had hoped that distance from her would help to reign in his longing to have her in his arms and in his bed. That wasn't to be.

One day, he and Keiko were talking in her office about his travel plans to return to the Detroit for the wedding and she mentioned she was also heading home. She couldn't wait to spend some quality time with her son who was staying with his father while she worked and lived on the island full-time. When she paused in explaining her reason for going home, he caught a weird expression on her face as if she were leaving something out that may be uncomfortable to reveal. When he asked her about it, she told him that she'd received an invitation to Tellum and Cheyenne's wedding. He knew that she and Cheyenne were acquaintances but didn't know that they were close enough for the small group that were invited to the wedding. He didn't question it, but instead, told her he was happy that she was going. Most of all, he was overjoyed that she would get the chance to see her son whom everyone knew she missed. Tru, five years old, was the light of her life. Her ex-husband, DeConnor, let Tru video chat with her every day; sometimes more than once a day. After months of intense angst while going through their divorce, she and DeConnor were finally in a good communicative space after they agreed it would be best for their son to stay in the states.

Twice a month, on the weekends, she would fly home to spend time with him before coming back to the island to lead the team that were doing the interviews for the large number of resort staff that needed to be hired and trained. Along with that, she was still the main person who kept up with his meeting and travel schedule. He offered to let her bring someone else on board to do it, but like him, she didn't trust anyone but herself to handle his personal business. He told her anytime she felt overwhelmed, she had his permission to get more help as she needed it.

When he left the resort to fly home a week ago in order to help Tellum with anything he needed for wedding preparations, he thought about her and the way she smiled at him when he headed out to the airport. He'd stopped by the office for one last check of his schedule. He wanted them on the same page. He said his goodbyes and as he walked out, she commented that she would see him at the wedding. He turned and saw a look in her eyes that he wondered about. Keiko may not know it but her eyes reflected deep feelings, even profound thoughts. They told many stories.

There was something in how they looked at each other that day that had him unable to sleep on his flight. He needed that few hours' nap after having back-to-back meetings the day before that went well into the night. Images of Keiko plagued his mind, shifting him off-kilter. He wanted her; there was no doubt about that. The idea of her sensually fulfilled him. He'd been here before. There had been another, years ago. He hadn't quite gotten over her even now. What he was feeling for Keiko was different but as desirous as it could be. This was a first for him after vowing his first love had crushed him to the point that he was never going to let another woman get that close to him ever again. He'd suffered quietly through a broken heart. There was a pull to Keiko that was the hardest fight in his life when it came to his heart.

"I see Keiko made it," Tellum leaned over and spoke.

Tellum bringing her up brought him into the present.

"Yeah. I was surprised you invited her. Not that it's a problem or anything. I didn't realize she and Cheyenne were that close."

"Don't ask me about it. I had nothing to do with the invite list outside of our family and my close friends. As for Keiko, that was all Cheyenne."

"Really?" Byrum questioned.

Tellum nodded and nudged Cheyenne to get her attention.

"Baby, Byrum has a question for you," he said, moving so that Cheyenne could lean over in Byrum's direction.

"You finished dancing? I saw you tearing something up out there. The women are still wondering if you'll be returning to delight them with your moves. You have a question for me?"

Byrum winked at his new sister-in-law. He rolled his eyes at Tellum knowing that the competition between the three of them, including their brother Callum, had been about who the best dancer was. They all knew it was him who had the moves. Cheyenne just confirmed that. No doubt, Tellum was questioning the idea.

"Not really. I was just chatting with your husband."

"Oh, I love the sound of that. *My HUSBAND!*

Tellum leaned over and kissed Cheyenne. Byrum waved them off.

"Get a room!" he declared.

"Oh, we will! If this party doesn't soon wrap up, y'all are about to be short one bride and one groom," Tellum exclaimed. "What was it about Keiko that you wanted to ask Cheyenne?"

"Byrum?" Cheyenne questioned.

"Right. I was telling your husband that I was surprised that Keiko was invited. Not that there is anything wrong with that since I know the two of you are friendly with each other. I was just wondering. I didn't see anyone else from my team here, though I see Tellum's entire staff."

"I won't keep you in suspense, brother-in-law. I received a special request to add her to the guest list."

Byrum perked up. He wondered who would make such a request.

"Who did that come from?" he asked.

"Your mother. My mother, your mother and I had our first meeting about the guest list months ago. After your mother confirmed I had everyone from your family, she wrote down Keiko's name and asked if I was okay with that. I didn't question it for one minute. Was that, okay? Is something wrong?"

Byrum didn't bother looking around to catch his mother's eye. He loved her but he felt like she had something up her s

"Oh, no – nothing is wrong."

"She looks amazing right? I cannot believe she's not a model. I asked her about that earlier when we were on the dance floor. She said she gets that question all the time. She's more beautiful than the prettiest model out there. She has the killer looks that talent scouts are looking for," Cheyenne said.

Byrum looked at Keiko as she stood from her table. He had tried talking to her when he had come across his parents when they were slipping out of the party but Keiko had been stopped by some guy who asked her to dance and she obliged him. That's when he decided to make his way back to his seat. He hoped he'd done a good job of tampering down his dislike of seeing Keiko enjoy herself in another man's arms. He was so used to seeing her in work mode that her having any kind of personal life never entered his mind; at least not until the reality of his desire for her surfaced. He finally stopped pushing it to the side.

His eyes stayed on Keiko this time as she gave hugs all around to Tellum's staff who sat at the same table. He knew he shouldn't, but he wanted to talk to her. He wanted to dance with her earlier, but he pushed that thought out of his head. He didn't want any gossip. Keiko was at the wedding without a guest and so was he. It's true that the women tried to sidle up to him, but he could only think of Keiko and the gorgeous mint green dress with gold accessories to set the look up right that she confidently moved about in. There wasn't an eye in the place of any man that didn't have a lust-filled look when they saw her. He assumed that for the next few days, she would be spending time with her son. If he was going to talk with her, he needed to do it now. He was way from work. They were far away from his team who were back at Silent Whisper, the Blackstone brothers second newest resort located on a private island in the Mediterranean. He didn't lack confidence, but he did question his intention. He wanted her, but to what extent he could have her was up to her.

"Are you good if I head out?" he asked Tellum.

"Yeah. Things are winding down a bit. Cheyenne and I are going to say our goodnights in the next ten minutes or so. Make your escape if you need to. You staying here at the hotel tonight?"

"I am. I wasn't sure how late we would be. I know the fellas are trying to hang after, but I could use a quiet night. The days and nights have been long at the resort. This is the first real break I'm getting in weeks. I'm booked here for tonight with a late checkout tomorrow. I'm then headed to the condo for another day of being at home. As much as I miss my home here in Detroit, I'm also ready to get back to the resort. When do you and Cheyenne fly out to the Amalfi Coast?"

"We're here in the Presidential Suite for the next two nights. When we checkout, we head straight for the airport. Two amazing weeks of loving on my wife. I love the sound that makes coming out of my mouth. We'll talk when I get back?" Tellum asked.

"Yes. Don't even think of doing anything work related while you're gone. I've already told every member of your team that I'm firing anyone who reaches out to you or takes a call, text or email from you. I mean it, Tell. Not *one* iota of work."

"You don't have to worry about that. I told him unless there is some kind of family or medical emergency, there is to be no communication for any other reason to the outside world. I plan to keep him too busy to be able to focus on work,"

Cheyenne laughed and winked at Tellum.

"You heard her. The wife is in charge," Tellum boasted.

"Cool. I'm out. Looks like the fellas are all on the floor. I'll holler at them tomorrow. Tonight, I'm heading to peace and quiet."

Byrum stood from the table. His eyes caught up with Keiko as she left out of the doors at the back of the room. He had to rush to keep up with her. Instead of going through the crowd and risking someone stopping him, he exited out of the side door and raced toward the elevator. He wasn't sure if she was staying the night at the hotel or not. If so, there were only two banks of elevators that went to the wing of rooms for their guests.

Rushing with hurried steps, he caught a glimpse of her green dress as she rounded a corner. He caught up with her before she reached the elevators.

"Leaving so soon?" he asked when he reached her.

"Oh, hey! My feet are killing me in these heels. I don't know what I was thinking wearing these. They look good but aren't good for my feet long-term. I have more comfortable shoes in my room that I should have brought down with me."

"Maybe it's not the shoes. It may be all that dancing. Every time you sat down, a new suitor reached out for a dance. Did you turn anyone down?"

"I love to dance. Besides, the band was great. They played all the hits. Then the DJ wowed us, and I couldn't resist. Are you leaving?" she asked.

"I'm hoping to catch up on some much-needed rest while I'm home. I don't know when I'll get home again with all that's going on at the resort."

"Your schedule has been hectic. Let me know if you want

me to reschedule anything once you return. You work too hard."

Byrum nodded and placed his hands in his pockets. He looked all around except for directly at her during the silence that lived between them.

"I do. I have to work on remedying that. Can I walk you to your room? I saw you and didn't have a chance to even say hello during the wedding or reception. Looks like we're headed in the same direction."

"Sure; that would be nice. You look nice in your black tuxedo and blue accents. The large wedding party looked fantastic. Did I see a photographer from Essence Magazine?" she asked.

"You did. I asked Tellum about that. The magazine inquired about doing a spread and article on their wedding. He agreed as long as Cheyenne was okay with it."

"I can't wait to see that issue."

The elevator door opened, and they got in.

"You look amazing in green. You are killing everything in that dress. I hope that's okay to say," Byrum said.

He wanted to say more but held back.

"Yes, it is and thank you."

Then it happened; they rode in silence to the eighth floor. Byrum kept his eye on the elevator number above the door as if it was the most interesting thing in the world. He was nervous. Who was he? Women didn't make him nervous. Keiko was no ordinary woman. She was the object of his desire; a desire that was growing by leaps and bounds every day. Before long, the door opened and he followed her out. He strolled with her with his hands in his pockets. He needed to keep them there in the safe zone.

"This hotel is nice. I've never seen the inside of it this way. I've been to a few events in the ballroom. I'm usually in and out, going home. Like everyone else, I figured I wouldn't feel like doing that tonight."

"It's very nice. This is my first time here. My room is amazing, all white and crisp everything. Well, this is me," Keiko alerted him and pointed to her door.

She turned to face him, and they stood, again, in silence. The gaze between them tore through his heart. What could he say at this moment? His mind raced with a lot, but nothing seemed appropriate considering their work relationship. He had so much he wanted to pour out to her but didn't. He shifted on his feet. For a split second, he felt like there was something Keiko wanted to say, but like him, she was holding something back. He saw it in her eyes.

"Well, I hope you enjoyed yourself. It was nice seeing you in an arena outside of work," he finally said.

"I guess we never really have before without the entire team being around. I'm glad I came for the wedding. Cheyenne was beautiful. Everything was amazing. Again, you wear a tuxedo well," she beamed.

"Thank you. I like to play dress up every now and then when I'm not at one construction site or another."

"I guess I better go in."

Keiko turned her back to him and searched for her room key. Once she found it, she placed it in the door and it opened. She walked inside slowly, turning to him with the door in her hand.

Byrum opened his mouth to say what was on his mind and then stopped. He repeated that action and stopped again.

"Okay," was all he could get out.

"Is there anything else? You look like you want to say something?" she asked.

Byrum let his shoulders sink. Now wasn't the time. Perhaps never was more like it.

"No, I'm good. I guess I'll see you when I get back. Have fun with Tru. I know he can't wait to see you."

"My parents are flying in tomorrow evening from Boston. When I pick them up at the airport, we're going to pick Tru up for the next few days. I'm excited. Okay, then I'll see you when you get back the day after me, right?"

"I don't even know. That's something the best executive assistant knows for sure. I have to check my calendar."

"I'll text a reminder to you tomorrow."

"Don't you dare. I'll figure it out. Have a good night, Keiko."

"You too, Byrum."

She looked down and closed the door leaving him standing there alone. His eyes stayed on the door for what seemed forever before he turned and walked back down the hall, kicking himself for a missed opportunity. Now it was too late; or was it.

Upcoming Releases

Get the next installment in 2025!
About *Desire for You*

Byrum Blackstone thought that years of protecting his heart would make him immune to falling for any woman again. That was until he found himself vulnerable to the one woman he knows he should stay away from; his executive assistant, Keiko Lee.

Keiko wasn't looking for love after her marriage crashed and burned. The last person she expected to fall for was her boss. They agreed to a secret affair as long as no one found out. Word getting out could destroy both of their lives.

Unbeknownst to them, Byrum's past comes back and discovers his secret affair. She's willing to destroy all that he has achieved in order to have him to herself.

Byrum is in the fight of his life to have a piece of the life he thought he'd left behind while holding onto the greatest desire he's ever encountered.

Leaks, Lies, Lust and Love
The Brothers of Chi-Town, Book 7
Coming - 2024

Carlos Kincaid is an irresistible, rugged loner who has always been that good guy who finishes last when it comes to women. Just when he is getting his life on track, his Achilles' heel shows up by the name of Everly Robinson. Along with her came memories of their inexhaustible, hot, steamy, lust-filled nights between the sheets.

Everly chose the wrong man one time too many in her life. Now, she's on the run from a dangerous man and in desperate need of help. With nothing but the clothes on her back, she returns to the only man she trusts. Carlos was also the only man she's ever loved despite toying with his heart and leaving him for his best friend.

Carlos is frustrated that old feelings could lead him back into the arms of the woman he needed to hate in order to forgive. He couldn't tell if her story was filled with lies or truths. Unfortunately for him, Everly is still the only woman he wants more than his next breath. Is he willing to risk his heart and his life for a woman who once betrayed him and his love for her?

The Law of Love
The Sullivans of Montana, Book 5
Coming - 2024

Brielle Sullivan, the youngest of the Sullivan's of Montana is caught up in an entanglement with her brother's best friend, Sheriff Marcus Coley. The drama of being sued by Marcus' ex-wife for ruining their marriage could reveal secrets that could cause her to lose the support of her family and the love of the first man who stole her heart.

Now Available

An Unexpected Destiny
Sister Act, Book 1

Destiny Lockhart's high school crush, Lincoln Cole, is again front and center in her life. She last saw him fifteen years ago when she threw him out of her bedroom after their one night together following the senior prom. That night had been her most embarrassing moment, leaving her feeling ashamed and undesirable.

There was no way entertainment mogul Lincoln Cole could ever forget the shy, yet beautiful butterfly that was Destiny from his years as a high school football star. The now feisty, sexy and self-confident executive who dripped in vibrant, dazzling appeal reminded him that they were never meant to only have a one-night-stand. They were always destined for forever.

For years, they lived on two different coasts unaware that soon, their past would become an unexpected present filled with unfinished desires that once looked like rejection.

For You, I Will
Sister Act, Book 2

Kasey Young discovered that a man would do anything to keep her in his grips, even if it's her ex-husband. She lived her life his way for years until she'd had enough and filed for divorce. He wants to insert himself back into her life with an ultimatum; take him back or lose custody of their kids. Kasey found herself between a rock and a hard place needing the help of a man she barely knew, but who stirred up deep carnal desires that had been lying dormant.

Attorney Darren Braxton stepped up to the plate to help Kasey with her child custody case as a favor for a friend. What he hadn't planned on was the hedonistic lust for a woman who could cause him to lose all he's gained because he can't say no to her. He did the one thing he could think of to save them both; he married her.

Kasey has to convince the court that their love is real or she could lose everything. Could she before it's too late?

More Than Friends
Sister Act, Book 3

A storm is brewing in Boston and her name is Nivea Lockhart. Boldly entering into a no-strings affair with her best friend, Jaxon Hightower, she thought she could put her true feelings aside. Her mind was on indulging in steamy nights of uncomplicated, noncommittal pleasure. She didn't count on her heart wanting more than that.

Jaxon is mesmerized by his best friend, an intense attraction he had done a good job of hiding since their early college years. He thought having a bevy of beauties instead of having her would lessen his attraction and not ruin the friendship he had come to rely on.

After an unexpected, mind-blowing encounter that surprised and shocked their socks off, Nivea and Jaxon danced around the inevitable, true love. What they didn't think about was a woman he had been involved with named Alicia, fighting for a permanent position in his life. She was a woman who had no plans of letting Jaxon go without a fight. What Alicia wasn't ready for was Nivea's response to her saying, It's On!

The Sweetest Revenge

Delaney Monroe had a secret. She thirsted for earth-shaking sex that being married for years never provided. Now divorced, she understood the assignment; to live life on her own terms. She'd never experienced the kind of racy, wild intimacy that she'd only dreamed of with her faceless fantasy man. She was sure he possessed all she wants and needs when it comes to her ultimate satisfaction.

Nashall Patterson was famously known for being a happily

single, salaciously sexy, and untamable stallion to every woman who has ever set eyes on him. He never had to worry about his heart being on the line because he never involved it when he indulged in women. That was until he met Delaney during a pre-wedding weekend meet and greet for his cousin's upcoming nuptials.

Delaney, the reserved businesswoman, and Nashall, the bad boy of hedonism had no idea that her secret hunger would lead to amorous encounters that were no longer just cravings of the body but drove them to the desires of their hearts as well.

Could what started out as voracious encounters lead to love of a permanent kind?

The Sweetest Temptation

As a teenager, Gabrielle Mann fell in love with strikingly handsome Adonis Duqette, an older, close family friend. He was the sweetest of temptations who helped her save face in front of her friends. He then broke her heart by rejecting her declaration of love.

Adonis is his given name; A.D. is what his friends call him. As a special forces operative, he was simply known as, Jaguar. When the Mann family is in need, Adonis drops everything to provide protection for Gabrielle, no longer a teenager, but a sexy, vibrant, damn-near irresistible woman. He once had no problem resisting his desire for her. Being back in her life, he was about to risk it all for the woman he had begrudgingly left behind.

Gabrielle's star-studded career as Hollywood's next "IT" girl is derailed when an unknown assailant targets her political family. Adonis reappears in her life to her chagrin. He once told her to forget about him and she did. Now he's back, looking hotter and hunkier than any man should legally be. While he's trying to save her life, she's trying to save her heart from the one man she vowed to never love again. Gabrielle is about to learn that some things are easier said than done.

It Should Have Been You

Karma:

Dr. Clayton Myers was never a believer in karma, but he did believe in fate. Both would soon collide and expose a secret that would impact the perfect life and relationship with the only woman he ever loved, but not the only woman he took to his bed. That revelation would put his life on a path he accepted while never forgetting what could have been.

Disappointment:

Dr. Donna Spencer had experienced one of the darkest days of her life at the hands of the man who made a promise of forever. She took the hit to her heart and realized nothing good lasts forever.

Fate:

After years of no contact, Clayton and Donna's paths would cross again, forcing them to face the past where their love resided, while wondering what should have been and if they could find their way back to love again.

Unforgettable

Baltimorean Reagan Kelly was expecting an uneventful weekend in New York City visiting her sister between Thanksgiving and Christmas. Though in the holiday spirit, the last thing she thought she'd find on a cold, wintery night was a chance at romance.

Two days in New York City for business and a chance to see his best friend was all Crime Novelist, Keith Jackson had time for, or so he thought. He soon found time to extend his stay when the chance of a lifetime to spend four incredible days with the most beautiful woman he'd ever encountered landed at his feet.

An unforgettable weekend is one thing, but can that weekend turn into a lifetime of unconditional love for Reagan and Keith, two self-professed workaholics, who didn't have a reason to slow down and smell the roses until now?

Seize the Moment

Aubree Campbell played a childish game with love and she lost. Ending her relationship with her live-in boyfriend, Russell Hall, because they became passing strangers in the night didn't have him begging and pleading for her to give him a second chance as she had hoped. Instead, the indomitable Russell made plans to move out and give her the space she desired, and then a world pandemic hit and they agreed to ride it out together under one roof.

Tensions brewed and so did their undeniable desire and passion for one other. Will their steamy nights lead them back to being on the same page in life and in love or will past hurt and jealousy return to put an end to their rekindling?

Get a bonus book, "Being Neighborly" when you get your copy of Seize the Moment! The fire doesn't stop!

The Power of Seduction

Bakery owner Raquel Hastings assumed her relationship was perfect in every way, both in and out of the bedroom where she had enjoyed the most tempting, titillating, and out-of-this-world sensual romps between the sheets with sexy engineer, Preston Sharpe, a man who knows his way around a woman's body. That was until he took a job in another country which left her only with memories and intoxicating desires to be loved like that again. Her world had been turned upside down until the day he returned with a plan to turn her world right side up.

Preston's alluring visions of Raquel haunted him at night, alone in his bed in a foreign country without the woman he loved. With the chance to return home and to her loving arms, he dreamed of once again sharing nights of satiating passion that only two hearts meant for each other could share. He knew he had to ready his game of seduction if he were ever going to again have Raquel back in his life and in his bed. This time, his plan was to make it last forever with the hope that Raquel could forgive him and give their love another chance.

Three's a Crowd
The Sullivans of Montana, Book 4

Businessman Shelton Sullivan was clear that as a kid, he loved life growing up on the Sullivan Ranch wrangling cattle and riding horses. As a man, he prefers big city life, wrangling expensive suits and most of all, riding sexy women. He was blindsided when a woman penetrated the wall of steel that surrounded, what some said was his black heart, when it came to being in love; he preferred lust.

Deputy Sheriff McKenna Gibson needed a fresh start in a new city. Escaping a life that was crafted for her had become old and dull. Sizzling, spicy encounters with Bozeman's most eligible bachelor was exactly what she needed to help her forget the secrets she was hoping to leave behind in her old life as a military wife.

Without warning, Shelton found himself swept up into McKenna's amorous sensualities that very much matched his own dalliances. Their steamy, seductive encounters led to even more explicit and erotic romps until Shelton's world crashed down like a Montana boulder. McKenna is injured in the line of duty and his world is rocked off of its axis when her military husband blew up the love he thought was blossoming from the one time he decided to let down his guard.

Is Shelton willing to forgive and forget and turn away from the red-hot stirring in his chest at the thought of her?

On the Right Track
The Sullivans of Montana, Book 3

Professional race car driver, Dayton Sullivan, is the youngest of the Sullivan boys out of Bozeman, Montana. He's found himself in a bit of a jam when he falls in love with Kima McDonald, the daughter of a man who could be responsible for the death of Kima's mother.

They ran to the Sullivan Ranch in order to escape the life she's being told she has to live to support her father's schemes.

It's discovered that her father has debts that can only be settled if he can get Dayton back on the race track and Kima married to a man she doesn't love.

Can their love sustain them through the ups and downs they'll face against her sinister father?

The Way You Love Me
The Sullivans of Montana, Book 2

Montana ranch owner, Perry Sullivan, befriended a woman who finds herself in dire need of his help. He doesn't hesitate to provide shelter and protection the way any man should for a woman who is in distress. What he had not planned on was in the midst of the turmoil that was her life, he would lose his heart and fall in love while at the same time putting the lives of his own family at risk. Gizelle Duncan had a tumultuous past she didn't want anyone to know about, but when that past, in the form of her abusive ex-husband, shows up in her life again, she has no choice but to accept help from one of those sexy Sullivan boys from the Sullivan Ranch. She thought she had lost all faith in real love until Perry showed her that she could trust him not only with her life, but with her heart.

"The Way You Love Me" will take you on a journey from the ashes of Gizelle's burned-out house and life and into the flames of passion that will not be contained even at the peril of a jealous ex-husband out for revenge.

Home for Thanksgiving
The Sullivans of Montana, Book 1

Firefighter Nicholas Sullivan is going home for the holiday after he was sidelined due to an injury on the job. Guilt over a life lost has kept him away from his family's ranch in Montana and now he's forced to face his past demons and deal with a self-imposed life of regret.

Veterinarian Parker Wingate's first encounter with the handsome firefighter was less than pleasurable. She sympathized with his hurt, understood his pain and before long, felt his love.

Knowing the holiday season is ending soon, can Nick go from living in love for the moment to allowing himself to finally live in love forever?

About the Author

Cheryl Barton lives in Maryland and in her spare time she loves to read espionage, crime and romance novels, cook, watch Sci-fi movies, spend time with family and friends and enjoy Maryland steamed crabs. Cheryl is celebrating over 30 years as a government employee and loves writing romance novels when she's not working.

Cheryl is the author of over thirty-one romance novels, four inspirational novels and is proud of six book compilation projects with several other incredible women. Cheryl was a 2019 Finalist for the Emma Award given by Romance Slam Jam and a 2018 Finalist for the Literary Trailblazer of the Year award by the Indie Author Legacy Award. Cheryl is a member of the Contemporary Romance Writers where she currently serves on the board as the secretary. Beginning in January 2024, Cheryl will serve on the same board but in her new position as the Vice President of Communications.

Connect with Cheryl Barton
Author Cheryl Barton website
www.cherylbarton.net
Amazon Author Page
www.amazon.com/author/cherylbarton
Instagram: @cherylbartonauthor
Facebook: @cherylbartonbooks
Threads: @cherylbartonbooks@threads.net

www.ingramcontent.com/pod-product-compliance
Lightning Source LLC
Chambersburg PA
CBHW030243030726
47493CB00023B/569